The Hapless Gonif

The Slater Ibáñez Books

That First Heady Burn
True Vermilion
The Dark Shill
A Stack of Sawbucks
The Hillside Roble
The Peroxide Pomp
The Incidental Twin
Brawl in Bardo
The Window-Shade Job
The Convenient Patsy
The Artisanal Grifter
Shrink in the Shadows
Project Chartreuse
From a Desert Playa
The Tired Canary
A Desperate Frame-up
Trail of the Blue Agave
The Saucer-Heads
The Satin Squeeze Play
Chiseler in Jade
The Eagle and the Weasel
The Mojave Gimmick
The Hapless Gonif

Subscribe to the Slater
Ibáñez Books newsletter:
slaternews.dagmarmiura.com

The Hapless Gonif

The Hapless Gonif

George Bixley

DAGMAR MIURA

LOS ANGELES

Published by Dagmar Miura
Los Angeles
www.dagmarmiura.com

The Hapless Gonif

First published 2025

ISBN: 979-8-89195-049-8

ONE

"YOU SHOULD DEFINITELY DO it," Pike said. "We can record your conversation with him. It might give us some insight."

The feds didn't really need his help, Slater knew, but Lenny had asked him to come see him in jail, and he was curious about what the guy wanted with him. He didn't mind Lenny, one of the bikers in the gang that Pike had infiltrated out in the Mojave Desert. Lenny's mistake had been mixing with the wrong kind of bikers and getting popped for cooking meth.

They were standing outside Pike's office building, the low winter sun barely over the surrounding towers.

"I don't even know when visiting hours are," Slater said.

Pike waved a hand. "I'm deep into this case, so it's

whenever I say they are."

Built thick, his dark hair was slicked back. It had been a huge relief when he'd finished the undercover job, and cut his hair, and shaved off the beard. The motorcycle was gone too, returned to some federal motor pool. Even the business-casual drag was a huge improvement over the saggy biker jeans and the leather jacket.

"You can head over there now," Pike went on. "I'll call to make sure they put you near a microphone."

"Does it seem odd to you that there's a big-ass federal prison in the middle of Downtown LA?" Slater said. "Don't they usually build those in the sticks? If somebody busts out, they can just fade into the city."

"The location is handy, I'd say. That's where Lenny is." He raised his eyebrows. "You can walk."

Stepping close, Slater met his mouth, lingering in it for a moment, then wrapped his arms around him and squeezed him hard.

When he stepped through the doors at the prison, there was a high counter with a guard parked behind it. As he approached, the guy greeted him in Spanish. He heard it all the time, as Slater had his father's dark hair and Latin coloring, but he hadn't managed to absorb much of his culture.

"I don't actually speak the language," he said.

The guard made him fill out a form, then asked for his ID. Once he'd handed it over, he waved Slater to a door at the side of the lobby. The lock snapped open as he approached it.

This wasn't even inside yet, just a room with a metal detector, and he went through the process of emptying his pockets. As he stepped through the frame, shrill beeping started.

"Feet apart, and spread your arms," the guard said.

Slater knew the drill, and stood with his arms extended. The guy ran the hand wand over him. It squealed when it passed his crotch.

"Take your belt off."

He coiled it up and put it in the tray with his phone and his keys. The guy waved the wand over his fly again, then pressed his latex-gloved fingers on his crotch.

"There's nothing there now."

"Oh, you know there's something there," Slater said. "Keep poking at it and it's going to get bigger."

He frowned. "Settle down, now."

"Can I take my phone?"

"No electronic devices. You can pick it up on your way out."

"What about the belt?"

"That'll be here when you leave too." His eyes flicked downward. "You don't really need it. Those pants are plenty snug."

"Say the word," Slater said. "If you've got a break coming up, I can ditch them."

"Move along now," he said, and jutted his chin.

Another guard rode up in the elevator with him, and directed him into a room with stainless-steel tables and stools bolted to the floor. A couple of guards were positioned at the sides of the room, and a handful of other inmates and visitors sat at the tables. It took a second to recognize Lenny, with his long hair in a crew cut now, already sitting at one. He was wearing bright orange, with his cut biceps and delts on display underneath. The guy was still totally fuckable.

Lenny sat up straighter when he spotted him. "Thanks for coming," he said as Slater took the stool across from him.

"How are you doing in here?"

"How do you think I'm doing? It's stir." He lowered his voice. "You never got picked up?"

"I did not."

"Lucky bastard. Is Yella still in?"

That was the nickname the bikers had given Pike when he'd been embedded with them.

"He's out," Slater said. "He's not sure if he's going to get charged with anything. I don't think they have enough evidence. Not yet, anyway."

"They got me on manufacturing and distribution."

"It sounds like they're throwing a wide net. From what I saw, you weren't really doing all that."

"Exactly," Lenny said. "I get why Yella doesn't want to come here, but maybe you can talk to him. He could explain to the prosecutors that I was just a runner. An errand boy. Pickups and drop-offs. I wasn't manufacturing anything."

"I'll ask him to do that. You know you can help yourself a lot if you turn state's evidence."

Lenny frowned. "I'm no rat. Besides, Memo wouldn't hesitate to croak me."

"Fuck Memo," Slater said. "He's going over for murder no matter what. That means he's not going to be worried about you." He watched him for a moment. "Do you have a decent lawyer at least?"

"I have a public defender, I think. I only met her once."

"Those people are stretched thin. You need to get a lawyer who has time for you."

"I don't have any money. My bike was confiscated."

"What about that piece of land you have out by Landers?"

"Who told you about that?"

"You did, genius. You also said you wished you'd never told Memo about it."

"I'm not really attached to it," Lenny said. "But how am I going to sell it from in here?"

"What's it worth?"

"I'd be real lucky to get fifty grand."

Slater waved a hand. "I'll buy it for fifty grand."

His brow furrowed. "Why? You've never even seen it."

"I know the Mojave. You told me there's no structures or roads on it."

"Just a dirt double-track along one side."

"And Memo did some digging," Slater said.

"I wasn't involved in that. I'm not even sure it's true."

Slater knew it was—he'd been out there himself, and had found the grave sites.

"Anyway, I can't really do bank-type transactions from in here."

"It's just about signing stupid pieces of paper. Like buying and selling a bike. Transfer the title to me, and I'll put the dough in your bank account. I'll get my lawyer to set it up."

"Why do you have a lawyer?"

"Because you need them sometimes." Slater waved at the room. "Like when the feds are trying to put you away."

"The property records are with the county. My name is on it."

"So are you staying sober?"

"There's not much choice in here." Lenny scoffed. "I can't believe I'm back in a place like this. I did it to myself. I just couldn't stay out of the racket."

"No one's beyond redemption. If you're not blaming somebody else, you're already halfway there."

"Tell that to my public defender."

Slater jabbed a finger at him. "Get a lawyer. I'll get the land transaction rolling as soon as I can."

"Talk to Yella for me," Lenny said as Slater got up and walked out.

In the lobby it took a minute to recover his belt and the contents of his pockets, and he finally walked out of the dank concrete box into the daylight, and took a deep breath.

He'd parked underground, in a garage slung between a courthouse and some other government building, and he trotted down the stairs and walked up on the Continental. It was easy to spot, sticking out a foot past the cars on either side, a classic early seventies land boat. He loved the cloudy blue paint job, and the spare tire profile built into the trunk lid, and the cherry interior. It was sheer swish, and there had never been anything as beautiful before or since.

Nosing up to the street, he drove to his office, a century-old building at the other end of Downtown in the Fashion District, and parked in the surface lot across the street. Most of the other tenants were small clothing factories, and when he strode through the lobby, a couple of day laborers were poring over the sticky notes advertising gig work cutting fabric and sewing and hauling garment racks. Upstairs he twisted his key in the office door, admiring the lettering on it:

SLATER IBÁÑEZ
MAXIMILLIAN CONROY
INVESTIGATIONS

The office was dark, and he flicked on the lights, and clicked his tongue to greet the little plaster statue of Rey Pascual perched on the front desk. A skeleton wearing a crown and holding a scythe, Rey had become a permanent fixture of the place, a de facto business mascot.

They had three small rooms, an office for him and one for Max, and the front office with a desk that their operatives sometimes used. He stuck his head into Max's office to make sure it was empty, then stepped over to his own, pulling his phone out of his jeans as he sat behind his desk.

Digging through his contact list, he found O'Dowd, the lawyer Max had hired to get their finances organized. She operated in a stratum that was ideal for them—not a crook, but just shady enough not to question their business practices. Slater sent her a text:

Can I come by today?

He pulled his keyboard close and peered at the computer monitor as he looked for the ownership record for Lenny's land. It was listed under his name on the county's website, and he printed it, then typed some notes about what he knew about Lenny, and printed that too.

On the desktop his phone buzzed, and he lifted it to look at the screen. The caller ID said WOODY. He didn't need to talk to that guy, but he couldn't blow him off either. Woody had paid him well for helping him out a while back. Slater picked up and said, "Ibáñez."

"I wanted to set up a meeting for you with an acquaintance of mine," Woody said. "A guy named Clyde. He owns the building where Greenleaf is. I think you might be able to help him."

"Is he a gangster?"

Woody laughed. "Why would you ask me that?"

"Lots of nightclub people are mixed up with the syndicate."

"Nobody at Greenleaf is a gangster. If he were, he wouldn't need you—he'd have his own button men. And Clyde doesn't have anything to do with Greenleaf. He's just the landlord."

"What does Clyde want me to do?"

"He can explain it to you. He asked me if I knew anybody who could dig into things discreetly. Maybe he thinks I have gangland connections because I work at a nightclub. I told him I had a guy."

"I'm definitely that guy."

"Don't feel obligated to work for him because of me," Woody said. "I don't know him that well."

"If Clyde is working at Greenleaf, my office is close. He could walk over here."

"The guy is a little fancy. He's not going to walk."

"You can tell him I'll be at my office in a couple hours," Slater said, and rattled off the address.

Once he'd ended the call, he saw that O'Dowd had replied to his text:

I'm here.

Swiveling around to the squat black safe in the

corner of his office, he dropped to one knee and twisted the combination into the dial. The century-old behemoth was bolted to the floor, and once he got it unlocked, and pulled open the heavy door, he took out the racks he'd need and loaded them into his satchel. The accounting envelope they kept inside had several extra pages taped to it, and he took it out, and wrote on it:

Slater –50G

He added the date and tossed it back inside, and locked the safe, then headed down to the street. The Continental's big engine purred once he got up to highway speed on the 10, and he navigated to West-wood, onto the stretch of Wilshire Boulevard that felt like a slot canyon amid all the office towers, and parked in the garage under O'Dowd's building.

When he stepped off the elevator and walked around to her office, the sign on the door with her name was gone. Slater pushed it open and stepped inside. The office looked bigger, with a doorway into another room, and different furniture. Sitting at a desk just inside was a guy with blond hair and dark roots, staring at a computer screen. Fuckable, he decided, but that hair. It was how people looked in the white part of Orange County.

As he stepped in, the guy looked up, his eyes flicking over him. "Can I help you?"

Slater stood in front of his desk. "Where's the lawyer?"

"Who are you?"

"The fuck do you care, Newport? I'm not here for you."

"There's no lawyers here. *No hay abogado.*"

"You're seriously going to patronize me like I just crossed the border, you racist fuck?" Reaching for a stack of file folders on the desk, he pushed them off the edge. They landed with a slap as paper splayed in an arc on the carpet.

The guy rolled his chair backward. "What the hell?" He was red-faced now. "Get the fuck out of my office."

Slater's instinct was to step around and punch him in the face, and it took everything he had to hold back. "You need to take a long hard look at yourself in the mirror, and fess up." He jabbed a finger at him. "You are the problem. Admit it to yourself." And louder, "It's you."

Walking out into the hall, Slater looked around. Maybe he was on the wrong floor. Once you got past ten or twelve all the numbers started to feel the same. It would be in the contact details he had for O'Dowd, but before he bothered to check, he stepped into the stairwell and hustled up to the next floor, and pulled open the door marked 25. The hallway here looked exactly the same, except there was a door with a plaque that bore O'Dowd's name followed by ESQ. He rapped on it with a knuckle and stepped inside.

The small office had paper piled everywhere, and behind the desk and the stacks on it sat O'Dowd. In her forties, at least, she had her Black hair styled in shaggy twists, most of it pulled back with a clip. Dressed in a cable-knit sweater, she greeted him and waved at the lone chair that wasn't piled with file folders and binders.

"Why are accountants always so messy?" Slater said.

She frowned, watching him sit. "I'm not messy. I know where everything is. Except your expense reports." She raised her eyebrows. "Because you never send them to me."

"I'm actually working on those. Right now I need to buy a piece of land. I printed out the details." He flipped open his satchel, and dug out the sheaf of paper, and handed it to her across the desk.

"I don't really do real estate stuff." She took the pages and leafed through them.

"But you can, can't you?" Slater said. "It's a simple transaction. The land description is there, and the name of the current owner. At the moment he's incarcerated at the federal prison in Downtown." Pulling out the five racks, he set them on the desk.

Her brow furrowed as she stared at the bundles. "And you want to pay cash."

"That's fifty grand."

"Oh, Slater."

"I figured you could lawyer it into his bank account. It's clean lettuce. From legitimate income."

"Not that you keep track of that for your tax preparer." She sighed. "Do you know how risky it is to have this sitting around?"

"So put it in a bank. I know you can do this."

"Has this jailbird agreed to the sale?"

"We worked it out this morning," Slater said.

O'Dowd pursed her lips for a moment. "It's going to cost you."

"I wouldn't have it any other way," he said, and got up.

TWO

ONCE SLATER WAS BACK at his office, he nosed the Continental into the surface lot and parked next to a little red Prius. That belonged to Etta, one of their operatives. He hustled across the street in a break in the traffic, and when he got upstairs, found Etta parked at the front desk. She'd turned Rey Pascual around to watch her work. Curvy, she kept her dark hair short, today wearing a vest over a plaid shirt. She greeted him as he stepped in.

"Isn't it a school day?" Slater said.

"I'm on winter break."

"You really do get to phone it in with that job."

"I actually earn the downtime." She raised her eyebrows. "Ten minutes in the classroom with middle-schoolers is equivalent to an hour of hard physical labor."

"I've got a new client meeting," Slater said. "You can sit in if you want."

"Tempting, but I'm supposed to talk to Max once he gets here. I might eavesdrop if you leave your door ajar."

In his office Slater sat behind his desk. Etta was learning the trade, and had a knack for it, and over time they were building trust. She worked a lot more for Max than for him, but not enough to give up her full-time job.

He started to sort through the pile of mail on his desk and soon heard a knock at the door. As he got up, he heard Etta pull it open and greet the guy. Pushing forty, maybe, he looked tired, his dark hair in a side part and cut short. Built thin, he was wearing a blue-gray dress shirt and tan chinos. Basically fuckable, Slater decided.

"Are you Clyde?"

He grinned. "You must be Ibáñez."

"Come in." Slater held his office door and let him step past, then left it open a few inches.

Clyde took the guest chair. "I thought I had the wrong building at first. It's all clothing businesses."

"It's like camouflage," Slater said, dropping into his chair and scooting up to the desk. "In this business we don't really want to stand out. Plus the rent is half what it would be over on Fig. So how do you know Woody?"

"I don't know him well. I've talked to him at my buildings. I know he performs at Greenleaf."

"Have you heard him sing? He's seriously talented."

"I'll have to go over there when he's working,"

Clyde said.

"He told me you owned the building where Sackett's and Greenleaf are."

"I don't actually own it. I take care of it and several other adjacent buildings. They're all historic structures."

"What do you mean, you take care of them?"

"I act as the landlord," Clyde said, holding his gaze. "Technically it's property management."

"So what do you want me to do?"

"Woody said you know how to look into things. Investigations, like it says on your door. One of my tenants is causing some trouble."

The guy was trying to project something like sincerity, or gravity, Slater saw, watching him talk. It might be authentic, but the heavier the sales job, the more likely it was jive.

Slater waved a hand. "What kind of trouble?"

"I'm not exactly sure, but I think she's stealing from some of the other tenants. I have a whole string of jewelry businesses in those buildings."

"Is that still the Jewelry District?"

"Totally. I have retailers on the street level, but also jewelers on the underground levels." He raised his eyebrows. "I don't have any solid evidence. But I know she's up to something."

"Tell me about this person."

"Her name is Les James."

Slater sat up and furrowed his brow to mask any reaction, any sign of recognition. He pulled open a drawer and took out a yellow notepad and a pen. Les James ran the nightclub where Woody performed, and Slater knew her. But this guy didn't need to know that.

"What have you seen her do that makes you suspicious?"

"Well," Clyde said, "she shouldn't have keys to access the floors where the jewelers work, but she does. I've seen her walking those halls."

"Did you confront her about that?"

"I wasn't sure if one of my people had given her keys. Later I found out they hadn't."

"Was this in the same building as her nightclub?"

"In the one next to it. But the buildings are connected internally in several places. From her building there's a connecting door on the floor below the nightclub."

"That would be the upstairs dining room at Sackett's," Slater said. "With the low ceiling."

"You've been there."

"My parents used to take me to Sackett's for lunch on Saturdays. We'd sit in the faux forest dining room downstairs."

"Apparently it hasn't changed in over a century."

"You don't mess with a classic."

Clyde grinned and held his gaze. "It sounds like you're a man who knows what he likes."

The guy was totally flirting with him, Slater realized, and sat back. "You're not shy."

"Woody said you were a man's man."

"Let's focus on the work. I'll need two grand to get started. We'll reassess in a few days."

Leaning back, Clyde dug in his pants pocket. "I assumed you'd want cash." He riffled through his wad and set a stack of C-notes on the desktop.

Slater scooped it up and folded it in half, not bothering to count it, and stuffed it in his jeans.

"I'll also need a written contract," Clyde said.

"Of course." Rising, Slater stepped to the door and pulled it open. "Can you bring in a printout of contract B?"

Etta swiveled in her chair and frowned at him. "B like bravo?"

"That's the one." He pulled the door closed and sat down again. "Tell me what else you've seen Les James doing that makes you suspicious."

"Some of the other tenants have mentioned that they see her hanging around," Clyde said. "That makes them nervous."

"Nobody's called the cops?"

"There's been no reason to. Not yet. Maybe you can find grounds to do that."

"Have you talked to her about any of this?"

"We discuss the rent, and routine maintenance. I never told her I thought she was a thief."

Etta knocked and then opened the door. "Unfortunately I'm having printer trouble."

"Rats." Slater looked to Clyde. "We'll figure it out, and get you a copy later."

As Etta pulled the door closed, he grabbed the pen and wrote on the pad:

Les James
Greenleaf
jewelers

"What's your last name, Clyde?"

"Park."

Slater wrote that at the top of the sheet and glanced up. "Like half the people in South Korea."

"It's actually more like twenty percent."

"That's still a lot of fricking Parks."

Clyde chuckled. "Not that it matters."

"What's your number?"

As he recited it, Slater tapped it into his phone, then texted him back with his name. A moment later he heard a muffled chime from Clyde's pants, and he dug it out and glanced at the screen.

"I've got yours now too."

"You need to show me around the place," Slater said. "Those hallways you talked about. And point out exactly what you've seen going on."

"I'll be in my office tomorrow." He told him how to find it, then rose.

"I'll come by in the morning."

Clyde held his gaze and spoke intently. "It's such a relief, knowing you'll be there. Knowing you can help me. I'd be lost without you."

Slater furrowed his brow. The guy was overselling it. "I'll do what I can."

Following Clyde out to the front door, he bolted it behind him. Etta waited a moment and then spoke in a low voice.

"You knucklehead. I'm not your damn secretary."

"I needed to look like I know what I'm doing. I knew you'd figure it out."

Keys rattled in the lock, and a moment later Max stepped in and greeted them. Burly and with mousy brown hair, today he was wearing his gray grid-pattern suit, his shirt collar open, the butt of his sidearm bulging under his jacket. He had a permit for it—unlike Slater, he was a licensed PI.

"This one basically just introduced me to a client as his secretary," Etta said.

"It was an on-the-fly type deal," Slater said. "I told her to print out contract B, and she knew exactly how to handle it." He eyed Etta. "Like a total *chingona*. She came in and explained to the client that there was a printer jam, and we'd get to it later."

Max furrowed his brow. "What's a *chingona*?"

"A badass." Slater threw up a hand. "A boss."

"What's contract B?" Max said.

Etta frowned. "Such a good question, Slater. What's contract B?"

"B for bullshit," he said. "A fictional document that precisely illustrates my point. You knew how to deal with it. You greased the wheels with the client, and helped me stall him, and didn't ask any dumb questions, like 'What's contract B?'"

"It probably doesn't sound like it," Max said, "but I think he's complimenting you on your skills here."

"I guess I'll take it, begrudgingly," Etta said. "Since you recognize the undeniable truth that I'm a badass."

Max waved a hand. "Or you could just take it without the grudge. You already know how to handle this guy. Use that."

Slater frowned. "What are you talking about? Nobody handles me. I don't need to be handled. Are you two saps ganging up on me?"

"It's just a figure of speech, buddy," Max said.

He scoffed. "The client wanted me to set up a contract. Do you do those on your window-shade jobs?"

"Office types ask for that sometimes," Max said. "I think having paperwork makes it more real for them. In my mind there's no great risk to signing one.

Most people don't want their confidential stuff publicized. Shady affairs and spying on their spouses and pending divorces. So even if they decide you broke the contract, they're never going to sue you and drag it into open court."

"That rings true. Do you have a document like that?"

Max nodded. "It's all legalese boilerplate. It's even on the letterhead. I'll email you a copy. From now on we'll call it contract B."

"All right. I'm out." Slater looked to Etta and raised his eyebrows. "Hold my calls."

She threw up her hands. "You just don't know when to quit."

His phone had buzzed in his pants a minute ago, and he pulled it out to check it on the way down to the street. It was a text from Reddy Kilowatt, the name he'd put in his contact list for Pike when they'd first met:

Still Downtown? Want to hit that brewpub on Grand?

Slater texted back:

On my way there, mi vida.

He drove the few blocks and found an open meter on the cross street, nosing into the space and then walking back to the brewpub. There was no sign of Pike inside, and no open booths. He went back out to the sidewalk to wait.

A minute later Pike stepped up, still dressed for the office in a creamy white shirt and tan chinos.

"Do you even know you're doing that?" Pike demanded.

"What are you talking about?"

"Standing there with your palm at your crotch. Like you're armed. Scanning the street like any second you're going to draw down on somebody."

"I'm not armed, officer."

"It doesn't matter," Pike said. "It's fricking hot." He mashed their mouths together for a moment, then under his breath, "With that dick swagger you look like a damn bandito."

"I'm not out here to merc anybody. The swagger is all for you, petal."

They went inside, and the host sent them to a booth that had opened up. The server approached and said, "What'll it be, boys?"

Pike set the menu down. "A small of the lager."

"Same for me," Slater said. "What's vegan?"

"Everything. We're fully plant-based now."

"That's great news. Burger me."

"The chili," Pike said.

Once she'd left, Slater eyed him. "Did you get anything useful from my prison visit?"

"I'm not sure yet. I only listened to it briefly."

"Lenny wanted your alter ego to point out to the prosecutors that he wasn't involved in manufacturing."

"I heard," Pike said. "That charge might get dropped later. For now it's a way to pressure him to be a witness. I'm glad you nudged him to do that. It would make his life a lot easier."

"Maybe a decent lawyer will point that out too."

"Were you serious about buying his land?"

"I've already set it in motion."

Pike laughed. "What do you want with twenty acres of empty desert?"

"It's beautiful, and it's pristine. Your people did retrieve all the bodies, didn't they? There's no clumps of gore left lying around?"

"Memo had them wrapped in canvas tarps and sisal rope. There's nothing left in that arroyo but sand and gravel."

"He didn't use plastic?" Slater said. "Maybe Memo's an environmentalist."

"I assume he used natural materials to promote decomposition."

Slater paused while the server set down their beer glasses. "Did you put the gravel back, at least?"

"I wasn't there." Pike tapped his glass to Slater's and took a sip. "It looked pretty level in the photos I saw. You might have to shovel some earth."

"Not anytime soon. I got a gig today." He told him about meeting Clyde.

After they'd eaten, Slater walked back to his car, and drove to his house, just a few minutes from Downtown. Pike had beaten him here, as his hooptie was already parked on the street. Nosing into the garage, he waited for the door to roll down, then headed up the stairs.

The bedrooms were above the garage, and on the floor above those was the kitchen and living space. It was a lot of house, a new construction in an old neighborhood, built by some idiot gentrifiers, but he needed it. He'd connected with Pike out in New Mexico and bought the house when Pike had started coming to stay. He needed the space for their narrative complex to unfold. It had been a good call— eventually Pike had moved here permanently, with all his clothes and his car and his job.

When he got up to the top floor, he walked through the kitchen into the big empty room. Some lounge furniture was clustered in a corner near the French doors onto the deck. He found Pike stretched out on the sofa.

"Do you want a belt?" Slater said.

Pike grinned. "Set me up."

Under his booze rules, that meant he could pour the good stuff, Pike's scotch, and leave the cheapo rotgut bourbon for when he was drinking alone. Walking back to the kitchen, he poured his ration into a tumbler, and one for Pike, and carried them to the sofa.

Pike sat up and took the glass, and Slater sat next to him, and clinked his on Pike's. Taking a slurp, Pike winced with the intensity of it.

"I love that burn."

"I love watching it hit you." Slater sipped at his own. It really was the good stuff, nutty and woody and smooth.

He leaned over to untie his boots and pull them off, then put his feet on the patch of faux Bermuda grass under the coffee table. It felt almost like real grass, except for the temperature.

"So I think the raccoons got into the trash bins," Pike said, sitting back.

"Seriously? How would they get them open?"

"They're smart. They were rooting around in the compost."

"I know there's one around. I've seen the scat."

"There's actually five of them. Tilly across the street sent me a video from her doorbell camera. In the middle of the night these five little fur balls waddle past her front door. She figures they must be siblings."

"I guess I should be glad you're making nice with the neighbors," Slater said, "so that I don't have to."

Pike chuckled. "It's not like we hold meetings or gossip over coffee. We just chat on that neighborhood app."

"There's an app for the neighborhood?"

"For every neighborhood."

"And here I thought I'd heard all the bad news there was for the day."

He gestured with his glass. "I'm not even going to tell you what Tilly said about your side yard."

"And lo, god shows me his *rachmones*," Slater said. "Do you want to read to me?"

Pike picked up the book they were reading, a modern translation of the *Theogony*. He didn't really care about classical Greece, but Pike had been reading a primer about the mythology when they'd met, and it had become their thing.

Shifting back to lean against him, he got comfortable, and Pike draped his arm around his chest.

"Where were we?"

"Reading about Nyx and her offspring," Pike said.

"Who's she again?"

"Nyx is the night. Daughter of Chaos."

"That's a logical combination." Slater slurped at his tumbler. "Fricking night. It's always night nowadays. The sun barely makes it above the horizon. No wonder the raccoons are running wild."

"Nyx is a hard-ass. In the *Iliad* even Zeus is afraid of her." He read from the book: "The home of Nyx is enveloped in dark clouds. It stands near the entrance to the underworld, and the abodes of Hypnos and Thanatos are nearby."

"Who are those saps?"

"Her sons, Sleep and Death."

"That must be quite the neighborhood."

"At the end of each day," Pike read, "Nyx prepares her chariot. Clad in a black robe, she drives its pair of horses across the sky, accompanied on her journey by the stars."

Sometime later he stirred as Pike set the book on the coffee table. "Was I out?"

"Hypnos got hold of you," Pike said. "So I'm going out of town tomorrow. Just overnight. I need to do some interviews."

Slater sat up to look him in the eye. "Are you going with Davis?"

"He's not trying to get with me. You need to smash that."

"He knows he wants to fuck you, and I know he wants to fuck you. I just can't understand why you don't see it."

"I don't see it because there's nothing to see."

"You say that now," Slater said, "but it starts with a work trip, and then you're playing tennis together, and then you're staying at his house. You buy a pair of French bulldog puppies, and matching sweaters, yours in blue, and you just know that rat-fuck sicko will want the same one in green. And he makes you laugh, and you're drinking lattes, and you wash your cars together on Saturday." He threw up a hand. "And meanwhile I'm tits-up on the pavement, tire tread marks all over me, trying to figure out what the hell I did wrong."

Pike massaged the back of his neck. "Where is this coming from? You want to get a dog? Is that what this is about?"

He dropped his chin, relishing the feeling of Pike's fingers. "Why would I want a dog?"

"I'm with you, and only you. You see that, don't you? I live here, and my stuff is here. I'm not going anywhere."

"I want to believe that."

"Belief is for stuff that has no evidence," Pike said. "Spread before you is a ton of evidence about me and what I want. It's as clear as Nyx and the stars crossing the sky."

He met his gaze. "It's actually hard to see her. Apparently she wears a lot of black."

Pike chuckled and got up, pushing him flat on his back, and climbed on top of him. It felt good, the weight of his body compressing him. Pike had intuitively figured out at some point that it tended to chill him out. Closing his eyes, he savored the sensation, the heat of Pike's body, the beating of his heart, his breath on his neck.

"Somebody's getting a stiffy," Pike said.

"How could I not? It's your messed-up pheromones. I'm totally in your thrall."

He mouthed his neck. "Want to fuck me?"

Grabbing his neck, Slater met his mouth, warm and firm and perfect. Eventually Pike got up, and he followed him downstairs. The bedroom at the back was quieter, and it had a bed in it, along with Pike's desk for when he worked remote, but they slept in the one facing the street.

Pike unbuttoned his shirt and dropped his trousers.

Once Slater was undressed, he pushed him back onto the bed, and climbed on top of him, and ground his woody into his thigh, mouthing his jaw and his face.

Reaching for the bedside table, he scrabbled in the drawer for lube, then positioned himself between Pike's knees and pressed into him. Pike winced as he got into it, and bit his lip. Shifting closer, Slater started thrusting deeper, then leaned over him, mauling his neck and his face. He built up the pace, pounding him for a minute, then grunted as he came. He lowered his weight onto him as he caught his breath, and eventually pulled up.

"Stay there." Pike grabbed his own cock, but Slater pushed his hand off and stroked him, slowly at first, building up speed, still pressing into him. Pike's face contorted as he climaxed, and Slater lowered himself onto his body again, relishing the intense heat, both of them still breathing hard. This moment, the satiety, didn't persist for very long, but it felt great.

THREE

MUTED DAYLIGHT FILTERED IN through the sheers as Slater woke, gradually swimming up to full consciousness. Pike was already gone. Eventually he got up and got dressed, in yesterday's jeans and a dark collared shirt.

Upstairs he found lukewarm coffee in the pot, and slurped down half a mugful, and grabbed a bagel, not bothering to toast it. He chewed on it on the way down to the garage.

He held the bagel in his teeth as he backed the Continental into the street, one hand on the wheel and the other on the seat back so he could see where he was going. As he popped the transmission into Drive and waited for the door to roll down, a woman walking up the street waved to him. That was Tilly, the neighbor, wearing a purple windbreaker even though it wasn't windy. Of course he'd look like a damn dog with a chew toy when he ran into her. He raised a palm in greeting and pulled the bagel out of his mouth. It didn't really matter—she already thought he was crazy.

Once the garage door was down, he drove to Glendale and parked in front of Svetlana's building. The growth of the ivy that mostly covered it had slowed down for winter, but it was still green, and the trees were filling in nicely. The goal had been to disguise the structure's shabbiness and decay, to get the city off her back about glowing it up. The sag in the roofline was still visible, and the steel-barred front door was still grungy, but overall the plantings had worked.

Slater walked around to the alley and looked up into the camera next to the back door. Svetlana's facial recognition system knew him, and the door lock quickly snapped open. Stepping into the antechamber, he waited for the machinery to do its thing. The scan for weapons was automated, but it took a minute longer to sniff for explosives, and he could hear the little fan pulling air across the sensors. Eventually the lock clicked open, and he stepped into the workshop.

Lining the sides of the room was a workbench, piled with plastic components and wire and circuit boards, and punctuated with stools and a few computer monitors. The place always smelled like solder and hot machine oil.

Svetlana walked toward him from the far end of the room. Curvy, she had her hair tied back, today wearing a dress in a bright-orange print.

"Do you know what egress means?" she said, and waved an arm.

"That's a lawyer type word. Is it about fire exits?"

"Exactly," she said, her Slavic accent flattening the vowels. "The fire department inspector insists that I have a point of egress in the front of this building."

"On the street side?" he said. "There's already a door there."

"It doesn't open. Now I have to turn it into one of these."

She gestured to the new crash door she'd put in the back wall, complete with a lighted exit sign and sensors wired into a little gray box. That was probably an alarm. There was a bulbous gray canister mounted above it.

"That looks the same as the ones you put on my garage door," Slater said. "You're prepared for break-ins."

"It's tear gas, the same as yours. Anyone who breaks in will need to wash their eyes before they can rob me. I didn't want to use knockout gas because I'm often working in this room. As far as the fire department is concerned, that canister is a fire-suppressing chemical connected to a heat sensor, not a break-in sensor."

"At least you have a starting point out front. There's already a door there."

"It's harassment." She raised her eyebrows. "I think the city doesn't like my business. They want to make me as uncomfortable as possible."

"Lots of jurisdictions would be fine with what you do. Some of those industrial warehouse towns are like the wild West."

"Such an elegant solution." She gestured to the vast room. "If you have some extra cardboard boxes, perhaps you could help me move."

He chuckled. "I get it. That would take a lot of effort."

"So what can I do for you today?"

"I need an audio bug that I can leave in somebody's office. You once sold me a calculator that had a mic in it."

"I have more of these." Svetlana walked to the side door and unlocked it by tapping her wrist on the reader. "You need just one?"

"Two, if you've got them."

She returned a minute later with the little devices and handed him one. It looked like a cheap desktop calculator, but thicker, and it was heavy. That was about the battery, he knew. When he tapped the buttons, the gray display flickered.

"It actually works as a calculator," he said.

"That makes it unlikely anyone will question its purpose. It's also unlikely to be thrown away. People don't tend to trash a device that is functioning. If you don't want it cluttering your desk, you'd toss it on a shelf or in a drawer."

"That's probably what I would do."

"Here is the power switch," she said, and pointed it out. "It should function for about a week. It communicates through the cell network."

Taking it back, she heaved herself onto the stool in front of her computer monitor, then scanned the bar code label on the back of the calculator with a wand tipped with a glowing red point. Next she tapped at the keyboard and peeled off the label. She did the same with the second one, then swiveled around and handed them to him.

"Both are connected to your account."

"What do I owe you?" Slater said.

"Two fifty each. For a good customer, two for four dollars."

Digging out his wad, he peeled off the C-notes and handed them over. "Good luck with the front door."

Svetlana tucked the cash into her bra and waved a hand. "I know that in the general picture, it's a detail. We must all compromise to live in this society."

It was interesting to hear her say that, given her business model, he thought, as he walked out and around to the street. So much of what she did and made, so many of the services she sold were totally on the down-low, and totally illegal.

Exiting the freeway into Downtown, he headed toward Broadway, and nosed into the parking structure across the street from Greenleaf. The ramp up was narrow because it was old, built sometime between the days when cars were a new technology and when they got huge in the 1950s. The outside of the building was clad in decorated terra-cotta and glass windows to make it look like an office block, but above street level all that was inside was six floors of parked cars.

Svetlana's calculators were too big to put in the pockets of his jeans, so he grabbed his canvas satchel from the back seat, and tucked them inside, and folded the flap closed. Climbing out, he looped the strap of the satchel over his opposite shoulder and shifted the bag around to his back.

Clyde had said his office was two doors down from Greenleaf, and once he was across the street, Slater saw that he meant it was two buildings down. At street level there were several shops in each one, and he walked past half a dozen before he found the doorway between them, marked only with the street number.

The door was locked, and on the intercom box he pressed the button labeled MANAGEMENT. A moment later the lock buzzed open, and he stepped inside. It was a little unstaffed lobby with some mailboxes, and a set of stairs leading up, and a century-old elevator like the one in his building. Those things were slow, and it was only a couple of flights up to Clyde's office, so he started up the stairs.

On the second landing a guy carrying a bicycle appeared above him and called, "Make way."

Slater scowled and stepped to the wall to let him pass. Wearing cycling shorts and an athletic top, he had his black Latin hair slicked back. A little skinny, but fuckable, he decided.

"Is that a fixie?" Slater said as he carried it past.

"It's got disc brakes. That's a new innovation since the nineteenth century." As he turned to descend the next set of steps, he bumped Slater's shin with his back tire.

"Watch it," Slater snapped.

"I told you to get out of the way, *paisa.*"

Stepping after him, Slater grabbed the collar of his shirt. The fabric was surprisingly stretchy, but yanking on it stopped him, and he pulled him backward. The guy dropped the bike, and it clattered against the railing.

"Let go of me." He spun around, lifting his arm in front of his face.

Slater shoved it aside and slapped him hard, left and right, a firm kovac. "Why do you make me do this to you?"

"Knock it off," he shouted, and stumbled down a few steps. "What is wrong with you?"

Lunging at him again, Slater shouted, "Why do you do it?"

The guy ducked and dragged his bike down a few steps, then looked back at him, his face red and contorted, shocked and angry that anyone would push back on the smack talk.

"Keep walking," Slater said through his teeth, "or I will crack you open." He watched as the guy hauled the bike around the landing and disappeared. "Stupe," he muttered, and resumed his ascent. He stepped into the hallway several flights up and found the door marked MANAGEMENT. Rapping on it, he pushed it open.

Clyde was sitting behind a cluttered desk, a long row of file cabinets along one side of the room and a credenza behind him. The furniture was utilitarian painted steel, just the basics, with no bougie finishes, all of it parked on well-worn linoleum.

"There's no windows in here," Slater said.

Dressed like he had been yesterday, in a light-blue dress shirt and chinos, Clyde smiled as he stood up. "Windows are for the revenue-generating suites. Let me show you around."

He'd planned to plant one of the calculator bugs here, but he wasn't going to get the opportunity, as Clyde waved him into the hall and pulled the door closed.

"I manage five buildings here. They're all contiguous."

Slater walked abreast as they headed up the hall. "Are they owned by the same people?"

"There's several different owners, but I manage them jointly. Most of them were built around 1910, but farther up the block a couple date to a little later."

He stopped at the end of the hall next to the stairs. A steel door ended the hallway, painted the same tan shade as the walls. It had lock hardware but no crash bar. It wasn't a way out—the exit sign above it pointed into the adjacent stairwell. Clyde dug out a key ring, and unlocked the door, then stepped through. The hallway continued beyond it.

"See how the paint looks different?" Clyde said. "This is a different building."

There was another stairwell right inside, he saw, just a few feet from the one he'd walked up. This one had an exit sign above it too.

"Is it odd that there's two sets of stairs so close together?" Slater said.

"Not really. When these buildings were put up, there was no door here, so each building had its own stairs." He pulled the door closed and motioned for Slater to walk with him.

"These are all offices?" he said, gesturing to one of the doorways spaced along the hall. They had suite numbers but no other signage.

"Small businesses," Clyde said.

"They're not customer-facing if they don't have their names on the door."

"Retail is on the ground floor. Some of these suites are used as storage space for those."

At the end of the corridor Clyde led him into a stairwell and descended several flights.

"This is the ground floor," he said. "The street is that way, but we won't walk through because it's a jewelry store. This way is the alley." Clyde walked down a side hallway and pushed on the crash bar of the door at the end. Slater followed him outside. The alley was narrow and dark, a slot amid the high-rises lining both sides.

"It must be gated at the ends," Slater said. "There's no tents or trash."

"That way is a dead end, but yeah, the other end is gated."

Dumpsters were parked tight to the buildings along the block, leaving just enough room for a vehicle to maneuver through. He stepped into the middle of the alley and looked up at Clyde's buildings. Most of the back doors were at street level, but behind one of the dumpsters he could see a flight of concrete steps leading down.

"The alley isn't used for much," Clyde said. "Furniture deliveries sometimes. The storefronts just use street delivery for their stock."

He opened the crash door, and waited for Slater to step inside, then pulled it closed. Back in the main hallway, he went to a stairwell that led below street level, and Slater followed him down. Clyde opened the fire door at the bottom with a key on his ring.

"Are there more offices down here?"

"Offices and workshops," he said. "The jewelers are happy that there's no windows. It makes for better security. Even so, it's not that secure. There are under-street delivery tunnels on this level."

"I've heard of those. Are they still used for any-thing?"

"They're abandoned."

As they walked past an open doorway, Slater glanced inside. The space was lit by old fluorescent tube fixtures, and a guy with gray hair was leaning over a worktable littered with tools, peering at some-thing out of view.

"Is this where you've seen Les James?" Slater said.

"Here, and on the floor where my office is." Clyde lowered his voice. "I need to know what she's moving around."

"You've seen her carrying stuff?"

"Canvas bags. About this big." He held his hands a foot apart, then waved Slater into another stairwell, and climbed back up to street level.

They walked down a narrow hallway to a door onto the sidewalk. The midday sun was on the buildings opposite, not quite managing to reach the pavement. Clyde gestured toward the corner where Sackett's was, and they walked abreast, and went into the cafeteria.

The place had been renovated, and the food looked to be more upscale than steam-table fare now, but it was still about loading trays. Clyde led him into the dining room, busy with the lunch crowd. Sur-rounding the tables were faux trees and foliage with taxidermy bears and badgers and raccoons. These conifers would never grow together in the real world. He hadn't known that as a child. Back then the room had felt magical, a little patch of lush wilderness in the heart of the city.

He followed Clyde to the stairs that led up to

another dining room. Fewer people were eating at the tables up here. The overflow for busy times, this space was functional and undecorated, with a drop ceiling like in an office. From here another staircase led up to the nightclub, Greenleaf. A chain across the stairs bore a metal sign that said CLOSED.

Clyde walked past the stairs to a door in the side wall. Painted the same flat beige as the walls, it wasn't marked as an exit or in any other way. It wasn't exactly hidden, but it was definitely easy to overlook. Digging out his key ring, Clyde unlocked it and twisted the handle.

It was another connecting door, opening into a long hallway. Once they'd stepped through, he locked it behind them and spoke in a low voice.

"This is a different building from Sackett's and Greenleaf. I've seen Les in here too."

"So she has a key to this door."

Clyde raised his eyebrows. "I didn't give her one."

He followed him down the hall, and up a flight of stairs, and through another locked door.

"This is a different building again," Slater said.

"Correct. My office is one flight up."

At the end of the hall he stepped into the stair-well, and they trudged down three flights. A sign said this was street level, and Clyde stepped into a short hallway, and unlocked a door at the end of it.

"You have to see this," he said as he stepped through and flicked on a light switch.

FOUR

T WAS A BIG empty room, Slater saw, following Clyde in. A long counter ran along the back wall, and the side where the street had to be was lined with raw wood framing backed by plywood, like the temporary construction they put over broken windows. The carpet had a dark blue and green pattern in it, stained and dusty with age.

"It looks like a hotel lobby," Slater said.

"It was. The hotel closed thirty years ago. I'm on the verge of renovating it."

Slater walked into the middle of the space and looked around. There was no furniture, and it hadn't been cleaned in a while, but it hadn't been squatted in or stripped for parts or vandalized either. The counter at the back was fronted by dark mahogany.

"Why is there no entrance from the street?"

"There used to be." Clyde gestured to the wall of unfinished plywood. "There's shops on the other side of that right now. We'll have to shut them down to regain street frontage."

"You're renovating it for the owners?"

"I partnered with the owners. We've got everything lined up. I just need to get the financing sorted out and we'll start work."

Watching him talk, Slater realized that he might have underestimated the guy. He'd assumed he was a nickel rat, but this made it sound like he had more going on.

"Are you going to open it as a hotel again?"

"That's the plan." Clyde crossed to the far side of the room and gestured to the wall. "Check this out."

A big patch of wallboard had been broken open and torn away, he saw, leaving some chalky debris and revealing a redbrick wall. It was odd, he decided. The bricks went up eight feet or so, and above them was a wooden beam. At the sides too, where the wallboard had been pulled off, the bricks ended at wooden posts. Unlike construction framing, they were polished and finished in a dark varnish.

"It looks like somebody bricked up a doorway," Slater said.

"That's exactly what happened."

"Is this an exterior wall?"

"The answer to that is yes and no."

Slater glared at him. "The fuck does that mean?"

He chuckled. "It's the end of this building. The owner of the land next door built a wing of the hotel a few years after this main part opened. They just tacked it on. It was small, so he didn't build stairs or an elevator on his property. The only way into his wing was through the main part of the hotel. It worked fine for a while, but then the pair of them had a disagreement. The owner of this building sealed it off, like this, with bricks." Clyde slapped them with his palm. "They did it on every floor. The wing on the other side of this hasn't been used since."

"Ouch. When did that happen?"

"In 1938."

"Seriously?" Slater demanded.

"The hotel operated for fifty years longer, but they never worked it out. Today both parts have new owners. They've agreed to collaborate on the renovation, so we're going to knock out all the bricks and open up the sealed wing."

"That's a crazy story."

He shrugged. "People can be petty."

Slater eyed the brick wall. "Looking at this, I'd say people can be fricking psycho."

Waving for him to follow, Clyde crossed to the door they'd come in, and killed the lights, and locked it once they were in the hallway. He started up the adjacent stairs.

"I hope I'm not wearing you out," he called back.

Slater looked up, admiring his athletic glutes. "It takes a lot of steps to get around here, considering the footprint of your buildings can't be that extensive."

"It's about half a city block."

He lost count of how many flights they ascended, at least five or six, until Clyde pushed open the door on the last landing. They stepped out into the daylight. This was the roof. It wasn't high enough for much of a view, and the buildings on either side were four or five floors taller, making it feel like a sheltered space.

The surface was sealed with that rubbery white stuff they used everywhere now. A couple of steel patio chairs and a table were set out next to one of the ancient skylights, a peaked metal frame with frosted glass panels embedded with wire mesh. Next to them were two narrow planter boxes and a tangle of dead foliage.

Breathing hard from the climb, Slater gestured to the boxes. "Was this you?"

"It's one of the tenants on the top floor. 604." He nodded to the patio table. "She eats her lunch up here. In summer those were blooming a lot. I think they were chrysanthemums."

"They're dahlias." Slater dropped to one knee next to the box and dug his fingers in the soil. The tubers were still here.

"How do you know that?" Clyde said. "There's no flowers, and everything's dead."

"Chrysanthemums have rounded leaves. These are pointed." He plucked a dry brown leaf and held it up.

Clyde furrowed his brow but didn't look closer. "They were pretty. Although 604 was the only one who got to enjoy them."

"If she did the work cultivating them, she earned it." He stood up and slapped the dust off his fingers against his jeans. "Dahlias are great. They come in tons of colors. They're a lot less work than chrysanthemums because they're perennial."

"I've heard that word."

"It means they come back after the winter. You

can just leave them in the ground."

"I hadn't pegged you for a flower guy."

"I trained in horticulture," Slater said. "That's just a ten-dollar word for gardening."

"That fits. I've never seen a non-Latin gardener in this town."

Slater scowled at him, but Clyde had already turned away to walk toward the stairwell. Slater followed him down.

"So how will you approach this?" Clyde said as they descended.

"I'll poke around, and talk to some people. You have to give me the keys to all these hallways and shared spaces."

"I can't do that. I can't have outsiders roaming around."

"You hired me to find out what's going on, man. I'm not going to rob the place. If any of your tenants ask, tell them I'm a plumber. Or tell them I'm working on getting better internet wired in. They'll be happy to hear it."

On the landing, Clyde stopped and turned back. Stepping close to him, he grasped his arms and leaned in to meet his lips. Slater flinched but went with it, and put his hands on the sides of Clyde's belt as he massaged his biceps. The guy was good at this, intent and firm and soft in the right ways. He could feel his dick tightening in his jeans.

Pulling back, Clyde nuzzled his neck, then nibbled his earlobe.

"Fresh," Slater murmured.

Eventually Clyde stepped back, and dropped his chin, and held his gaze. "Come downstairs."

They'd been on so many floors and doors and stairwells that Slater's reckoning was off. He thought the office was somewhere else, but here it was, with the MANAGEMENT sign on it. Clyde stepped behind his desk, and unlocked one of the file cabinets, and rolled out a drawer. Digging around, he produced a key ring and tossed it to him. Slater snagged it out of the air. It only had half a dozen keys on it.

"These fit all the doors between the buildings?"

"It should cover most of them," Clyde said. "Not the hotel lobby, but you won't need to go in there. Those will also open any of the doors from the street."

Slater tucked them into his front pocket and frowned. If the guy would sit that foxy caboose down for a minute, he could plant the calculator bug.

"You don't need to tell people you're a plumber," Clyde said. "You can say you're working for me. You're doing a structural inspection. That gives you a reason to be prowling."

"I'll check in later." He turned to leave.

"Ibáñez."

Slater turned back and raised his eyebrows.

"Don't make me regret giving you the keys to my kingdom."

He scoffed and walked out.

Once he'd descended the stairs to the little space with the mailboxes, he went out to the street and walked toward the hotel building. From the sidewalk there was no indication it had ever been a hotel, just a couple of storefronts with clothing and jewelry. These merchants were not going to be happy to get evicted to make the lobby accessible again.

Crossing Broadway, he paused on the sidewalk

to get a better look. He could see where the hotel building ended and the sealed wing started. The two adjoined, like all the buildings along the block, but they had different facing. The windows were at the same level but in a different style. There were just two shops on the street level of the sealed wing, a jeweler next to a quinceañera place.

Slater walked farther north. Andy's loft was several blocks up but not far enough to make it worth moving his car. He strode into the lobby of Andy's building, and went up to his floor, and knocked on his door.

When Andy pulled it open, he had a few days' stubble on his face, his shaggy brown hair looking wilder than usual. He was wearing boxers and a tank top, even though it was winter, revealing his wiry musculature.

Andy frowned at him. "You're supposed to text first."

"You're here, aren't you? I was in the neighborhood. It's work."

He waved him into the room, a studio loft with his bed and a kitchen counter and big tattersall windows that looked over the square. They'd left those for atmosphere when the building had been converted from its original incarnation as a textile warehouse.

Dropping into his gaming chair, Andy swiveled from his desk and its array of computer monitors.

"I mostly just … work here these days. I sleep at Kyle's pad."

"It's your pad too now." Slater raised his eyebrows. "You married that high-fructose cupcake."

"You make it sound like I've ... done something wrong."

"You don't need me to point that out. Did you know exposure to too much sugar can actually induce diabetes? That guy definitely gives me a toothache."

"Slater, why are you here?"

"Can you look into somebody for me? Her name is Les James. She runs a nightclub called Greenleaf. It's a few blocks down Broadway."

"Text me her name. What do you ... need to know?"

"The basics," Slater said, digging out his phone and tapping at it. "Is she a lowlife, arrests and convictions, who's sued her."

"I'll see what I can find out."

He sent him the text and tucked the phone away. "So am I still on the no-fly list?"

Andy's random muscle movements intensified a little. It was a side effect of his CP, a giveaway of his emotional state. "Every time you come in here, you ... hit on me."

"It used to work. Until you went on the cupcake diet."

"You have to go. I've got work to do."

Slater watched him for a moment. "Bye, beautiful."

Back on the street, he walked to the entrance to Sackett's, and into the dining room, through the faux spruces and pines. The crowd had thinned out as it was well past the lunch hour. He mounted the stairs to the upper dining room, and approached the staircase leading up, and stepped over the chain with the CLOSED sign.

He knew there was an elevator from street level

to Greenleaf, but he usually came up this way. The nightclub was a sprawling open room interrupted by regular columns. The bar ran the length of the far wall, finished in ornate dark wood. That had to be original. Near the stairs was the alcove with the bandstand, and facing it was an array of tables. Opposite the bar was a row of windows with arched tops that looked over Broadway, and in the middle of it all was a parquet floor for dancing.

As he strode in, the guy behind the bar stood erect and eyed him. He had his hair in a ponytail. It looked like he was mopping the floor.

"What's up?" he called.

Slater gestured to the swinging doors next to the bar marked STAFF ONLY. "I'm here to see Les."

It was pure bluster, and she might not even be here, but the guy didn't say anything and went back to mopping.

He pushed through the doors into a wide hallway. There was no decoration or pretense back here, with fluorescent lighting, and scuffed linoleum, and pale green walls that could use a coat of paint. The first entryway was on the same side as the bar, and it didn't have a door. It looked like the way into the kitchen. Farther along was a row of blue lockers, and past them one of the doors hung open. Slater stepped over to it.

It was a small office with no windows, like Clyde's but darker, and less cluttered. It had wainscotting in the same wood paneling that fronted the bar along with an incongruent dark-red carpet. Parked behind the desk was Les James, gazing at a laptop screen, her long dark hair tied back. She had to be pushing fifty.

Les looked up at him, not quite startled, but

clearly he'd interrupted her concentration.

"I know you," she said, "but the name escapes me."

"Slater Ibáñez. I come in here sometimes."

"You're a friend of Woody's."

"I'd say more like an acquaintance of Woody's."

She chuckled. "I've seen you in here. Sit down, if you want."

Slater pulled his bag off as he took one of the guest chairs. "I'm not interrupting your work?"

"You're absolutely interrupting my work. But I'm a sucker for distraction. How do you know Woody?"

"I met him in a thrift store, oddly enough."

"That guy is a pain sometimes, but he's talented."

"That voice."

Les raised her eyebrows. "Tell me about it."

"What kind of pain is he?"

With his satchel in his lap, Slater reached inside, and found one of the calculators. Feeling for the power switch, he clicked it on with a fingernail.

"He's got lots of ideas about how a nightclub should be run, even though that's not his job. Lately he seems to have chilled out a little. It feels like he's more focused on the music."

Slater knew why—he'd helped the guy claim a sizeable insurance payout. That meant Woody was a lot less concerned about money these days.

On the wall behind Les was an oversize painting, and Slater gestured to it with his free hand. "That's a dramatic scene."

As she turned to glance at it, he sat up and dropped the calculator on the carpet. It landed noiselessly, and he pushed it under the desk with the toe of his boot.

"That's Mount Ararat," Les said. "I wish I knew what it was worth. I paid enough for it." She raised her eyebrows. "So are you here for any specific purpose besides gossiping about my performers and admiring my wall art?"

"I'm told you've been having trouble with the jewelers."

"Woody said that?"

"I was chatting with some of your neighbors."

She suddenly looked tired. "Tell me you're not working for Woody."

"I'm working for Clyde Park. He has me doing some inspections."

"And that includes gossiping with his tenants?"

"You know how it goes," Slater said. "People like to talk."

"Do you drink?"

She rolled open a desk drawer, and pulled out a fifth, and set it on the desktop. It was bourbon, he saw, but he didn't know the label.

"I don't mind a belt once in a while."

"There's glasses on those shelves."

Rising, he stepped over to the wall. A quartet of lowball tumblers sat next to a row of binders. He grabbed a couple and set them on the desk. Lying in a tray in the desk drawer, still rolled open, he could see an ugly black handgun.

"Is that the nine mil?" he said. "Isn't that supposed to be in a gun safe?"

"I usually lock my desk."

She pushed the drawer closed, then poured a decent slug for each of them. Lifting one of the glasses, she tapped it on the other, and sat back and sipped at it, not waiting for him. Reaching for the other glass, Slater sat down and took a sip. It was absolutely delicious stuff. He closed his eyes for a moment to savor the heady flavors.

"It's such a bad habit for somebody who runs a bar," Les said.

"Day drinking?"

"Drinking period. Although, if I was going to develop a problem, it would have happened already, don't you think?"

"Personally I drink to make all this tolerable." Slater waved vaguely at the room.

"I hear you, brother." She chuckled. "Did somebody send you to talk to me? Woody or Clyde?"

He took another sip. "Negative. I'm just poking around. The guy behind the bar said you were back here."

"Well, the only conflicts I have are with people who work for me. Even then it's not really juicy. They say, 'Pay me more,' and I say no." She gestured with her glass. "Running this place feels like one of my floor show acts. This woman who juggles chainsaws. Three of them at a time."

"Yikes. That's hard-core."

"She's adorable. Wears a cute little dress. They're electric, so they're not as bulky or as heavy as the old-school ones. The downside is there's no point in having them running. It would be more engaging if you could hear the motors. Anyway, it's complicated, like my crazy life." She slammed the contents of her glass and set it down. "You don't need to be listening to gossip, and I don't need to explain myself to you. But I will say, I'm not really beefing with anyone." She raised her eyebrows. "And stay out of my business."

"Got it." Slater drained his glass and set it on the edge of the desk as he stood up. "I'm no connoisseur, but that was possibly the best bourbon I've ever had."

Les chuckled. "That's one of the perks of running a bar. You figure out what the good stuff is." She sat back and waved a hand. "Bring your friends around."

FIVE

WALKING OUT OF LES's office, Slater strode through the empty nightclub and headed for the stairs. He couldn't really just wander the halls and knock on doors, but he knew a guy who might know some of the jewelers.

Once he was out on the street, he walked up to Sixth, and into a jewelry store with brilliant white spotlights blazing down on the display cases, making everything sparkle and gleam. The armed guard at the door, a burly guy in a black jacket, gave him the once-over but didn't attempt to slow him down. It was a big place, with several vendors, and a woman behind one of the counters greeted him.

"I'm looking for Vahan," Slater said.

"I think he's in the back." She stepped over to the doorway and disappeared.

It was quiet in here. One of the other staffers was leaning on a counter, talking to the lone customer, a tray of rings between them, and another staffer stood at the far side of the room, his hands behind him, idly watching Slater.

A moment later the woman stepped out of the back, followed by Vahan. The guy had a beautiful big nose and dark coloring. A little chunky, he was wearing an ugly brown suit and had an awful haircut, neglected and covering his ears. You'd think his wife would make him cut it once in a while. His face cracked into a gummy smile of recognition, and Slater stepped over to him.

"You're looking good," Vahan said.

"You need a haircut."

He guffawed. "What can I do for you today?"

"Do you know other jewelers in the neighborhood? I need to meet some of the ones who work on Broadway. On the opposite side."

"Where Sackett's is? Sure, I know people over there."

"Can you introduce me to some of them?"

"What do I get out of it?"

Slater raised his eyebrows. "If you help me out, I won't call your wife and explain your sex life to her."

His eyes bright, he lowered his voice. "You come in here and threaten me? You're a damn hoodlum. You can suck my dick."

He jutted his chin. "Make me."

"Come in the back, and I will."

Slater waved a hand. "Bring it."

Vahan chuckled. "I wasn't sure that was going to work." He lifted the gate in the counter and led him into the narrow corridor.

The guy might not have been certain, but Slater knew it would play out exactly this way. Vahan stepped into a small office. There was no jewelry or tools in here, just a desk and a chair on the grimy linoleum, and piles of plastic binders and loose paper. He flipped the deadbolt, and as he turned to face him, Slater stepped close enough to make him flinch, and jutted his chin.

"What were you saying?"

He put a meaty paw on Slater's shoulder and pushed him down. Dropping to his knees, he could see the guy was already getting hard. Having the illusion of power over him was a turn-on.

Slater looked up at him and made his eyes wide. "Please don't make me."

Vahan cackled and grabbed the back of his head, pulling his face into his pants. "Suck my dick."

Zipping open his fly, Slater pulled out his junk and started to smoke him. As Vahan got into it, he ran a hand into his hair, thrusting into him.

"You filthy little slut," Vahan growled.

It didn't take him long to come, with a yelp, and he pushed him back. As Slater got to his feet, he saw that Vahan had a stupid grin on his face.

"I can't believe you blew me to get a couple of business introductions."

"I've done a lot more for a lot less."

He zipped up his fly and adjusted his crotch, breathing hard. "Give me a minute here."

Slater folded his arms. "Ticktock."

He laughed at that. "You're such a dick."

Flipping the bolt, he led him out into the store,

and said something to the woman at the counter in Armenian. He had no way to identify the language, but it was a reasonable assumption, as he knew Vahan was Armenian. He followed Slater out to the street and they walked toward Greenleaf.

"You want to meet the retailers, or the people in the back offices doing the manufacturing?"

"Whoever's around."

"Should I tell them how I know you?"

"As long as you're comfortable with me telling your wife how I know you."

Vahan laughed. "You're not that guy."

He didn't know him very well, Slater thought, eyeing him sidelong, but he didn't need to point that out.

"So what should I say?" Vahan said.

"I'm working for the building management. Doing some property inspections. I want to meet some of the people who work here so they won't think I'm a burglar."

"Is any of that true?"

"Actually it is." Slater pointed out the quinceañera store across the street. "Anywhere from here to the corner."

"There's lots of industry people in these buildings."

They crossed the street, and Vahan knew where the doors were, walking in between the shops. He leaned in to look at the intercom buttons.

"I have a key." Slater dug it out and tried a couple before he found the one that fit.

Inside, Vahan led the way down a flight, and into the hallway, and knocked on a door.

"Nobody here," he said finally.

Farther down the hall, he stopped at an open doorway and greeted the guy inside. Working at a desk and wearing thick-lensed glasses, he pulled them off when they stepped in.

"This is Slater," Vahan said. "He's working for the landlord."

He frowned. "Do you need to get in here?"

"I don't," Slater said. "I'm inspecting the shared spaces. Hallways and stairwells. I just wanted to meet some of the tenants."

"You're working for Park?"

"That's right."

"I'm not surprised you came with Vahan. Park doesn't have a lot of friends around here."

"Does he make trouble for you?"

"Are you going to report what I say back to him?"

Slater chuckled. "He hired me, but I'm no rat."

"Let's just say he's a difficult person."

"I could see that. Do you know the woman who runs the nightclub? Les James."

He shrugged. "Never heard of her."

"Well, if you see me around, don't shoot."

Back in the hallway, Vahan led him out to the street and to another entrance, in the next building. Slater used his key again, and Vahan headed downstairs. He knew there was a connecting doorway from where they'd just been, but obviously Vahan didn't.

They talked to several more manufacturers, among them a father and son team, and made small talk, then went to another office. This guy claimed he didn't know Les James, but his reaction to the name said the opposite.

Walking back up to street level and out onto the

sidewalk, Vahan gestured to a shop window. "This woman specializes in silver. Let's talk to her."

The narrow space had brightly lit displays, and Vahan exchanged a few words with the woman. The guy could almost be pleasant when he wasn't trying to score. Somewhere under the sleazy veneer there was actually a glimmer of charm.

The woman behind the counter had her dark hair tied back, wearing a black turtleneck with several silver chains over it. From the lines on her face she had to be in her sixties.

"This is Milena," Vahan said. "She designs all these pieces."

Slater looked into one of the cases. "You make beautiful things."

Vahan's phone tweedled in his pants, and he dug it out. "I have to go," he said, tucking it away again, and stepped out to the street.

"My mother wears a piece just like this," Slater said, and pointed to a necklace of silver scrollwork embedded with three red glass discs.

"Then she bought it from me," Milena said. "The red comes from cadmium and selenium."

"Is that safe?" He frowned. "It sounds like it might be radioactive."

She laughed. "There's no danger. It's inside the glass."

A guy stepped into the doorway from the back of the store and stood there, watching them. His black hair slicked back, he had a roman nose, and his dark beard was trimmed tightly. Basically fuckable, Slater decided, and ignored him, even though he could feel his eyes on him.

Finally the guy spoke: "Where did you go to middle school?"

"Why are you asking me that?" Slater said.

Milena said something to him in another language, and the guy frowned.

"This is my son, Erik," she said. "He pretends he doesn't understand Armenian. This is Slater."

"Were you in wrestling?" Erik said. "We used to go up against the public schools. I think you might have given me an oil check back in the day."

"I wrestled, but I never did that. It wasn't allowed on our team."

"What's an oil check?" Milena said.

Erik waved a hand. "A wrestling maneuver."

Slater had to suppress a grin. Specifically it meant grabbing hold of your opponent by the ass, and grinding a finger into his anus. It was an underhanded way to break somebody's concentration.

"I remember you were scrappy," Erik said.

"I didn't win all that many matches."

A woman walked in from the street, and Milena called out a greeting. She and Erik both shifted focus to the newcomer, and Slater walked out.

It was already getting dark, and it felt cold. Crossing to the parking structure, he fired up the Continental, and flicked on the headlights, and drove to the Arts District. In front of the Swati Gallery he nosed into a street space, then walked inside.

A big space with high ceilings and walls painted flat white, a century ago it had probably been a small factory or a warehouse. Today overpriced paintings hung on the walls. Sitting at the glass-topped front desk was Celeste. He knew she pronounced it the

Spanish way, "Ce-les-*tay*." Curvy, she had long black hair, and was wearing a dressy blouse that showed her clavicles.

Celeste looked up as he stepped in. "Deliveries are around the back."

"I'm not the help, sister," he snapped.

She laughed and sat back. "I'm just playing. I know you, Ibáñez. You're the guy who recovered *Peasant with Hay Fork*."

"I'm also the guy who cut you in for ten large on the reward for that job."

"I'm very grateful for that."

"And I repotted your *Aglaonema*." He gestured to the potted plant next to her desk. "You're welcome."

"So many clients have commented on how healthy it looks."

"That sounds a lot like a lie," Slater said. "But I can see it's thriving."

"Are you here to shop for fine art?"

"I have a gig for you, if you've got a minute." He put his hands on his hips. "I need to butter up a patsy. I figured you could give her the dope about her painting, and I can soak up the gravy."

Celeste's eyes narrowed. "It sounds like you want me to cook dinner for her."

"I want to pay you for your expertise in this world." He waved at the gallery. "I'm investigating this woman. She has a painting in her office that she knows nothing about. I figured you could look at it and tell her whether it came from a printing factory in Guangzhou or got lifted from the Musée d'Orsay."

"I could probably give her a general sense of what it is."

"If you do that, it'll make me look like I'm doing her a favor. Build some trust, lower the defenses."

"What do you want me to tell her about the art?"

"It doesn't matter." He waved a hand. "The truth is probably the easiest route. That way you don't have to make stuff up."

Celeste chuckled. "I can do that."

"How much lead time do you need to get over to Broadway?"

"If I'm here, twenty minutes."

"Does tomorrow work?"

"Probably," she said. "Hit me up."

Slater walked out and drove to his office. The surface lot was mostly empty at this hour, and he hustled across the street. As he flicked on the lights he double-clicked his tongue to greet the statue of Rey Pascual on the front desk, positioned now to watch the front door with his bony empty eye sockets.

It was too early for Greenleaf, he decided, and sat at his desk, and spent time reading about Clyde's buildings. The public library had some records about the neighborhood. What Clyde had told him looked to be accurate, that the row had been built in the early twentieth century.

He found a couple of articles about the sealed-off hotel wing. Even though it sounded like a folktale, that was true too. *The Bugle* had interviewed the original owner's daughter in 1971. She explained what had happened, the falling-out between her father and the hotel owner, and complained that she was still paying property taxes on a building she couldn't get into without a ladder.

Eventually Slater got up and stepped into Max's

office. They had a little wardrobe in the corner, in the same art deco style as the desks, dark wood with a chevron motif on the rounded corner. Etta had set all this up when she renovated the place for them. She'd had the walls painted and even found classic deco light fixtures. The place looked legit now, like they'd actually moved in.

They both kept some clothes in the wardrobe, including a classic 1970s suit Slater had bought from a stash of dead stock in one of the factories upstairs. It was in a broad red-and-purple plaid, and had the sheen of polyester, and absurdly wide lapels. Taking it over to his office, he hung it on the back of the door. It would work with the shirt he was wearing, he decided. It was green but so dark that it was almost black.

Pulling on the pants and the suit jacket, they felt light and thin, like he was half naked. He moved his wallet and keys and phone from his jeans, then tossed them on his desk chair. There was a pair of shoes in the wardrobe to go with the suit, but his boots looked OK. The main thing was passing the dress code at Greenleaf. That was a hard no denim.

It was close enough to walk, and he left his wheels where they were, and headed up the street. In the next block a row of tents filled half the sidewalk. They collected like tumbleweeds anywhere without active ground-floor retail. He crossed the street to avoid them. It wasn't about being afraid of the occupants, but he didn't need to be inhaling the stench of the urine-soaked concrete.

SIX

WHEN SLATER WALKED INTO Sackett's, the cafeteria was closed, and he rode the elevator up to Greenleaf. The doors opened at the top of the stairs, where a burly guy in a black suit was perched on a stool. Giving Slater the once-over as he stepped off, he grunted "ID." Once he'd given his card a cursory glance, he handed it back and looked away.

In the alcove fronting the dance floor the bandstand was lit up, with powder-blue walls that stretched onto the coved ceiling. There was a drum kit and a grand piano, and music stands with a logo attached to the fronts that read GREENLEAF. Nobody was on stage right now, but recorded music came through the sound system.

People were occupying some of the tables, and

half the barstools. Slater crossed the room and sat at one. Eventually a woman with her hair pinned back stepped over, clad in the white shirt and black vest of her profession.

"A tonic water," Slater said.

"Do you want me to slip some gin into that, honey?"

"Not at this time."

She grinned and stepped away.

His booze rules said he could have one, since he was working and it was after dark, but he didn't know how long he was going to be here. He needed to stay sharp, and he might need to have that one later.

Digging out a twenty, he set it on the bar top, and once he had the drink in hand, swiveled to look over the room. A couple of musicians were on the stage now, a guy messing with a trombone and another at the piano. Over the canned music he could hear them warming up. Both of them were wearing the house band jackets, in a green velvet fabric with black trim.

Over by the doors into the back he saw Les James step out. She looked completely different from earlier in the day, wearing a long dress, black or maybe midnight blue, her hair styled to look unstyled and down on her shoulders, and heavy evening makeup. Jewelry sparkled at her neck and her ears.

Next to her was a twink, in his twenties maybe, his red hair in a little pomp. They were talking, he realized, even though they were both facing the room. He was wearing the green jacket of the house band. The drummer, Slater remembered. Woody had been macking on the guy when he'd first come in here. What was his name? Something Anglo and

Midwest. Finally it came to him: Lars.

Watching them talk, they seemed familiar, more than boss and employee. He knew the guy had been sleeping with Woody at some point. Maybe he was sleeping with Les too.

He sipped his tonic water and watched the room as more people gradually wandered in. The bouncer carded everyone, and at one point he turned away a pair of college-age men. They didn't look underage but they were dressed down, one in a polo and one in a T-shirt and a ball cap. Both of them looked pissed, and they walked out again. LA was mostly a casual place, and having a dress code at all was exceptional. People weren't expecting it.

The rest of the band got set up, gradually taking their places. He'd forgotten how much brass there was. Eventually they started into a song. It was slow and romantic, but it sounded great. After a few tunes, when Slater was well into his second tonic water, Les strode out onto the stage, her jewelry glittering in the spotlight. She stood at the mike and spoke.

"It's so lovely to see you all here this evening. Please welcome Mr. Woody Newkirk."

There was scattered applause as Woody stepped out, wearing a dark-red suit. He hadn't seen him in a while, and his Black hair was a little longer, styled in knobby curls now. As Les walked off stage, he stepped up to the mike and flashed a beatific smile. This guy was totally fuckable.

Woody launched into a song, accompanied by the band. It sounded old, like a classic, but Slater had never heard it before. The lyrics were romantic, and Woody's tone was pure, his delivery smooth and so confident. It made him easy to watch.

After a few more songs, talking over the applause, Woody said, "Thank you," and raised a hand, then walked off-stage. The band was taking a break too, it seemed, as they broke formation, and the stage lights dimmed, and the recorded music came up.

Digging out his phone, Slater called Woody, glad that he picked up.

"Are you done for the evening?" Slater said.

"I'm at Greenleaf tonight."

"I know that, man. I just watched you perform. That last number really put lead in the pencil."

Woody laughed. "I didn't see you. I'm actually not on again tonight."

"Have you got a minute?"

"I have to change, and talk to Les. Do you know that diner on Eighth? It's open late. I can meet you there in a few minutes."

Slater did know the place. It was just a couple of blocks away. He finished his tonic water, and left some singles for the bartender, then walked out.

Stepping onto the sidewalk it felt cold, and he shoved his hands in the pockets of the thin suit pants. He rounded the corner and saw that the cross street was blocked off with K-rail. There was always something going on down here, the densest part of the metropolis. He started across Spring Street, but as he stepped off the curb, a guy with his hair in bushy spikes, maybe still a teenager, stepped in front of him. He was holding a walkie-talkie, and held up his other hand.

"You have to wait here a minute."

"I've got the light, toots, so unless you've got a

badge or a rod, that's not going to happen."

"It'll just be a couple minutes. We're filming here. It's fun to watch."

"A commercial for a fabulous new shampoo, I'm thinking," Slater said, "or yet another superhero movie? I'm not interested in helping enrich your corporate masters."

"Come on, man." He stepped in front of him, briefly putting a hand on his shoulder.

Slater held his gaze and spoke slowly. "If you touch me again, I'll dislocate your arm."

He frowned but didn't move to escalate, and Slater stepped past him into the street. Behind him he heard the guy speak into his walkie.

"Hold, hold, hold," he said, followed by the snarl of static as he released the transmit key.

Slater wasn't even halfway across when an electric-blue blur raced up the street, engine roaring, and passed just a few feet in front of him. He stopped short and looked after it. It was some modern low-slung sports car. He could feel a surge of adrenaline, his heart pounding. If he'd been a second faster it would have knocked him in the air like a bowling pin.

Back at the curb, the guy on the walkie was shouting now. "Are you not listening to me? I said hold."

That had been close. Slater took a breath and looked both directions. The car had stopped in the middle of the next block, and someone was standing next to it now, leaning in to talk to the driver. Of more concern was that these yahoos usually had a cop around, moonlighting as private security but still wearing the uniform and the sidearm. They were off the taxpayers' clock but they still had the power to throw him in the clink. But there was no sign of anybody like that as he reached the curb.

When he walked into the diner, only one table was occupied. A guy with dark Latin hair and wearing a food-stained apron stepped out from the counter. "How many?"

"I'm alone."

The guy waved him to a table, and Slater sat in a booth opposite where he'd pointed. He knew this place, and if he'd said he was with someone, they'd make him wait out on the street. He didn't need that kind of static. It wasn't exactly a rug joint, but it was hard to blame them. On the edge of Skid Row they had to deal with all the homeless people who'd come in to warm up and claim to be waiting for a friend before they ordered anything.

The guy approached a minute later. "What'll it be?"

"Is that barley soup still vegan?"

Slater was halfway through the bowl when Woody walked in, and smiled as he sat across from him.

"I love that suit," Woody said.

"It's vintage."

The server stepped over, and Woody eyed him. "Can you do decaf?"

Slater pushed his bowl aside. "Tell me about Les James."

"Why are you asking?"

"She came up in an investigation."

"Is that what you're doing for Clyde?"

He waved a hand. "It's unrelated."

"So what are you investigating? You think Les is a crook?"

"That's confidential."

Woody's brow furrowed. "I'm not sure what you want me to say."

"I don't know her. You do." Slater raised his voice. "Sing, brother."

He waited as the server set down his coffee, then picked up the cup.

"I haven't really done business with her," Woody said. "I was trying to get that rolling when I came into some capital."

"I remember."

He chuckled. "That money means I can set up my own business. In the meantime I'm still working for her. She's pretty easy to get along with."

"Meaning what?" Slater said. "You can work when you want to?"

"The roster has to be locked down way ahead, but she'll say what flavor of music she wants to do, and I can pick the songs. She's open to different ideas. Like she wants the music to be sweet early on, then hard later so that people will dance. I figured we could add a sweet stretch later too, so that people could take a breather and order drinks. She actually tried that."

"What about her personal life? Who's she sleeping with?"

"No idea," Woody said. "I'm pretty sure she's cis-het. I've seen her flirt with men but not with women. There's no husband or boyfriend that I know of."

"You asked if I thought Les was a lowlife. Have you seen anything to suggest that?"

"She pays her staff on time. I know she has secrets, but so does everybody. What makes you think she's a lowlife?"

"Nothing, really." Slater watched him for a moment. "I think I'm biased."

"You said you don't know her."

"I've seen her at work. When she dresses up for the evening, she looks like a million bucks. That sets the tone for the place." He gestured helplessly. "It seems like she knows what she's doing."

"That just means she's competent. Lots of crooks are competent."

"She's also never high-hatted me," Slater said, "even though she's a swell. She never kicked me out of Greenleaf even though her bouncers have tried to eighty-six me more than once."

"That's because you respect the place."

"How would she know that?"

"You dress for it. Way beyond the minimum." Woody gestured to his jacket. "Like the vintage threads. That demonstrates respect. Besides, you're hot, and when somebody looks good, it lifts the atmosphere of the whole nightclub."

"Now I know you're yanking my chain." Slater folded his arms. "When is she usually in her office?"

"Not mornings. Most days from around noon, I'd say. On weekends she comes in later."

"How's Lars?"

"A total snack, as you know," Woody said. "But the guy is such an airhead."

"The bloom is off the rose?"

He sipped his java. "It's more than that. I'm over Lars. He has some weird-ass ideas about the world."

"Like what?"

"It's about paranormal stuff." He waggled his fingers next to his temple and said "woo-woo" in a falsetto tone. "He's also a rigorous twelve-stepper. I don't mind that, but it takes up a lot of his time. He goes to meetings a dozen times a week. Do you know that new Skid Row building over on Main? It has homeless housing upstairs and meeting rooms on the ground floor."

"Sure." Slater had had to go over there regularly, when a judge had ordered him into an anger management class, but he didn't need to tell Woody about that.

"It's right near the nightclub. Lars does a meeting there and insists on going even though that's the only opportunity I have to eat before work. So he'll never eat with me." Woody gestured. "It's important, breaking bread together."

"I guess sobriety has a price tag," Slater said. "Is he sleeping with Les?"

He frowned. "I seriously doubt that. Lars is a twink through and through. But I think they get along. You know, not everything is about sex."

"On that, Woody, you're misinformed." Slater waved at the guy behind the counter and called to him: "Check."

Woody dug in his pocket, and Slater waved a hand.

"I can buy your damn Sanka."

Once Slater had settled up, and said good-bye to Woody on the sidewalk, he walked back to the parking structure across from Greenleaf.

The blue sports car was in the middle of the block, balanced on its side now, with chunks of black debris littering the pavement. Half a dozen people were standing around it. It was hard to tell whether that was an intentional part of the film shoot, as a dramatic way to shill exciting new products, or it was just an accident. He wondered idly if they'd actually killed anybody. But he didn't need to stop to ask. Either way, it was just raw stupidity.

Back at his office he changed into his jeans, and hung the suit in the wardrobe, then went down to the Continental and drove to his house. Climbing the stairs from the garage, the place was dark and quiet. This was the time of day to arrange a hookup. But maybe he could skip it. He was still a little skeeved out from that nebbishy dope Vahan.

In the kitchen he grabbed the bourbon bottle and poured out his ration. It didn't really matter that he was drinking this applejack instead of the good stuff. He was used to it. Pike's scotch was meant to be savored, intended for people who didn't need booze rules.

He slammed the paltry dribble, closing his eyes to savor the heady burn. It was hard to believe how little of it there was. Once he'd poured another couple of fingers into the glass, he put the bottle away. He deserved a premium snort, he reasoned, since he'd been left alone like this, deserted by Pike.

The music got good late, and he put on the radio. Pulling off his boots, he left them on the faux grass and stretched out on the sofa. Grabbing one of the throw pillows, he sniffed it, hoping for a hint of Pike's scent, but he couldn't detect it. He took a slug of bourbon and shuddered at the intensity.

His phone buzzed, and when he checked the screen, it said REDDY KILOWATT. He picked up.

"I hear music," Pike said. "Where are you?"

"I'm at the house. You must have left the radio on."

"You're just relaxing?"

"I'm sitting bolt upright in a hardback chair. In the dark. It's cold."

He chuckled. "Did you eat?"

"I found a candy bar under the seat in my car," Slater said. "It was a little melted. It must have been there over the summer. It tasted weird. How do you know if peanuts have gone rancid?"

"At least there's bourbon to comfort you."

"There's only a dribble left in the bottom."

"I saw a new bottle in the pantry a couple of days ago," Pike said.

"A rat got into it."

"My heart bleeds for your hardship."

"I'm not the one who left town with a strange man."

"Davis didn't make it," Pike said. "I'm with Brewster on this trip."

"Is she trying to get into your pants now too?"

"That would be no."

"Where are you?"

"Lompoc."

"It's pronounced lom-*poke*."

"That's what Brewster said. She calls it 'slow-poke.'"

"Funny. Were you at the prison?"

"That's tomorrow. How's your case?"

Slater told him a little about prowling around the buildings on Broadway, and going to Greenleaf. "Do you have a separate hotel room, at least? Put the extra lock on your door. You never know what Brewster might try to pull."

"She's in a relationship now. I heard all about it on the drive. Brewster's not coming for me."

"It's easy to assume that, until she gets all liquored up, and then you're right there. Listen, if you go out to the snack machine, put your pants on. Strutting around in those hoochie-daddy underpants, she'll try to jump your bones for sure."

Pike laughed. "I don't run around in my skivvies. The only person who's going to jump me tonight is Hypnos, and he's about to deliver a haymaker. So I'm hanging up. I love you, forty-niner."

"Forever, *mi vida*. Wear pants."

SEVEN

SLATER WOKE WITH A headache. That would be from imbibing that third chapter last night. At least the room wasn't spinning. Forcing himself to sit up, he planted his feet on the floor. The air felt cold. He shivered and stood up, taking a deep breath. It didn't qualify as a full-on katzenjammer, he decided.

In the bathroom he looked at himself in the mirror before he showered. His eyes looked a little bloodshot, the skin under them dark and blotchy. He spoke through his teeth. "Stumblebum."

Once he was dressed he went upstairs and put half a bagel in the toaster. He couldn't bring himself to fire up the coffeemaker. Pike did better with that. He could get java out somewhere.

It looked bright out, and he carried his bagel onto

the deck. The cold air felt good, waking him up as he sat and munched on it.

A couple of alerts had come from Svetlana's software, and both said only NEW TALKING. That had to mean that the audio bug under Les James's desk had recorded voices. Svetlana spoke better English than that. It was more evidence that she outsourced her coding to the motherland.

Tapping at the screen, he listened to what it had picked up. The first clip was half a phone call, Les's voice talking about beer. The inaudible person she was talking to must have been a liquor distributor. Next was Les's voice again with another woman. They were talking about the song lineup. He knew that voice. She was the band leader, and played sax, but he couldn't recall her name. None of that was informative. He texted Celeste:

Noon at Sackett's?

Hustling down to the garage, he backed the Continental into the street. As he waited for the door to roll down, Celeste's reply buzzed his phone:

I'll be there.

Nosing into the parking structure on Broadway, he eased up the ramp, the ancient construction leaving just a few inches to spare around the big vehicle. He pulled into a stall next to a sweet little Pacer. You didn't see those every day.

As he climbed out, he pulled on his satchel and looked over the vehicle. It was two-tone, in a bright maroon shade and creamy yellow. This model was famous for those expansive windows, and they had no tint, so he knew someone was sitting behind the wheel. When the driver opened the door and got out, he saw that it was Clyde.

"I love your ride," Clyde said, gesturing to the Continental. "It's a '74?"

"Close. A '73. What are you doing with the Pacer, man? It's too early in the day for me to be walking around with a stiffy in my pants."

He laughed. "You like it?"

"It's a total dick magnet."

"His name is Milton. He's a '78."

Slater walked up to the front end, parked next to the building's crazed and dust-hazed faux office windows, and admired the recessed headlights. "Is this factory paint?"

"Not original," Clyde said, "but the colors match the factory paint."

"This is perhaps the most perfect car ever built."

"Better than your ride? Why don't you get one? There's a few around. If you don't have room for it, trade in the Lincoln."

"I don't think I could live up to all this. I'd be like Icarus, flying too close to the sun." Slater met his gaze. "Plus it's got a gutless engine."

"This one has the two-barrel 258. If you keep it tuned right, it does just fine."

Slater walked with him to the stairs and followed him down to the street. At the corner Slater paused on the sidewalk.

"You're not coming over?" Clyde said.

"Not yet."

"Come by my office later."

Up the block he walked into a little alley that led

off the street. Most of them around here were piss-stained and littered with trash and worse, but this one dead-ended and had several storefronts. Somehow they'd kept the tents and sleeping bags out. He walked into the little food market.

They did Greek coffee, he knew, and he ordered a couple of them, and watched as the woman made it. Andy once told him you could draw a line on the map of Europe, and west of it people drank Italian coffee, and east was Greek style. Whether these people were Armenian or not, Armenia was definitely east of that line.

As Slater walked up on Milena's shop, the little paper cups in hand, a guy in a navy-blue suit stepped out just as he was reaching for the door. Burly and dark-skinned, his hair buzzed short, the guy was fuckable, but he reeked of law enforcement, and gave Slater a pointed once-over. Slater shot him a look and stepped around him.

Inside, he set the paper cups on the counter. Milena came out of the back and smiled in recognition.

"You look tired. What's this?"

"Greek coffee," Slater said. "I thought it might be close to Armenian coffee."

She leaned toward him over the counter. "Don't tell anyone it was me who said it, but it's basically the same thing."

"It's from that little place in the alley. I don't know where they're from."

"I'm just glad you didn't call it Turkish coffee. The Ottomans murdered plenty of my ancestors."

"Yeah, I know that's still pretty raw."

Milena raised her voice. "That's because they never admitted to it. You can't expect people to move on if you won't even admit what you've done. The Germans at least have faced up to what they did."

"That one's still a little raw too. I'm Jewish, and you won't catch me riding around in a Volkswagen."

"You're Jewish." She raised her eyebrows. "That wouldn't have been my first guess."

Slater picked up one of the cups and pulled the lid off. "One of my uncles said my role in the family was to fill in the low-achieving end of the bell curve."

She laughed, and took the other cup, then took a delicate sip. "So what are you doing here, treating me to coffee, still hot from the *jezve*?"

"What do you know about Les James?"

"I know Les. She's my trashy neighbor."

"I get it. Nightclub people are a little rough around the edges." He gestured with the little cup. "It's not a clip joint, though. She puts on good music. Have you been up there?"

"I just meant that we share the dumpster in the alley. We call each other the trashy neighbors."

"So you're friends."

"Why are you asking? And why were you with Vahan yesterday? I know you were prowling the back hallways and downstairs."

"You sound like a cop."

Milena chuckled. "Other people met you yesterday. Jewelers have lots of valuable inventory. You can understand why we're wary."

"The building manager hired me to look around," Slater said.

She didn't react to that, Slater saw. He hadn't

told her that yesterday, but obviously she'd already heard it.

"Is it for Park's hotel project? That seems like a pipe dream to me. He claims he has all the permits, but I haven't seen any work happening. Is that what you're doing, surveying for the construction?"

"For now I'm looking at all the points of egress. Where the fire exits have to be, that kind of thing."

"You're with the fire department?"

"I'm not."

"So tight-lipped," Milena said. "I guess it's none of my business. Have you been in the old delivery tunnels?"

"Where are those, exactly?"

"Under the street. If you're examining the exit doors, you should look at those too. I'll show you."

She slammed the last of her coffee, then stepped out from the counter, and flipped the sign in the door to CLOSED, and set the bolt. Waggling her fingers for his cup, she took it from him and waved him into the back. It was a smaller room than the shop, with a desk with a laptop on it, and a worktable piled with plastic trays and tubs, and a couple of chairs. Milena dropped the cups in the trash, then herded him out the back door into the hall.

He'd probably walked past here with Vahan or with Clyde, but it all looked the same. As she locked the back door with her key, he saw there was no name on it, just the suite number.

Milena led him to the top of a stairwell and started down. The ones leading down all started at street level, he realized, just like the stairs going up. They were usually near each other, but none of them were connected. Maybe that was a safety thing, so that all the stairs ended at the ground floor. It made sense—in a panic after an earthquake or in a fire you wouldn't mistakenly pass the exit floor and evacuate into the basement. If he was posing as an inspector he should probably be aware of stuff like that.

He followed Milena down a flight, and she walked back in the direction of her shop. There were offices on either side. He'd spoken to people in some of these with Vahan.

Milena turned into a side hallway, toward the street, and at the end stopped in front of a set of double doors. Made of steel and painted yellowy-tan like the walls, they looked old, and weren't marked or numbered.

"This is the way into the tunnels," she said. "Probably each of the buildings has an entrance, but this is the only one I know about."

Slater tried the handle, but it was firmly locked. "Nobody uses them?"

"Nobody needs them. It's cheap and easy to move things with trucks now. These tunnels were for times when everything was done with manual labor."

"I don't suppose you have keys to this door."

"Mr. Park should. Ask him."

They walked back to the stairwell and to the back door to her shop. When they went inside, Erik was standing behind the counter, and frowned at the sight of him. As Slater stepped around the counter, the sound of a phone ringing came from the back office.

"I'll get it," Milena said. "Thanks again, Slater."

Erik waited for the ringing to stop, then eyed

him. "What were you two up to?"

"I asked her to show me the door into the old delivery tunnels."

"Don't they keep those locked? I've never been in there."

"They were definitely locked today."

"So you don't remember me at all from wrestling."

"It was a long time ago," Slater said. "My memory is patchy. I had a lot on my plate."

"We should grab a beer and catch up."

"I can't really do that. I'm embroiled in a multi-dimensional narrative complex." He held up his left hand and wiggled his ring finger.

Erik briefly took hold of his hand and peered at the ring. "I bet you bought that around here."

"You'd win that bet."

"I'm not asking you on a date, Ibáñez. Just to hang out. And what's a narrative complex?"

"Like a relationship, only more intense, and more meaningful." He dug a business card from his hip pocket and set it on the counter. "That's my cell."

"It says you're an insurance investigator," Erik said, peering at it. "I heard you were a building inspector."

"It's not that different. I work whatever gigs I can get. None of it pays enough to call myself anything specific."

Milena stepped out of the back. "Slater's mother is a customer. She has a piece of the sterling and cadmium glass."

"Sweet." Erik nodded. "People love those."

"There's an idea," Slater said. "I should get something to match. For the next time I need to give her a gift."

"Such a considerate son." Milena eyed Erik. "Are you paying attention?"

Slater waved a hand. "It's not about being considerate. If I give her some bling, it'll cool her out, and keep her off my back."

"Now I'm listening." Erik chuckled. "What piece does she have?"

Looking into the display case, Slater pointed out the necklace that looked like the one Doris wore. A minute later he'd paid them for a piece that matched, a pin with a red glass disk surrounded by silverwork, and walked out with the little paper shopping bag in hand. He pulled his satchel around and tucked it inside.

Down the block he walked into Sackett's, and into the dining room. The place was busy with the lunch crowd. Celeste was already here, parked at a table for two along the wall, a coffee cup in front of her. She was gazing at her phone, but looked up as he approached, and tucked it away as he sat across from her.

"What happened to you?"

Slater frowned. "Nothing happened to me. What are you talking about?"

"You look a little haggard."

"It might be the stomach flu."

"Or maybe a hangover."

He scoffed and folded his arms.

"I haven't been in here since they renovated," Celeste said, glancing around the room. "I'm glad they kept the forest and the critters. I loved it when I was a kid."

"Me too. It's been here forever."

"Tell me about your target."

"Her name is Les James. She runs the nightclub upstairs. Don't let on that I hired you. She needs to think it's just a thoughtful favor."

She nodded. "Got it."

They rose, and he waited as she put her cup on the return rack. Slater led the way upstairs, and at the flight that led up to Greenleaf, he stepped over the chain.

"Did you miss this?" Celeste said, pointing at the CLOSED sign.

"It's fine."

"You're a scofflaw, Ibáñez," she said as she stepped over. At the top she paused and took in the room. "Oh, I like this."

"There's live music, and a floor show. It's where the hep cats come to groove."

From behind the bar, a guy called to them. "We're closed."

"I have a meeting with Les," Slater said, and gestured toward the doors into the back.

The office door was open, and Les was sitting behind her desk with her tennis shoes propped up on it, looking at her phone. Slater knocked as they stepped in, and Les sat up.

"I ran into Celeste," he said. "I thought you should meet her."

"Were you downstairs at Sackett's?"

"I love that place," Celeste said. "Although it's gotten pricey lately."

Les chuckled. "They need to pay for the kitchen upgrades."

"Slater said you had a painting I should look at.

I'm thinking it's this one."

"Celeste is in the art world," he said.

"Mount Ararat." Celeste stepped over to it.

"The one and only." Les swiveled her chair toward her. "Can you put a price on it?"

"Value is subjective. It's worth whatever it means to you." She leaned in to peer at the canvas. "I can tell you it's not a mass-produced job. A painter did this, and looking at the brushstrokes, they took time with it."

"I know the artist is from there."

"Armenia?"

"That's right."

Celeste stepped back. "Well, whatever you paid for it, someone put their heart into this."

"Good to know."

"Have you been?"

"Some of my friends have," Les said, "and one of my uncles. You work in art?"

"I'm at the Swati Gallery. In the Arts District."

"What are the trends in art right now?"

"It's kind of like fashion," Celeste said. "It changes all the time, and my sense is that the pace of change is accelerating. The market is always looking for something new. We sell mostly to investors."

"That means big-ticket pieces?"

"More like they're betting that specific works will get more valuable. It's like playing the stock market. The number-one question I'm asked is, 'What will this piece be worth in ten years?'"

Les nodded. "So it's the realm of the very wealthy. That sounds a little depressing."

"I still get to work with art, and play a role in

figuring out what's going to catch on."

"You probably don't see a lot of these." She nodded to Ararat.

"Once in a while we do an exhibition of landscapes."

The pair of them chatted a moment longer, then Celeste stepped toward the door. "Thanks for letting me see it."

EIGHT

⌐⌐⌐⌐⌐⌐⌐⌐⌐⌐⌐

S LATER FOLLOWED CELESTE OUT of Les's office. They didn't speak as they crossed the parquet toward the stairs. A couple of steps down a guy was working with a mop, and he looked up as they approached, and frowned at them. "Can you take the elevator?"

They went over to it, and once the doors rolled closed, Slater spoke. "I knew you were the one."

"You liked what I told her?"

"You pulled out stuff I didn't know. Like Les is Armenian."

"Does that matter?"

"I'm not sure yet. It seems like there's lots of Armenians working in this neighborhood."

As the elevator doors rolled open, Celeste paused. "I hit the wrong button. This is the upstairs dining room."

"We can go this way. You won't have to walk all the way through the faux forest." Slater stepped out and walked over to the subtle door Clyde had showed him.

Digging out his key ring, it took a couple of tries, but eventually he found the one that unlocked it. They stepped through, and he locked it again.

"There's another stairwell here," Celeste said. "Is this a different building? Who gave you that key?"

"I'm working with the guy who manages both." He led the way into the stairs down.

"I love this old place. I wonder if either of these buildings are connected to the delivery tunnels."

"This one is. Somebody showed me the access door."

"I've actually been in them. They go all over. The problem is the access points are always locked."

Slater stopped on the ground floor. "The door was locked when I saw it, but I might have a key."

"Are you serious?" She waved a hand. "You have to try it."

They walked around to the stairs leading down. This looked like the right hallway, and from his reckoning Milena's shop was just above them. A minute later he found the side corridor with the doors at the end.

"This is it." He dug out the key ring as they walked up to the door, and tried one, and then another. It worked, flipping the bolt with a metallic *clank*. It was easy to remember which key it was—the only one on the ring that was brass.

"Score," Celeste said, and stepped through as he

heaved open the heavy door.

Slater followed her in. It was dimly lit and smelled earthy, like when you were digging up an old garden. Only a few yards wide, the concrete walls were unfinished, and the floor was gritty. The illumination was daylight, filtering in from a grid of opaque glass squares in the ceiling, a few feet overhead.

"I've seen those." He gestured to them. "The blocks in the sidewalk. I wondered what they were for."

A dark mass floated along the array, momentarily dimming the squares, followed by a lighter shadow moving in the opposite direction. Pedestrians on the sidewalk, he realized.

"Now you know," Celeste said. "Want to explore?"

"Hell, yeah." He closed the door and locked it with the key. It had the street number of the building on it, he saw, hand-painted and fading with age. "Which way?"

Celeste gestured, and they walked abreast. The doors were spaced about as far apart as the buildings upstairs, each with a street number on it. It looked like every building had access to this. A few doors along, they came to a cross-tunnel.

"This has to be under Seventh Street," Celeste said. "Let's go that way."

The stretch of overhead glass blocks ended, and Slater turned on the flashlight on his phone, holding it at waist level. A minute's walk farther, the light fixtures on the wall were illuminated, and he killed it again. When they got to the next corner, the wall was marked SPRING ST.

"I think I know where we are," Celeste said.

"So do I. It's painted on the damn wall."

"I mean I've been down here before. Come on."

She led the way up the tunnel. There was light from more glass blocks overhead, then a stretch where the light fixtures were working. The tunnel opened into a wide space at one side, and Celeste stopped.

"See the color?"

Slater looked around. Unlike the bare tunnels, there were remnants of green paint on the walls here, peeling and stained but visible, and on the ceiling intact patches of blue.

"My theory is that this was a speakeasy during Prohibition," she said. "If it was just a storeroom, why would you paint it? A shop owner showed me this. Her place is a little farther up that way. She found a hidden door in her store that leads right here. Built into the hallway with an invisible seam in the wainscotting. It could have been concealed for some other reason, but based on the date it was built, she's sure it was about secret access to booze."

"I guess it's like dope is today," Slater said. "You can make it illegal, but people are still going to do it."

"She wanted to bring some tables down here and start serving drinks, but it's impossible. There's no plumbing, so the health department would never sign off on it. And imagine a bar with no exits—the fire inspector would have an aneurysm."

"I get it. Nobody wants drunk influencer trash running around down here."

They walked back the way they'd come, and Celeste stopped at one of the doorways.

"I can see light inside," she said, her voice low, and stepped up to it.

The double doors were battered, and the projecting

strip on the left one that covered the gap between them had been bent outward. Slater watched as she tried the handle. The door opened, revealing a hallway inside, the walls painted pale green. The lights were on, and he could hear the hum of machinery.

"Slow down, Seabiscuit," he said. "You don't want to get popped."

"I'm not going in. But why is this open? I wonder if they still use the tunnels for some purpose."

"Maybe somebody just forgot to lock it."

She pushed the door closed and gestured to the number painted on it. "Do you know the address?"

"I have no clue where this is. But it looks like every building was connected to this tunnel."

Pulling out her phone, she snapped a photo of the number, then tucked it away. "In case I need to come back."

"Hey, smoke 'em if you've got 'em."

As they walked back to the junction, Celeste pointed farther down. "There's an interesting place at the end of this tunnel too."

"Like what?"

"You have to experience it for yourself. Like a painting or a sculpture. If someone tells you about it before you see it, that biases your thinking."

"Do you want to show me?"

"I should get back to the gallery," she said. "You can walk it on your own. There's no snakes or bear traps."

Once they were back at the doorway they'd started from, Slater unlocked the door.

"What do I owe you?"

"I should probably say nothing. You did cut me in

on the bounty for *Peasant with Hay Fork.*"

"That's an unrelated matter."

"It wasn't that much work," Celeste said. "Would you be pissed if I said a hundo?"

"I would not." He dug out his wad and peeled off a C-note. He would have paid her two or three yards if she'd asked. Just one seemed like a bargain.

"I'm thinking you're going to keep exploring," she said as she pocketed it.

"I have to now, since you won't come across with what's at the end of that tunnel. Can you find your way out of the building?"

Celeste chuckled. "I should be able to handle it."

Once she'd gone inside, he locked the door again and walked back to the junction marked Spring Street, then walked the way Celeste had pointed out. He didn't need his flashlight very often, as most of the overhead fixtures were working.

It was hard to estimate how far he'd walked, several blocks at least, when the tunnel got wider again. Here it looked like it was being maintained, with smooth newer concrete, and less dust and grit on the ground, and modern light fixtures. On one side a set of doors looked contemporary, unlike anything else he'd seen, and had a key-card reader mounted next to it. That had definitely been installed since Prohibition. He tried the handle, but it was locked.

A little farther along, a set of doors blocked the way forward. They had a lighted exit sign above and a crash bar on this side. That meant they'd lock again, and he wouldn't be able to get back into the tunnels. He pressed on the bar, and pushed it open, but no alarm sounded. This was a hallway, he saw, with institutional carpeting and a drop ceiling. It felt like he'd stepped into an office building. He let the door close behind him and walked up the hall.

A pasty guy in black chinos and a dress shirt appeared from a doorway and walked toward him. This was the first person he'd seen since he'd left Celeste. He stopped in front of Slater.

"Are you an intern?" He lifted the card hanging from the lanyard around his neck. "You have to wear your ID."

"And you don't have to have a shiner," Slater said, "but you definitely will if I have to punch you in the face."

The guy frowned and stood up straighter, and Slater walked past him. A few yards farther was a lighted exit sign, and he stopped to look through the glass in the door. This was a stairwell leading up. He stepped inside and mounted the stairs, pushing open the door at the top.

It was like stepping into the past again, but this space was ornate, dotted with classical columns and lit by daylight, with a polished marble floor and a high arched ceiling. Looking up, he studied the murals on the walls. He'd been in this rotunda before, long ago. In his mind, city hall was on the next street over. But it filled the whole block, so it made sense it was on Spring Street too.

Walking toward the entrance, he thought about it. The tunnels were about more than just deliveries. Celeste had pointed out a speakeasy. The politicos of a hundred years ago could sneak back to that space to get their booze on.

Outside on the wide steps down to the street, he

stopped for a moment and blinked to adjust to the bright daylight. On the sidewalk, a guy with wild hair and a ripped-up ski jacket was staggering toward him. Slater waited to let him pass before he descended the last few steps.

A woman paused on the steps next to him, watching the guy. "It's like the zombie apocalypse."

Slater eyed her sidelong. Wearing a royal-blue suit and pearls, this was an upscale desk jockey. She looked a little familiar, but he couldn't read the ID card hanging around her neck.

"An apocalypse is going to take more than one junkie," he said.

"Why is he all hunched over like that?"

"It's fetty and tranq."

She briefly glanced at him. "What are you talking about?"

"The fentanyl on the streets is laced with xylazine now. It's a tranquilizer that attacks their muscles and makes them walk with a stoop."

"It looks like it attacks his skin too."

"He's been scratching at his face because he can't really feel it," Slater said. "I'm surprised you people let them come around your fancy office building."

"It's not just an office building. City hall is in the middle of the city. That's the point."

"I'm sure they want it to appear that way. But the politicians try to keep the hopheads over by Mac-Arthur Park, where they don't have to look at them. That actually makes Westlake the core of the apocalypse."

"Are you not concerned that you might be talking to an elected official right now?"

"What, you're offended by the truth? If you're a politician, you should be used to that. You're not the moron who represents my district. I know what that trash bag looks like. Beyond that, I don't really care who works here."

"You do realize there are whole teams of people on the streets every day dealing with this problem."

"Not very effectively, I'd say." Slater gestured to the guy, who'd stopped walking and stood there in front of them, swaying on his feet. "Lo, the zombies have breached the Civic Center."

The guy turned toward them, maybe reacting to Slater's movement. He looked more lucid than his gait had implied, but his eyes were glassy. Mounting a couple of steps, he flashed a gap-toothed leer.

"What you got for me?"

"Spread out," Slater said.

"For a twenty I will."

He raised his voice. "I said beat it."

He reached for Slater's shoulder with an unsteady hand, and Slater threw a quick rabbit punch to his jaw. His head snapped sideways, and he yowled, and stumbled down a few steps. Shaking his head, he continued on his shuffling trajectory.

"What are you doing?" the woman demanded. "You can't just punch people."

"Says the woman who's standing around wearing three strands of pearls while sixty thousand of these birds are sleeping rough."

"You don't get to judge me."

"With any luck the voters in your district will. You and all the other piggies at the trough."

Before she could snap back, he walked away. He

wasn't even sure she was on the council. Those grifters wouldn't be caught dead in public without their bodyguards, and she was outside on her own. But he'd seen that face somewhere.

It was easier walking above ground, as there were familiar landmarks, and the distance felt shorter than it had in the tunnel. Soon he was back on the block with Clyde's buildings. He let himself in the entrance he'd first used, and walked the corridor on the ground floor, then tried the keys in the door at the end. One of them worked, and he stepped through into the next building. Pulling it closed, he walked the length of the building. This end had to be right up against Sackett's, but there was no door here, just a blank wall. Unless he was missing something, that meant the only connecting door between these two buildings was in that upstairs dining room.

He stepped into the stairwell and descended a level, passing a guy he hadn't seen before. Not even trying to be subtle, he looked Slater over as they passed. Milena's explanation felt accurate—the jewelry business had a concentration of valuable stuff. It made sense they were wary.

Mounting the stairs again, he went to Clyde's office, and pulled his satchel around, ready to dig out the calculator with the bug. Knocking on the door, he stepped in.

Behind his desk, Clyde grinned and sat back. "So what progress have you made?"

"I've had a look around, and talked to some of your tenants. I'm feeling things out."

"Has that given you any indications about what Les is up to?"

"It's early days."

Rising, Clyde stepped close, then dropped his chin, and held his gaze. "I know you won't let me down."

It would be so easy to pull him into a kiss. He knew that's what the guy was angling for, and it was hard to resist. Fuck it, he decided, and put a hand on the back of his neck, and mashed their lips together. Clyde was warm, his mouth firm. He ran his hands into Slater's hair.

Eventually Slater pulled back. "You're quite the wolf."

"You're just saying that."

He adjusted his crotch. "First it was Milton, and now you. The pair of you are intent on making me chubby."

"We broke through into the sealed wing of the hotel. Do you want to check it out?"

Slater took a breath. "Totally."

NINE

SLATER SHIFTED HIS SATCHEL onto his back as he stepped into the hall, and waited as Clyde locked his office door. Right across the hall he unlocked another door and flicked on the lights as he stepped in. It was a storeroom, Slater saw, with metal shelves, and mops and brooms, and a stack of five-gallon buckets. From a shelf Clyde pulled out a folded-up pile of canvas, off-white with dark scuffs and stains, and tucked it under his arm. It looked like a moving blanket or a painter's drop cloth.

Slater followed him to the next building, and down a flight, and through another locked doorway. This had to be upstairs in the main part of the hotel. Unlike the utilitarian office suites in the other corridors, the doors here were dark wood, with finished frames, and decorative numbers next to them—these were guest rooms.

The hallway jogged into an elevator lobby and continued farther. He could see it now, at the end of the hall, a doorway into a darker space. The bricks were gone, but it was obvious where they had been, with dusty pink residue and bits of mortar clinging to the polished wood of the frame. He followed Clyde through.

The vibe was different here. This hallway was lit only by daylight filtering in from the doorways on the street side. Most of them hung open, and each had a frosted glass transom above it. The walls had an orangey-brown wallpaper in a scrolly floral pattern, water-stained and mottled and peeling in places. The board floor was dark and grimy. Everything felt like it was slowly decaying back to black.

"The floors feel solid, don't they?" Clyde said. "My guy says we can probably just sand and stain and put down a layer of resin. They don't need to be replaced."

"I can't believe anyone could afford to just let this sit here for so long."

"The shops on the ground floor pay enough rent to cover the property taxes. Those haven't gone up since Prop 13 in the seventies." Clyde pointed to the glass above one of the guest room doors, hanging open at an angle. "My guy called those transom windows. He said they used them for ventilation in the days before air conditioning."

Slater stepped into the room below it, then into the one across the hall. They'd been cleared of furniture, but this one still had a little desk with an antique typewriter on it. Both were covered in enough dust to imply they'd been here since the brick barrier went up.

Stepping out again, he walked to the end of the hallway. "It's not a very big footprint."

"I haven't broken into the other floors yet, but I flew a drone outside the windows to look in."

"They have the same vibe as here?"

"Even the same wallpaper. It looks like the pigeons got in on the top floor, because there's some guano around, but it's all still intact, and I know the roof is good."

"Who owns it now?"

"The main part is a local company, and the new owners of this wing are in Shanghai. We're finalizing the details now, and soon we'll be renovating the whole thing."

Clyde stepped into one of the guest rooms and spread the canvas sheet on the floor. Standing in the doorway, Slater watched him work. Clyde stepped over to him, and nuzzled his neck, then met his mouth. When he pulled back, he held his gaze.

"We could be the first people to rock this place in ninety years."

"I wondered what the tarp was for."

He mouthed his neck and whispered, "Make love to me, Slater."

When Slater pushed him toward the tarp, Clyde crouched, then stretched out on his back and dug in his pocket, and handed him a little container. It was lube. He'd totally planned this.

Slater straddled his hips, and dropped to his knees, and massaged his chest. The guy had some definition in his pecs. He unbuttoned his shirt, and mouthed his neck and his chest. Eventually he sat up and unbuckled his belt. Clyde shoved his trousers down and pulled them off. He had a raging stiffy. Kneeling between his legs, Slater popped his fly, and pulled out his junk, already hard.

"You're not going to take your jeans off?" Clyde said.

"Do you want me to?"

"It's fine. It's hot."

Once he'd lubed up, Slater pressed into him, moving slowly, his hands on his waist, drawing him closer. Eventually he started pounding him, and Clyde reached for the back of his neck, pulling him in, kissing his mouth. Slater pulled back as he came, groaning and straining into him. A minute later, he sat back on his knees and grabbed Clyde's cock.

"What do you want me to do with this?"

"Do you want to smoke me?"

Slater shifted down and took him into his mouth. The guy was rock-hard, and he worked him for a while. Clyde climaxed with a spasm, and a shudder ran through his body.

Shifting onto his back, Slater stretched out beside him and caught his breath. The floor felt hard under the thin canvas. He looked up at the stained ceiling. It must have been white at some point. Now it was a mess of reddish-brown stain patterns and dark patches of mold and peeling paint.

"You're so good at that," Clyde said.

"And you're a pistol, son."

He rose, and buckled his belt, and waited for Clyde to pull his pants on. Once he was dressed, Clyde grinned and paused to kiss him.

"Grab the other end."

They folded up the tarp, then walked out to the main part of the hotel. Once Clyde had unlocked the door into the next building, and they'd stepped through, Slater stopped at the stairwell.

"I'm going out this way."

"That was a blast," Clyde said.

Slater trotted down to the door to the street, then crossed to the parking lot. He felt a little guilty about fucking the guy. Pike hated that he did stuff like that, and he knew it was stupid to stick his dick into his work. But the sex rules said he could hook up when Pike was out of town, or if he needed to do it for work, and technically it was work-related.

Pausing on the sidewalk before he went into the parking structure, he thought about how far it was to Della's office. It couldn't be more than ten minutes' walk over to the Financial District. He could leave his car here.

The tone of the city changed as he got closer to the new office towers. The old Downtown of Sackett's and Greenleaf had a gritty vibe, the same as where his office was. That whole area bordered Skid Row. Over here the new Downtown was bland and sterile, with glass-curtain skyscrapers and car-centric design where street level was mostly about parking access.

In the lobby of Della's building he walked over to the elevators. They hadn't put up card-key gates like some of these towers had. He didn't know how many floors Cudahy Mutual rented, but they weren't likely to be as security conscious as the bankers and lawyers and consultants in this neighborhood.

Stepping off on 34, he walked into Della's office.

An unfamiliar guy was on the front desk. In his twenties, his dark hair was in a natty style, and he was wearing a powder-blue shirt and a red necktie.

"What happened to Crystal?" Slater said.

The guy gave him the once-over. "Are you looking for the mail room? It's two floors down."

"What is it with this place?" Slater demanded. "Everybody's a wise guy. Do they pay you extra to throw shade?"

He raised his eyebrows. "If you need emergency housing, the shelter is over on Main."

Leaning in, Slater slapped him, left and then right, a rapid kovac. "I've had enough of your guff."

He raised his arms and rolled his chair backward and bumped into the cabinet behind him. "Stop it," he shouted.

"You'll take it and you'll like it," Slater said through his teeth, and leaned in to pull the guy's arm down and land one more blow.

As he stepped back, Della walked out. Pushing sixty, she had her hair in a money style, and wore a print blouse and a black skirt that emphasized her narrow waist.

"What are you doing?" she said. "You can't manhandle my staff."

"I'm calling security," the guy said.

Slater jabbed a finger at him. "Stay away from that phone."

"Jacob, settle down. You don't need to call anybody." She frowned at Slater and beckoned him to follow.

Walking into her office, Della let him step in, then closed the door. She had a great view from up here, the concrete and asphalt and greenery of the basin stretching to the hazy horizon.

Della stepped behind her desk. "I pay you to do that in the field, not in here."

"You haven't been paying me at all lately." He dropped into one of the guest chairs. "Where's Betty Burnout?"

"You mean Crystal? I know you two enjoyed needling each other. She got promoted. Her new position is assessing claims."

"She'd be good at that. I know she's no idiot. No scammer will be able to lay a snow job on her." He sat up. "So when somebody's doing a big commercial building renovation, with permits and financing and all that, they need to get insurance too."

"Construction and real estate aren't my field, but I'd say that's probably accurate."

"Can you get a look at the documentation for a specific project? It's tangential to the case I'm working, but I want to know what's involved."

"If they applied for insurance," Della said, "I can probably dig up something."

"Will you need a reason or an excuse for doing that?"

She smiled. "Government works that way. We don't." She rolled open a desk drawer and pulled out a little pad with coil binding at the top. "What do you know about it?"

He rattled off the address of the hotel, and Clyde's name. "It's a hotel renovation project. I don't know the name of the company that's doing the work, but there's more than one property owner."

"I'll see what I can find out." She set down her

pen. "I wish I had some work for you, but it sounds like you've got other things to do."

"I still need work. I'm in the middle of buying a chunk of empty land out in the Mojave. Twenty acres of pristine desert landscape. It's not going to pay for itself."

She sat back. "What is your deal with the Mojave? You keep sending my people out there. To recover the Kawada necklace, and then that pallet of palladium."

"The palladium was actually in the Great Basin Desert, and I didn't put it there. But you're right. I kind of love it out there."

"Is that dreamboat of yours on board with this purchase?"

He frowned. "Pike doesn't tell me what to do."

"If that's the case, he sounds like a keeper." As he stood up, she held his gaze. "Don't rough up my receptionist. Jacob is a gentle soul."

"You could have fooled me." Slater flashed his palms. "It's really up to him. If he chooses his words wisely, he won't force me to react."

As he walked out to the elevators, Jacob glared at him.

"What happened to your face?" Slater said. "It looks painful."

"Prick," he growled.

Not looking back, Slater called to him, "See you next Tuesday."

His phone had buzzed a minute ago, and in the elevator he pulled it out to check. The notification said NEW TALKING. Svetlana's bug had recorded sound in Les James's office. There were two clips, he saw, one of them from earlier today that he hadn't noticed.

No one else was in the elevator, so he tapped to listen to them. The newest one was Les's voice, speaking another language. That had to be Armenian. Only Les was audible. She was on a phone call. The second clip was in English.

"Spill the tea, girlfriend," Les said.

"He wouldn't say," a man's voice said. "I think he knows something, but he wasn't about to tell me. That guy has an ego the size of his Bronco."

"I guess I can take a run at him myself. But he likes you better."

"Only because I put out. Listen, I've got to get to my meeting."

"Go on, then," Les said. "One day at a time."

That was the end of it, and he tucked his phone away. It felt like the recording had started in the middle of the conversation. Maybe they'd walked into the office at that point. They were talking about twelve-step. He'd never heard Lars's voice, but thinking about it, it had to be him. Lars was a twelve-stepper, and the only person in their orbit that he knew drove a Bronco was Woody.

Pausing in the lobby, Slater checked the listings for twelve-step meetings, and found the one Woody had mentioned, in the building on Skid Row. It was happening soon—that's where Lars was headed. He could make it if he hustled.

Assuming a rapid pace, he headed back toward the old Downtown, as the last dregs of sunlight faded to the gray of dusk. He turned onto the street with the new building. Technically this was just outside Skid Row. There used to be a string of restaurants on this block and the next one, but the pandemic had killed most of them. The unguarded doorways and sidewalk space had quickly filled with tents and sleeping bags.

At least the street trees on this block hadn't died with the eateries. There was an old established jacaranda and newer pink tab trees. Those were delicate but they looked to be in good shape, in contrast to the stark derelict neighborhood. In a couple of months they'd bust out in pink flowers, especially dramatic because they didn't produce leaves until later.

When he tried the door, it was locked. The guard at the desk inside looked up at him, and the door lock buzzed open. Slater walked in, and the guy looked him over, but he must have decided he didn't look like he was going to bust up the place, as he soon turned his focus back to the blue glow of his phone screen.

In the wide hallway with the meeting rooms, taped to a closed door he found a sheet of printer paper that read WOMEN'S ENCOUNTER GROUP. Lars wasn't going to be in that one. Farther down, a similar sheet taped to a half-open door said NA. He'd assumed Lars was in AA, but he could easily be a junkie rather than a drunk. It was hard to detect it in people after they got clean. Looking in, he spotted Lars, then stepped inside.

The room had a long table in the middle with a dozen stackable chairs around it, and more chairs lining the walls. The meeting hadn't started, it seemed, but a dozen or so people were sitting at the table and chatting. There was a range of gender and young and old people alike. Some of them could easily be on the skids, but others looked like they weren't disenfranchised—office drones and blue-collar types. Wearing a blue plaid shirt, Lars was one of those. His red hair stood out like the light bar on a fire truck.

Slater took a chair opposite him and farther down the table. The guy in the seat next to him, with a scruffy gray beard and wild hair, greeted him as he sat. Slater nodded and mumbled "Hey" in acknowledgment.

Watching Lars talk to the woman next to him, the guy looked tired, like it took effort to stay awake. In other circumstances he'd assume he was strung out on opioids, but it made no sense to come to a twelve-step meeting when you were high.

At the end of the table a guy stood up and introduced himself. "I want to welcome everyone. It's great to see you mugs here. First of all, there will be no crosstalk in this meeting." He looked pointedly around the table.

It made sense he'd have to read the riot act. Some of these fools could be permanently addled. That happened with dusters and speed freaks, even cokeheads. The guy read from a book, a couple of pages about taking a personal inventory, and next they all listened to a different guy talk. Wearing a heavy jacket, his hair was in little dreads. Slater couldn't decide if he was homeless or just a little rough. His voice was deep and gravelly.

"Back in the day, I was strung out on Quaaludes. We called them disco biscuits."

It was hard to imagine this guy in a discotheque. He didn't look like he had the stamina to make it across the street, never mind shaking his booty on the dance floor. It must have been a while ago.

"When you couldn't get 'ludes anymore," he went on, "I thought I could get clean. But then somebody started importing them from India. That's when I had a revelation." He made his eyes wide. "The 'ludes weren't the problem. It was me."

Slater folded his arms and took a breath. The guy talked a little more, and eventually wound it up.

"I have to remind myself that I'm not a bad person who needs to behave. I'm a sick person, and I want to heal."

As he sat down, people around the table clapped for him. Slater stifled a scoff. He knew you weren't supposed to give feedback. That was considered crosstalk. It seemed like a wasted opportunity, considering this guy really needed it.

A couple of other people spoke, not including Lars, who sat there listening. At one point he started blinking rapidly, and inhaled sharply, and sat up. A minute later he shook his head like he was groggy. The guy was clearly struggling to stay awake.

Finally the meeting ended, and some of the crowd got up and moved toward the coffee urn on the table by the door. Lars rose and stood chatting with the guy who'd spoken first, with the heavy coat and the dreads. Slater had seen enough, he decided, and stood up, and headed for the door.

The guy who'd started the meeting had a paper coffee cup in hand, and stepped into his path, and introduced himself. "Thanks for coming. I know sometimes that's the hardest step."

"It was actually easy," Slater said. "The door wasn't locked."

He laughed. "Stay for coffee, if you want."

"I've got stuff to do."

"I hope we'll see you again."

He walked out. That wasn't going to happen. These patsies were sitting around trying not to get high. Slater had to drink to make all this tolerable.

TEN

THE FASHION DISTRICT WAS only a few blocks from here, closer than going back for his car, so Slater walked. Upstairs in his office the lights were off, and the statue of Rey Pascual sat on the front desk, silently watching the door.

"How you doing, Rey?" he said.

He sat at his desk, and leaned back, and heaved his boots up. He'd hoped to find Max here, but it would have to be a text instead of a face-to-face. He tapped at his phone:

> Do you know an Armenian speaker that you trust? I need somebody to listen to a recording.

A minute later Max's response came:

> I've had some Armenian clients, but nobody I could ask for something like that.

He really hated to get into it, as it could bear an exorbitant price, but he gritted his teeth and texted Doris:

Does any of your posse speak Armenian? I need a brief recording translated.

Her reply came soon after:

Probably. I'll check.

Slater texted back:

Ticktock. This needs to happen soon.

Setting his phone in his lap, he closed his eyes and massaged his temples. He still hadn't completely recovered from last night. He'd started to drift off when his phone buzzed with the worst ring tone of all: *No wire hangers! … What's wire hangers doing in this closet when I told you no wire hangers, ever!*

"Damn it," he snapped, and picked up. "What do you need, Doris?"

"What do *I* need? My beloved son, the *gantse macher*, asked me for an urgent favor. I'm following up."

"That was a while ago, but I guess I remember."

She laughed. "It was a few minutes ago. So is this recording something that'll traumatize my friend?"

"I don't speak Armenian," Slater said, "so I have no idea. Is this someone you trust?"

"You don't need to question that. Her name is Nara. She said you can stop by her place in the morning. I'll text you her address."

"Send her name too."

"I'm looking forward to celebrating Hannukah," Doris said.

"You say that because you think I'm going to flake. It's in my calendar."

"I know Pike will remind you."

Once he'd ended the call, he pushed himself out of the chair, and stepped into Max's office, and pulled out the other seventies vintage suit he kept in the wardrobe. This one was heavier, in a fake wool fabric, with an oversize houndstooth pattern in warm green and brown.

After he changed into it, he locked up the office and stepped into the men's room down the hall to check his look. It was such a wild suit. The lapels were huge, and the pants flared at the bottom. He rode down to the street and walked back to Clyde's buildings. It was cold out, and the faux wool didn't keep him very warm. It was still a little early to go up to Greenleaf, he decided, and walked past it, past the jewelry stores shuttered for the night, to the street entrance of the building where Clyde's office was. Digging out the key ring he'd given him, he let himself in.

Slater spent a few minutes prowling the corridors. He wanted to see the place after hours, and it was quiet now, and felt like nobody was around. He descended to the level below the street. All the office doors were closed. Clearly nobody was working.

Back on the ground floor, he went around to the stairwell up, and climbed to the floor above Clyde's office. In this corridor he saw light from an open office door. A guy with gray hair and a bald patch on top was peering at a computer monitor, and looked up at him when Slater paused in the doorway.

"Are you looking for the nightclub?"

"I was looking for Les James," Slater said. "Have you seen her around?"

"Not tonight. She'll be at work now. Are you the surveyor that Park hired?"

"That's right. You're in the jewelry business?"

"I'm a bookkeeper. Why are you here so late?"

"I'm headed to Greenleaf," Slater said. "What are you doing here at this hour?"

"Tax season is coming up."

"Have fun with that."

The guy was right, he realized, as he walked away. Les would be working. Whatever skulduggery she was up to would happen earlier in the day, or after the bars closed.

In the stairwell he descended to the level that connected to Sackett's upstairs dining room. He used the keys to get through the connecting door into the next building. Sackett's was still another building along, and as he walked, he realized he'd picked the wrong floor. That access point was another level down.

When he stepped into the stairwell, a woman was descending, and paused a few steps above him. Wearing a black dress that hugged her curvy figure, her hair was in a tidy tight Afro, and she was wearing a vibrant pink dahlia.

"You must be 604," Slater said.

She frowned. "How do you know where I live?"

He had assumed it was an office, but there were lots of live-work spaces around. "I saw your dahlias on the roof, and now you're wearing one. How did you get it to bloom so late in the year?"

"I have a planter box in my unit." She stepped

down to the landing. "I started them late. They turned out kind of perfect. Is it weird to be wearing a fresh flower in the middle of the winter?"

"Not even a little," Slater said. "You look like a million bucks."

"So who told you the ones on the roof were mine?"

"Clyde Park."

Her expression hardened. "That little creep."

"You're not a fan?"

"He's nosy. What's your name?"

"Slater."

"Talisha. Tali when I want it to sound white."

"It's fine to leave the tubers in the soil," Slater said, "but you should cut back the foliage."

Her brow furrowed. "I thought it didn't matter. It's all dead. The tubers are dormant."

"If you cut them down, you won't get any spurious growth in March. More important, right now you can tell what they are, and if somebody from Oaxaca notices, they'll dig up the tubers and have them for lunch."

"I didn't know they were edible."

"Lots of people do."

She nodded. "That sounds like good intel. Are you working for Clyde?"

"I'm doing some assessments for him."

"If you're planning to come into my unit, I need twenty-four hours' notice."

"I'm not going to do that," Slater said. "Do you know one of the other tenants named Les James?"

"I've seen her around," Talisha said. "I'm actually going to her club tonight. Greenleaf."

"Where have you seen her around?"

"Her business is here, so she's at Sackett's some-times, and upstairs in her own place." She waved a hand. "And out by the dumpster, and weirdly, in the incinerator room."

"Why is that weird?"

"There's no incinerators anymore. Some of the machinery is still there, but you can't burn your trash. Not since the 1950s. It's completely disused."

"What was she doing?"

"Who knows? I saw her walking out."

"Was anybody else down there?"

"I didn't see anyone, but I didn't really hang out. Just long enough to figure out what it was."

"What were you doing there?"

Talisha shrugged. "Getting to know the building."

"That sounds like a lie."

She laughed. "You're nervy, Slater, calling me a liar to my face."

"What were you really doing down there?"

Lowering her voice, even though there was no one else in the stairwell, she held his gaze. "Apparently there are these old tunnels connecting the buildings in this neighborhood. Just below street level. I was looking for a way in."

He watched her for a moment. That actually had the ring of truth, he decided.

"Do you want to walk with me to Greenleaf? I'm on my way there myself."

"You're definitely dressed for it," Talisha said. "I dig the houndstooth. The thing is, I've got a girl-friend, or an almost girlfriend. I'm meeting her there. So I'm not going to drink with you, or dance with you, or sit and listen to your man stuff."

He frowned. "I asked you to walk over there, woman, not to get engaged. Besides, I'm exclusively on dick."

"So that settles that." She gestured down the stairs. "Let's go, then, dick hound."

Slater trotted down a flight and stepped into the hallway. "We can go this way." As they walked abreast, he scoffed. "She thinks I want to dance with her. Let's hope your ego will fit through the door." Digging out the key ring, he found the one that fit.

"Why do you have keys for this?" Talisha said.

"Like I said, I'm working for Clyde Park." He got it open, and they stepped into the upstairs dining room at Sackett's.

"I did not know this doorway was here."

"They painted it to blend in. It's not a fire exit, so it's not marked, and there's no crash bar."

A few people were at the tables, eating from trays, and the stairway leading up didn't have the chain across it now.

"This sounds like the house band," Talisha said as they ascended. "That's so much more fun than a DJ."

The bouncer on the stool at the top carded them both, and after he took a perfunctory glance at their IDs, they walked in, and Talisha strode toward the bar. Slater paused to survey the room. There were lots of people here, especially along the bar. It seemed early for a crowd, but maybe there was a headliner tonight that he hadn't heard about. There was no sign of Les James.

The band was playing a hard tune, but nobody was up dancing. Eight musicians were on stage, all wearing the green velvet band jacket. He'd met the woman on sax. She was thin, with black hair, and he knew she was the band leader. The bug in Les's office had picked up her and Les yammering about the song list. On the drum kit was Lars, his arms flailing maniacally with the fast beat.

At the bar, Talisha was standing next to a woman on a stool, leaning close to her. That had to be her date. The woman was dark, maybe South Asian, and had bleached part of her hair blond, and was wearing gold jewelry. The pair of them were talking intently, ignoring the music and the crowd, fully absorbed in each other. He remembered that phase with Pike, and how that felt. When there was nothing else in the world to do or see or think about except that big mook.

Walking over to the service area, he ordered a soda water. While he was waiting for it, he felt eyes on him, and looked down the bar. A guy was watching him. He'd seen this blockhead before, walking out of Milena's place. He was beefy, and basically fuckable, but he looked like a cop. That suit could have easily come out of a police station undercover staging closet. Even the way the guy was looking at him felt like law enforcement—open and intent, with zero mack or flirt factor.

Once he had his soda water, he shot the guy a look and threw up his free hand, a tacit *What the fuck,* then walked to the opposite end of the bar, closer to the stage. Over here he had a good view of the door into the back. He planted his feet apart and stood watching the band. Talisha was right: They were way more engaging than canned music.

The pianist did a solo as part of the song, and then it drifted into a solo by the guy with the trumpet. He saw Les appear from the back, glowed up again, in a dark-blue dress that showed cleavage, her hair down. She stood watching the band for a while, then went back inside.

After the band had run through its set, the stage lights dimmed, and they started to vacate as the recorded music came up. At the service area he ordered another soda water, and watched as Les walked out onto the floor. She approached a table with a pair of straight couples and stood chatting with them. He couldn't hear them over the music and all the other voices, but it looked like a prosaic conversation, just Les making the rounds and schmoozing with her clientele.

Looking down the bar, he saw that the cop was still here, and he was watching Les now. Why was the same cop who'd been talking to Milena hanging around Greenleaf? It felt like it had to be connected to Clyde's ask—the overlap was too much to be coincidental.

From the double doors, Lars walked out, and strode past the bar. He glanced at Slater standing there, then did a double-take, and smiled as he stepped over.

"I saw you in my meeting tonight. You were dressed differently."

"This isn't a denim kind of place," Slater said.

"Tell me about it." He pulled open the lapel of the green jacket. "The band wears velour. I'm Lars."

"Slater. So is it hard to stay sober when you work in a bar?"

"Sober is a goal, not my current reality. But I am clean. Almost three years now." Lars gestured at the room. "This place isn't really triggering for me. How long have you been hitting up meetings?"

"Not that long."

"Well, that's a really good one. You get people from both ends of the economy."

"Skid Row types, I'm thinking," Slater said, "and the people who live in the residential conversions around here."

"Lots of people come into the neighborhood for work too. So there's ethnic diversity, and different generations. At meetings in WeHo everybody looks just like me."

"I'm impressed you're aware that it doesn't have to be that way."

"When you're in the rooms in other neighborhoods, you either act like an entitled dick, or you realize you have white privilege." Lars grinned. "Anyway, you should keep coming back."

"I saw you on the drums tonight."

"This is a great place to perform. I love the music we do."

Slater put his hands on his hips. "I'd say it knocks you on your ass."

"Do I look that wiped out?"

"Like you haven't slept in days."

"I haven't," he said intently. "I'm in the middle of a research project, but the plan fell through."

"What kind of research?"

Lars raised his eyebrows. "The most important kind of all. Metaphysical research. Exploring the very nature of reality."

"Does that mean ghost hunting?"

"Ghosts are for dilettantes. What I'm doing is a

whole paranormal thing. I need a VCR."

"Of course," Slater said. "A VCR is the first thing I think of when I hear the words 'paranormal research.'"

Woody stepped up to them and clapped Slater on the shoulder. "Is Lars hitting on you?"

"I don't think so," Slater said, "but if he is, I can probably handle it."

"Watch yourself," Woody said. "He's got rhythm, but he's slick."

Lars flashed him a thin smile as he walked away. "So you're a friend of Bill's and a friend of Dorothy's."

"I'm a booze hag and I'm on dick," Slater said, "if that's what you mean."

He chuckled. "In that suit no one is going to call you a hag."

Lars hadn't asked him how he knew Woody. That meant either he was totally oblivious and self-involved, like lots of people were, or he already knew.

"Listen," Slater said. "You need a VCR. I have a VCR. It's sitting on a shelf in my garage. I've been meaning to take it to the thrift store."

"I appreciate the offer, but that's only part of the problem. I also need a bed, or even a couch in a quiet place. And I have to do it tonight. My roommate decided to paint today. Everything at my place is messed up. I can't even get in the door."

"I have a spare room. It's technically an office, but it has a bed in it. You can close the door and do whatever you need to do." Slater frowned. "It's not messy, is it? Like taxidermy, or throwing perfume around, or fabric dye?"

"It's nothing crazy. You'd do that for me? I don't even know you."

"Well, I know you're clean, and I know Les. If she hired you, I know you're not going to rob me." He shrugged. "There's nothing to steal anyway."

"This is amazing," Lars said. "The band is done for the evening. I can go whenever you're ready."

Slater pulled out his phone. "Let me check with the old ball and chain."

"It sounds like you're in a bar," Pike said when he picked up. "Are you at Greenleaf?"

"How would you feel about a one-time overnight guest sleeping in your office?"

"It's your house, so it's your call. It's fine by me. Who is it? Do I need to lock up my laptop?"

"You can assess that for yourself. We'll be there soon." He ended the call and eyed Lars. "Green light. We can go."

"Give me a minute to change. I'll meet you out front."

ELEVEN

WHEN LARS APPEARED ON the sidewalk, he'd changed back into jeans and the plaid shirt, his day pack slung over his shoulder. They crossed to the parking structure, and Slater unlocked the passenger door of the Continental for him.

"This is quite the car."

Slater stepped around the trunk. "I know."

"How old is it?"

"It's not old," he said, climbing in. "It's classic. Early seventies."

"Why does it only have two doors?" Lars said. "It needs about six. You could seat the whole band in here. Their instruments too."

"It was meant for commuting to work, not hauling rugrats around."

Slater maneuvered out of the lot and headed north.

"So who's the ball and chain?" Lars said.

"His name is Pike."

"What's he like?"

"He's all gravy," Slater said. "Then you look under the gravy, and there's more gravy. All the way down. You'll probably meet him. He likes people."

"He's gravy? As in he's brown and salty?"

"As in he puts up with my crazy. He doesn't put demands on me. I still haven't completely figured him out." He waved a hand. "He's optimistic but he's not stupid. To me that seems like a contradiction, but it's who he is. He likes to dance, and he reads books. It's weird."

"That's what I need," Lars said. "Someone who builds me up, not tears me down."

He accelerated onto the freeway, and minutes later turned onto his street.

"What is this, Angelino Heights?"

"Close. Echo Park." Slater nosed into the garage and climbed out. Stepping over to the workbench, he picked up the VCR, and set the old mini TV that came with it on top. Nodding for Lars to follow, he carried them up the stairs, and into the back bedroom, and set them on the bed.

Lars walked in behind him. "This looks so inviting right now." He set his backpack on the end of the bed and went into the adjoining bathroom.

"Hey, forty-niner," Pike said, stepping into the room. He was wearing a black T-shirt and sweat pants. "Groovy threads. Where's your guest?"

Lars came out of the bathroom, and Pike introduced himself.

"Why do you call him forty-niner?" Lars said.

"He only likes pants that were invented during the gold rush."

"That's a very sweet pet name. What does Slater call you?"

"Reddy Kilowatt. Because I had to tase him when we first met."

"That's intense."

Slater frowned. "You didn't actually have to. It was a choice." He raised his eyebrows and jabbed two fingers at him. "Zap."

"It worked out, though," Pike said. "Lars, can I offer you a beer?"

"I'm actually on the wagon, like Slater."

His eyebrows shot up. "Oh, really?"

"We were at the same twelve-step meeting tonight."

"Well, viva sobriety." He eyed Slater. "What's with the old TV?"

"I can explain all that," Lars said, "but can we sit somewhere?"

Pike beckoned him to follow, and they trudged upstairs, and through the kitchen.

"Why don't you have furniture in here?" Lars said, looking over the big empty room.

"Why does everybody always say that?" Slater said. "I need it to be open. Space to breathe, and space to think." He gestured to the French doors. "There's chairs farther in."

In the kitchen Pike poured soda water into three glasses, and Slater led them to the lounge furniture. He sat in one of the easy chairs, and Pike took the other, setting his glass on the coffee table. Lars sat at one end of the sofa.

"I like the outdoor turf," he said, reaching down to feel it. "It kind of works."

"That's Pike's decorating chops," Slater said. "So what do you need the VCR for?"

He sipped his water before he spoke. "It's called psycho-electroid dream recording. You have to stay awake for at least twenty-four hours so that your dreams will be extra strength."

"Ouch," Pike said, his brow furrowing.

"Then you attach a bare copper wire to your third eye." He tapped the middle of his forehead. "You plug the other end into the recorder. The in port."

"That makes a lot of sense," Slater said. "You wouldn't go connecting it to the out port."

"You start recording with the VCR as you fall asleep," Lars went on, "and it tapes two hours of your intense dreams."

Pike picked up his glass. "What comes out on the tape?"

"I'll find out tomorrow."

"Did you come up with this exercise?"

"It was in a book I read about quartz."

"I'm surprised that it came from a book," Slater said. "I assumed it was from some influencer who made it up last Tuesday." He frowned. "Although the fact that it was in a book doesn't make it any more plausible."

"It's totally plausible." Lars's tone was intent. "The unseen world is all around you all the time. You need to wake up."

"So how does quartz relate to psycho-electroid dreaming?" Pike said.

"It's a natural recording system. Because of the shape of the crystals, apparently. Quartz can replay events that have happened in proximity to it. It's called the stone tape phenomenon." He raised his eyebrows. "That means crystals and rocks can record and replay things, especially traumatic events. It's one theory about what ghosts are—playback of stuff that happened long ago. Quartz is especially good at it."

"Why not just record your dreams with quartz?" Pike said.

"Because there's no play button," he said slowly, as if maybe Pike hadn't been paying attention, "like there is on a VCR."

"I wonder if you could do it with newer technology."

"I should look into that." Lars sipped at his soda water. "That book came out in the nineties. There might be an easier way by now."

"Isn't there some paranormal thing where metal records information too?" Slater said. "I've seen people read rings and keys."

"That's called psychometry. You can read metal to get feelings and impressions. It's not scientific like the stone tape phenomenon, though. It's way more out-there."

"I get it," Slater said. "It sounds completely improbable compared to taping a VCR wire to your forehead."

"I can actually do psychometry, although I don't make a habit of it. Drummers already have a reputation." He shrugged. "If I advertised my psychic power, it would just amplify that stereotype."

"What reputation?" Slater said.

"That we're all flaky, and we're OCD, and we're emotionally messy. It's not true."

"Is that your job?" Pike said. "You're a drummer?"

"I'm in the house band at Greenleaf."

"We go there sometimes. I'll look for you." Pike dug in the pocket of his sweat pants and held out his keys. "Can you read these?"

Lars didn't reach for them, but set down his glass. "Before I handle them, you should pick the key that you've had the longest."

He messed with the ring for a moment, and pulled one of them off. "This key—"

"Don't tell me anything about it," Lars said, cutting him off. He sat forward. "Give me a second to get ready." He closed his eyes. "You can't cross your legs. That interferes with the flow of psychic energy."

Slater stifled a scoff. "Where did you learn all this?"

"Pipe down for a minute. I need to concentrate."

Slater folded his arms and watched him sitting there, taking slow deep breaths. Eventually Lars extended his hand, not opening his eyes. Pike leaned across and set the key on his palm, and he folded his other hand over it. He sat that way for a minute before he spoke, eyes still closed.

"I see you with another man. Not Slater. A Black dude. You're sitting on blue folding chairs. At a concert hall or a stadium."

"Busted," Slater said.

Pike laughed. "That's pretty vague."

"When I first met Davis, you were going to a baseball game with him. And here's the cold hard evidence recorded by your keys. His lust for you is burned into the metal."

"I can also see the night sky," Lars said, furrowing his brow. "There's a few stars around. Two of them are brighter than the others. Not far from the horizon. The impression I get is that they're in the northeast. One is kind of blueish, and the other is more yellow."

"Castor and Pollux." Pike eyed Slater and raised his eyebrows. "That's cold hard evidence about you and me."

Lars opened his eyes, and handed the key back. "That's all I got. You can see it's imprecise. With the VCR you get actual scientific data, not just impressions." He waved a hand. "My psychic insights might be a little hazier than usual because I'm so tired."

"I can't believe you've been awake for twenty-four hours," Slater said.

"Longer. Since yesterday morning."

Pike sat up. "You'll want to get to it, then. Hit that record button and fall into the sweet embrace of Morpheus."

"I thought Hypnos was sleep," Slater said, rising with him.

"He is. Morpheus is his son. He brings the dreams."

"Hold up," Lars said. "Are you guys exclusive? Maybe we can mess around before dreamtime."

Pike frowned. "Did Slater advise you to suggest that?"

"I came up with it on my own."

Pike eyed Slater and raised his eyebrows.

"It's your call," Slater said.

"I guess we can do that. As long as you don't fall asleep halfway through."

Lars dropped his chin. "How could I, with a smoke-show like you involved?"

Pike laughed and walked toward the kitchen.

"Weren't you seeing Woody?" Slater said.

"Why does that matter?"

"I can't sleep with you if you're emotionally entangled with him."

"I'm done with that guy," Lars said. "He's way too full of himself."

Downstairs, in the front bedroom, Pike started to undress, ditching his sweat pants. He'd quickly become comfortable with the threesome thing, Slater realized. Lars pulled off his shirt. He was actually buff, unexpectedly, and for a twink he had great delts and biceps. It must be the drumming.

Slater draped his suit jacket on the chair, then the pants. Pike stepped up to Lars, running his hands up and down his arms, and leaned in to kiss him. Watching them made Slater's heart pound. He knew he couldn't get pissed. He'd signed up for this.

Stepping behind Lars, he ground his burgeoning woody into his butt cheek, and grabbed Pike's arms, and pulled him close, compressing Lars between them.

"This is so hot," Lars said.

Slater stepped back. "So what do you want to do?"

"I want to fuck this guy." He jutted his chin at Pike. "Can you handle that?"

Pike's eyes narrowed. "I can try."

"If you're doing that, I'm going to do you," Slater said.

"Right on." Lars climbed onto the bed. "I get to be the man in the middle."

Moving next to him, Pike stroked his cock, and pressed their mouths together. Slater climbed on the other side of Lars and ran his hands along his torso.

He had great pecs too.

"Man, your body hair," Slater said. "Even your pubes. It's all electric orange."

Pike pulled away and grabbed a condom. When he rolled back, he squeezed Lars's cock. "Safety first."

Lars giggled and let him roll it on. Slater put a hand behind his neck and leaned in to kiss him, exploring his mouth, warm and taut. Eventually Lars pulled back and eyed Pike.

"Can you lie on your belly?"

Slater watched as Pike flipped over, and Lars shifted close to him, and pressed into him. He was hard now too, and grabbed the lube, and slowly eased his way into Lars. Groaning, Lars shifted position, and in a minute he'd worked up to pounding Pike. It didn't take much work for Slater, just finding the right position. Wrapping a hand around his chest, he pulled himself close, and buried his nose in his red mane. Inhaling the scent of his heady sweat, he gradually built up to it, then came.

A moment later Lars groaned and spasmed, straining into Pike, then climbed off. As Pike rolled onto his side, Lars stroked Pike's cock, mouthing his jaw and kissing him. A minute later Pike came, a shudder running through his body. Shifting onto his back, with the heat of Lars's skin next to him, Slater could feel his heartbeat starting to slow.

Suddenly Lars sat up and gasped. "I can't fall asleep."

"You'd better get plugged in," Pike said.

"Can I use the shower in there?"

"Knock yourself out."

Lars climbed off the bed, and scooped up his

clothes, and walked out. Slater heard the back bed-room door close.

Lying on his side, Pike ran his hand on his chest. "You picked him up at a twelve-step meeting?"

"I was surveilling him. He's part of my case."

"Why are you sleeping with somebody from your case?"

"Hey, the gunsel came up with that idea. I'm thinking it was mostly about you, mister smoke-show."

"The smoke is built in. I can't really switch it off."

"Dangerous tools need to be wielded responsibly," Slater said. "I probably should have said no. My policy is to keep my dick out of my work."

"Good thing it's just a policy," Pike said, "and not a rule with any consequences. It tends to get fractured pretty regularly."

"I'd call it an aspirational policy."

He chuckled and nuzzled Slater's neck. They spent a minute close together, and Slater relished the feeling of his warm skin. Eventually he got up, and went upstairs, and poured his ration into a tumbler. Once he'd slammed it, he took a brief supplementary pull from the bottle before he put it away.

Killing the lights, he went down and climbed into bed with Pike.

"You smell like bourbon." Pike wrapped his arms around him, and notched his knees behind Slater's. "That's so odd. I heard you were on the wagon."

"I was playing a role for investigative purposes. It's not nearly as disruptive as you growing your hair out like a damn hippie and riding around on that hog."

"Long hair never hurt anyone."

"Tell that to the shower drain."

Pike chuckled and squeezed him tight.

As his mind descended toward sleep, he savored the feeling, fleeting though it was, of being sated and warm. It was the best thing in the world.

TWELVE

I N THE MORNING MUTED daylight filtered in through the sheers. Slater lay in bed, enjoying the hazy feeling of consciousness gradually returning. Pike wasn't here. A moment later it all came crashing back into his mind. They had a house guest. Pushing himself out of bed, he washed up and pulled on a shirt and a clean pair of jeans. When he walked out, the door to the back bedroom was closed.

He found Pike at the dining table next to the kitchen, wearing a gray buttoned shirt for the office, coffee and cut-up fruit in front of him, his phone in hand.

"Did you hear Lars?" Pike said. "He's snoring like a chainsaw in there. That boy needs a sleep apnea test."

"Maybe that'll show up on the videotape."

He poured a mug of joe from the carafe, and

grabbed an apple, and sat with Pike. He was half-way through it when Lars stepped into the kitchen, dressed and carrying his backpack.

"Did it work?" Pike said.

"I haven't watched the tape yet, but everything will be on it. I'm hoping for a breakthrough."

Pike reached for his hand. "What's this?"

Lars let him take hold of it. There was something written in black ink on the back of his hand, Slater saw.

Pike peered at it. "It says, 'Am I recording this dream?'"

"I probably shouldn't have written it in Sharpie." Lars pulled his hand back. "I didn't want it to come off in bed, but then it wouldn't wash off in the shower."

"Why did you write that?" Slater said.

"It's for the dream recording. If you wake up inside the dream, you look at your hand to see if it's written there."

"Of course it's not going to be there," Slater said. "You're dreaming."

Lars raised his eyebrows. "Are you sure about that?"

"There's java in the pot," Pike said. "Help yourself."

"I don't have time, but listen, guys—do you need a redhead in your polycule?"

Pike furrowed his brow. "We're not really poly. Although Slater does have a high sex drive."

"That's a diplomatic way to say I'm sleazy," Slater said.

"Well, maybe we can do whatever we did last night again sometime. I'm down for mindless casual sex."

"I do like your hair," Pike said. "It looks lighter this morning."

Slater frowned at him. "Red means stop."

"It's because I washed all the product out of it." Lars ran his hand through it. "So can I get your digits?"

As Pike recited his cell number, Lars tapped it into his phone. Slater had to bite his tongue. Pike didn't need to be hanging out with this guy. In a way it was his own damn fault. Slater had brought him here.

"Give me your number, and I'll text you back," Slater said, and thumb-typed it as he recited it.

"I should go." Lars tucked his phone away. "How far is the metro?"

"If you're headed to Downtown, I can give you a lift," Pike said.

"Right on."

Slater scowled as Pike got up. It felt like this guy was a little too interested. Pike must have read his face, as he paused to lean in and kiss him, and in a low voice said, "It's fine."

With the sound of their feet on the stairs, then the front door closing, he finished his apple and sat listening to the quiet house for a minute. Digging out his phone, he saw that O'Dowd had messaged him earlier:

Call me when you get a chance.

He dialed her number, and O'Dowd picked up.

"I went to the federal prison yesterday," she said. "You have some interesting friends."

"He's not really my friend."

"Leonard signed off on the sale, and the title is clear."

"What does that mean?"

"There's no mortgages or loans or liens against the

property. You just need to sign some stuff and it's all yours. Once we do that, Leonard will have the funds."

"Can I sign electronically?"

"It has to be notarized," O'Dowd said, "so you need to come in to my office."

He went down to his gear cabinet, bolted to the floor at the back of the garage. It was actually a gun safe disguised to look like a regular office-supply storage unit, hiding in plain sight to evade the interest of anyone who broke in. He kept all his illicit tech from Svetlana inside, and once he got it open, he pulled a vehicle tracker off its charging cable. A matte-black plastic box about the size of a cell phone, one side was studded with magnetic ribs. Opening the trunk of the Continental, he tucked it out of sight next to the spare tire.

Backing into the street, he waited for the door to roll down, then drove to Westwood, and parked under O'Dowd's building. This time he found the right floor on the first try, and knocked on the door as he stepped in. O'Dowd was dressed up today, in a somber gray suit and plain jewelry.

"Are you going to court later?" Slater said.

She smiled and sat back. "I almost never appear before the court. I have a meeting. Sit down."

They got into it, and O'Dowd had him sign a series of documents, one after another. Some of them seemed stupid and pointless, like the one to waive a property inspection. There was nothing to inspect— it was open undeveloped desert.

Finally O'Dowd shuffled the pages together. "That's all of them."

"When will Lenny get the dough?"

She rose and put the sheaf of paper into the photocopier that sat on the credenza, raising her voice over the noise of it clanking out copies.

"I'll put it through as soon as I've filed everything. It'll hit his bank account tomorrow. Leonard thinks you're doing him a big favor. From what I saw, you're probably overpaying for it."

"I'm not actually on his sucker list. It's a beautiful piece of land."

"You know it's miles off the electric grid," O'Dowd said, raising her eyebrows. "It would cost you a hundred grand just to get wires out there, maybe half that to put up solar panels and a battery. Digging wells in that area is hit and miss, so you'd likely have to put in a tank and get water trucked in."

"How do you know all that?"

She pulled the paper off the machine and sat down again. "It's part of the real estate transaction. As the purchaser, you should be aware of it too."

"I know it's not arcadia. And I'm not planning to live there."

Tucking the sheaf of copies into a manila envelope, O'Dowd frowned. "Isn't Arcadia where the horse track is?"

"Before that one, it was where Pan lived. The god of the wilderness. It was the ideal countryside with the simple life. Green and lush and idyllic."

She handed him the envelope. "That's definitely not what you just bought."

———

DOWNSTAIRS IN THE GARAGE, Slater climbed into the Continental, and checked Doris's text about her friend. Her name was Nara. Probably another teacher. Lots of Doris's confederates were. He put the address into his navigation. It was in the damn Valley, but the freeways must be moving, as it said it would only take half an hour or so.

He rolled through the Sepulveda pass and transitioned onto the 101. It was always warmer out here, and he cracked the window for the air. As he turned onto Nara's street, he realized he knew this neighborhood, a little bubble of wealth surrounded by middle-class sprawl. He pulled up at Nara's address and climbed out. The gate in the low wooden fence along the sidewalk was unlocked, and he stepped through and paused to look over the plantings in the yard. She'd put in dryland native ground cover to replace the lawn.

A woman stepped out the front door. With dark hair, she was in Doris's general age bracket, and wore a chunky necklace in yellow and orange glass over a light sweater, and baggy black pants. She called out a greeting in a husky voice.

"This isn't half bad," Slater said, nodding to the yard.

"It shouldn't be. It cost enough. I remember you're a gardener."

"Not full time. Do you know what kind of *Salvia* this is?"

"My landscaper told me it was sage."

"*Salvia* is a kind of sage. There's lots of species."

"To me it looks a little ratty here and there," Nara said.

"It's a native, so it's in exactly the shape it needs to be. If it doesn't rain much this winter, you can put some water on it." He gestured to the taller plant next to the porch. "The sagebrush doesn't need it, though."

"It's a different kind of sage?"

"There's no relation. It's in a completely different order."

"My landscaper said I could make tea with that one. Apparently it's good for menstrual cramps."

Slater frowned. It was hard to believe she still had that problem. "Don't go nuts with that. It can mess up your liver."

"Come inside."

Nara led him into the kitchen, to a high table with bar chairs around it, next to a big bright window.

"Nice house for a public school teacher," Slater said.

"My husband was the high earner, not me. And for Toluca Lake this house is actually modest."

He took the chair opposite her. "It's such an odd neighborhood. There's no gates, but it has gated community energy."

"Meaning what?"

"Well, your neighborhood welcome sign says 'armed response on patrol.' Like it was Beverly. It's still the freaking Valley."

Nara frowned. "There are a lot of break-ins. Doris said you needed something translated."

"An audio recording of a phone conversation." He dug out his phone and met her gaze. "Whatever you hear, you need to keep it to yourself."

"You think I'll gossip about your business on social media?" She chuckled. "You were always that kid. Truculent. The pugilist. I was so glad when Doris got you into wrestling. It gave you an outlet for all that aggression. Your anger at the world. It gave her a chance to breathe."

"I wasn't actually angry at the world. Just the rampant bottomless human stupidity that fills it."

"I know you had it rough, losing your father at that age," Nara said. "You must have been in middle school. That would make anyone angry. I always wondered if maybe you were addicted to it. The anger, and the surge of hormones that comes with it."

"I thought you taught in the classroom." He raised his eyebrows. "Did you also obtain a psychiatry degree?"

She gestured to his phone. "Play your recording."

He tapped at it, and Nara leaned over the table to listen, her brow furrowed. Once it had played through, she sat back.

"I can't hear the other side of the conversation, but this person implies that she's acquiring something."

"Acquiring what?" Slater said.

"That's not clear. Goods or money, maybe. This person is not really a native speaker. Maybe she learned the language in the family. So her way of speaking is a little rough. She said it was about Artsakh."

"Who's that?"

"Artsakh is part of Armenia that's currently occupied by a neighboring country," Nara said. "There have been armed struggles over it. Currently the conflict is only verbal, but it flares up now and then. The Armenians aren't just going to let it go."

"You think this person is involved in that?"

"These issues have a variety of participants, and the diaspora has a lot of resources."

"Who was she acquiring whatever it is from?"

"That's not clear," Nara said. "But I don't think it was the person she was talking to."

"Who was she talking to?"

"Someone she was trying to convince of something. But again, I have no idea what that was." She waved a hand. "I know it sounds vague. That's what I got."

Slater slid off the chair and tucked his phone away. "Do you want me to pay you?"

"I'm not going to take money." She stood up. "Give my best to your mother."

He held her gaze. "Loose lips sink ships."

Nara laughed. "Things work differently outside your dark world. I don't gossip because it's rude. You don't need to threaten me."

Walking out through the *Salvia,* he climbed into the Continental. Nara was like Doris, all comfy and settled in a verdant place where flowers were always blooming, and people were basically decent and moral and honest. From Slater's stratum of reality, people were basically fucking crazy.

The traffic was still flowing, and he rolled over the hill into the city, and parked across from his building. When he got up to his floor, a tall guy with short dark hair was standing outside his office.

"What do you need, Stretch?" Slater said.

"Who are you?"

Slater scoffed and stepped past him to his office door.

"I asked you a question."

The guy was way too close, standing right behind him. Slater turned around, and delivered a rapid kovac, slapping him left and then right.

"Why do you make me do this to you?" he demanded.

The guy raised his arms in front of his face. Why did they always do that? The predictability of it made it easy to work around. He planted a palm on the guy's chest and shoved him toward the door to the stairwell. As he stumbled backward, Slater could see the surprise and anger on his face. It was always the same with these birds.

"There's nothing to steal here. Keep moving."

Stepping into his office, he bolted the door behind him before the guy could come after him. The lights were on, and Max was at his desk, his head cocked, his cell phone mashed against his ear. He raised a hand in greeting.

At his own desk, Slater dug out his phone. Andy had texted:

Drop by.

He pulled O'Dowd's envelope out of his satchel and leafed through the real estate documents. It was copies of all the stuff that he'd signed. The digital versions were the official ones, he knew, but the title was here, a single sheet with the land description and his name on it. This tangible format, something he could hold in his hands, made it more real. Shuffling it all back into the envelope, he squatted in front of the safe behind his desk, and twisted the dial to get it unlocked, and heaved on the handle.

As he was stuffing the envelope inside, wedging it in among the stacks of bright-yellow bundles of euros, he heard a sharp knock at the front door. Twisting the handle to close the safe, he spun the dial to clear the wheels, and heard Max open the door.

As he stood up, Max appeared in his office doorway. "You have visitors. This is Agent Roscoe."

THIRTEEN

R OSCOE WALKED INTO SLATER'S office, his
hefty bulk filling the door frame. This was
the law-enforcement putz who'd been hanging around Greenleaf last night. He was even wearing the same fugly suit. Behind him was the tall guy
who'd been lurking in the hall a minute ago.

"Didn't I just tell you there was nothing here to
steal?" Slater said, eyeing the guy.

"I'm not a thief, you dick."

"Are you a pill popper, though? You seem a little
wound up."

"What is wrong with you?" he demanded.

Slater put his hands on his hips. "Cool it, baby, or
I'll break your nose."

"Let's all just calm down, shall we?" Roscoe said.
He had a deep voice, and vaguely Southern intonation.

"The pill-head doesn't look like a cop," Slater said, eyeing Roscoe, "but you definitely do. The fuck are you idiots?"

"Like your partner said, the name is Roscoe. Ramírez is a civilian consultant with us."

Slater spoke louder. "The fuck is 'us'?"

Reaching into his jacket, Roscoe pulled out an ID wallet, and held it open at arm's length.

"Treasury?" Slater said, peering at it.

"I know you know what that means," Roscoe said, "if you're a wannabe gum-heel."

"You don't get to condescend to me, G-man. I know you losers look into counterfeiting and bank fraud. I'm not doing that."

"Can we sit?"

Slater made a wide gesture. "By all means. Would the agent like an espresso as well, with a slice of lemon rind to spritz in it? Perhaps a biscotti, or a chilled soda water?"

Roscoe frowned. "No thanks." He turned to Ramírez. "Grab a chair."

Stepping into the front office, Ramírez rolled in the one from the front desk. Roscoe closed the door and dropped into the guest chair.

"I heard you were a handful."

"I saw you at Greenleaf," Slater said, sitting behind his desk, "and now you're here. How did you find me?"

"It's my job."

"What are you investigating specifically?"

"My wheelhouse is financial crimes."

Slater waved a hand. "I don't do those."

"Who's this?" Roscoe lifted the statue that sat at

the side of his desk, a plaster rendering of a naked guy with great hair, standing with a horse.

"Careful with that."

He read the name etched on the base: "Pollux."

"Like Castor and Pollux?" Ramírez said. "I thought those were stars."

"In antiquity they were badass horsemen."

He set it down. "So where's Castor?"

"Sitting on my boyfriend's desk."

"Aw. That's so sweet."

"Why are you here," Slater said, raising his voice, "getting up in my grill, and selling wolf tickets?"

Roscoe sat back and gestured with both hands. "We live in a diverse multicultural country. That means the problems that other places have tend to show up here too."

"You can skip ahead a little." Slater rolled his finger in the air. "I know what kind of country we live in."

He frowned. "What do you know about Zebulon Pike?"

Pike had a flag on Slater's name, he knew. Anyone who pulled up records about him would see Pike's request to be looped in.

"He was an interesting guy," Slater said. "The Spanish held him captive for a while in Santa Fe, when it was still part of Mexico. He finally bought it in the War of 1812. Although I know you people don't like to talk about that, since you lost that war and all."

"What does that mean, 'you people'?" Ramírez said.

"Uncle Sam. The government. The man. Whatever you call yourselves."

"You sound like a seditionist," Roscoe said.

"When you're the hammer, Roscoe, everybody looks like a nail." He jutted his chin at Ramírez. "If you're a consultant, I assume you're not packing a badge. You're just a drug-addled banking-industry dirtbag?"

"Fuck you," Ramírez snapped.

"Normally I would, but you're a stupe. I'm afraid I'd get charged with sexual assault. Stupid is a spectrum, right—it's easy to detect but hard to measure objectively." Slater threw up his hands. "Where's the line between just plain stupid and legally incapable of giving consent?"

"You are such an asshole."

"I don't see how that tracks. I'm just telling it like it is."

Ramírez leaned toward him. "If you can't figure out who's being the asshole, it's you."

"Did you run out of Quaaludes, Stretch? Apparently you can still get them from India."

Roscoe held up a hand and looked sidelong at Ramírez. "Would you let me talk for a second?" He eyed Slater. "I'm asking about a different Zebulon Pike. This one is still breathing."

"Why are you hanging around Greenleaf anyway? You know it's a total buzz kill to find a cop lurking in there. Nobody needs to see that."

"I'm the one asking the questions."

"I saw you at one of the jewelry stores too," Slater said. "Why are you hassling those people? They seem like regular working folks. I'm sure they don't need Big Brother getting up in their business."

He huffed and raised his voice. It was the first

sign that he might be getting rattled. "Why are *you* hanging around there? What do you know about Les James and her operation?"

"Greenleaf is a blast. Les puts on an amazing floor show. The place is pure hotcha."

"You know what I'm talking about."

"I actually don't," Slater said. "And unless you have a subpoena or a warrant, I really see no advantage in talking to you about anything."

Roscoe rose. "Americans can't conduct their own foreign policy, Ibáñez."

"Who knew?"

"It's illegal. Ignorance of the law is no excuse." He fished a business card out of his pocket and set it on the desk.

"I'll keep that in mind."

After he walked out, Slater rose and picked up the card. His office was in one of the federal buildings in the Civic Center. As the front door closed, Max stepped out of his office.

"You went at them hard. At least the part that I heard."

"I wanted them to explain themselves," Slater said. "They didn't do much of that."

"That guy was a Treasury agent. Was it about the half million in euros you've got parked in the safe?"

"Nobody knows about that but you and me. And it's only four hundred grand. We need to figure out a way to turn that into something else. In cash it's just sitting there depreciating."

Max chuckled. "I never thought I'd have the problem of having too much money lying around. So what does Treasury want with you?"

"It's about the case I'm on. These historic build-ings on Broadway. I saw him hanging around there more than once. It makes me think I've stumbled into something I don't quite understand yet."

He told Max a little about it, in broad strokes, then headed down to the street and across to the Continental. Driving to Andy's building, he parked in the surface lot behind it, and went upstairs, and rapped on the door.

Andy pulled it open, wearing his usual boxers and a T-shirt, and flashed that perfect smile. Slater followed him inside and watched him drop into his gaming chair.

"Les James never got arrested for anything," Andy said, "but there's … plenty of stuff about her out there."

"Like what?"

"For a few years she ran a bar called the Blue Finch."

"I remember that place. Over on Beverly, or maybe Third. It was always crowded."

"It's still there. On Beverly. Les was like a … neighborhood celebrity. Eventually she sold the place to … somebody else, and opened Greenleaf."

"Would that have given her enough capital? She renovated Greenleaf before it opened."

"The Blue Finch is popular," Andy said. "She probably sold high. I didn't see … anything about other investors in Greenleaf."

"If Les partnered with gangsters, it wouldn't be in the records."

"Did somebody imply she was … in bed with the syndicate? I never saw any … sign of that."

"If they were involved, they'd be hanging around the place," Slater said. "They're easy to spot. I've never seen anyone like that."

"Do you need photos of her?"

"Show me anyway."

Andy swiveled to his screens and slid his arms into his black gauntlets. They were an input device for his computer that compensated for his lack of fine motor control. He pulled up a photo of a woman with dark hair and a big smile, standing behind a bar, an array of bottles behind her. She was wearing jeans, and a blouse that showed some cleavage, and a lot less makeup than she wore at Greenleaf.

"There's less mileage on her," Slater said, "and the look she's working is ratchet, but that's definitely Les."

"The look is for the Blue Finch. I know … Greenleaf is high-tone, with a band and a … dress code, but the vibe at the Blue Finch was kind of hipster honky-tonk." He clicked through several more photos of her at the bar.

"Was there any hint about political stuff? Groups or causes she was involved in?"

"Nothing like that. But I didn't … look for it specifically."

"It's new information since we talked. Who runs the Blue Finch now?"

"A dude. His name is … here somewhere."

"Text it to me." Slater dug out his wad of cash. "What do I owe you?"

"For the research, three dollars."

"That seems extortionate, especially since I'm not allowed to hit on you anymore." He counted out the C-notes and set them on the desk.

"Cha-ching," Andy said. "You know you'd be … lost without me."

"That doesn't mean you're not a chiseler." He tucked his cash away. "Bye, beautiful."

It was a short drive down Broadway to the structure across from Greenleaf, and he cruised each level, moving upward, until he spotted the Pacer. He pulled into a stall farther down the row, then retrieved the tracker from the trunk of the Continental, and clicked on the recessed power switch with a fingernail.

Clyde hadn't even let him sit down in his office, so he'd had no chance to plant the audio bug. This would give him an alternate source of information, a way to shag the guy remotely.

Squatting at the Pacer's rear tire, he realized he'd forgotten to put on gloves. He pulled out his handkerchief and wiped his prints off the device, then held it with the hankie as he reached up into the wheel well. There was lots of steel on this classic machine, and the magnetic ribs adhered almost instantly.

Slater rose and tucked his hankie away. Clyde was walking over from the direction of the stairs, his brow knotted.

"What are you doing to Milton?"

"Looking at his undercarriage."

"Do you approve?" Clyde paused at the Pacer's rear bumper.

"You keep him in pristine condition."

"Not on my own." He nodded to the row of cars, where the Continental's sweet blue tail end stuck out past the other vehicles. "Do you do the wrenching on the Lincoln?"

"I don't have enough time, or enough brains. I've

got a guy. But I like to look."

Clyde dropped his chin. "I understand that. I like to look at you. You're so handsome, Slater."

"Thanks," he said, and put his hands on his hips.

His expression sobered. It was hard to maintain that level of mack when Slater wasn't returning it. "So what are you doing up here?"

"Working for you, big guy. I just pulled in."

"Do you want to take Milton for a spin?"

"I'm afraid my wings would get singed by his brilliance."

Clyde chuckled. "I have to run over to the hardware store in Westlake. It's not far." He handed Slater the keys and stepped around to the passenger side.

Climbing in, Slater adjusted the seat and the mirrors, then backed out of the stall. "The engine sounds amazing."

"When you've got anything with a carburetor, it's all about keeping it in tune."

"I love all the glass," he said, pulling into the street. "You can see what's coming. The crap cars they put out nowadays are like prison cells, with the slitty little windows."

"No computers required for Milton," Clyde said. "No bogus autonomous horseshit, no screens, no distractions. It's just driving."

"Preach, brother." He braked for a stoplight. "I love the acceleration. It's totally smooth, and almost ponderous, but not quite. Like, 'I hear you. I'll get you there. No stress.'"

Clyde laughed. "You totally understand Milton. So what have you learned about Les James?"

"There are some anomalies. Most of the jewelers

claim they know who she is, but that they don't really know her. It feels like they're obfuscating. I think there's something in that."

"I wish you could figure out specifically what she was doing. Can you do surveillance or something?"

"I'm going to poke around more today."

When he pulled into the parking lot of the hardware store, they both climbed out and walked in.

"I need to find somebody who works here," Clyde said, and strode up one of the cavernous aisles.

There was an automated key copying machine right here, Slater saw. Those worked fast—there should be time. He dug out the key ring Clyde had given him, and fed the keys into the machine one by one. It rapidly spit out the copies. Thinking about it, he made a second copy of the brass key that opened the door into the tunnels.

He'd finished and stuffed them all in his jeans by the time Clyde reappeared, and he followed him to the checkout. It looked like the only thing Clyde was buying was a real estate lockbox.

When they walked out to the parking lot, Slater handed him his car keys.

"You don't want to drive?" Clyde said.

"I definitely want to. I just don't think I'm worthy."

FOURTEEN

⊏⊐⊏⊐⊏⊐⊏⊐⊏⊐⊏⊐

CLYDE WAS LESS GENTLE with Milton on the drive back, punching the accelerator when he had the opportunity, braking hard before he made a right turn. Milton could handle it, and responded appropriately. They rolled into the parking structure, and climbed out, and went down the stairs to the street.

As they were waiting for the crossing signal, Clyde opened the real estate box. "I'm going to need a magnifying glass and a Mandarin translator to figure out the instructions on how to set the lock code."

"I've got one of those," Slater said. "Exactly the same one. I can show you how it works."

"Great." He closed the box's compartment. "Come up to my office."

When they got upstairs, Clyde set the box on his desk.

"It's all mechanical," Slater said, and flipped it open. "You set this switch first." He showed him, then closed the little door. "What year was this building put up?"

"Construction started in 1908."

On the mechanical keys, he punched in the numbers. "One, nine, zero, eight. Four digits." He opened the box again. "Then you flip the switch back. Now you can close it up, and press this button when you want to lock it."

Clyde took hold of it, and tried to open the door, then punched in the code, and pulled it open. "Amazing."

"You should put in your own code," Slater said. "You don't need people knowing it."

"You're not going to jack my ride."

"You know I want to."

Dropping into his desk chair, he rolled open a drawer, and dug out a pair of keys, one square and one round. Those were for the Pacer, the same as the ones he'd just handed back to him. Clyde dropped them into the box, and locked it, then swiveled to set it on the credenza.

"Sit down." He waved to the chair across the desk.

Of course he'd invite him to lounge around here when he didn't have the audio bug with him.

Slater sat and gestured to the lockbox. "Why do you need to lock up your car keys?"

"It's a spare set. I lost them a while ago, and it was a huge pain. The auto club couldn't help me. Milton is too old. If I had a new EV, the guy said, he could open it in a hot second."

"So is everybody in these buildings in the jewelry business? What have they told you about Les?"

"Most of my tenants are jewelers," Clyde said. "You might have seen the pawn shop, and those clothing stores. I'm kind of sick of them all. The hotel renovation was supposed to lift me out of it, but it's so damn slow. It keeps getting stalled." He waved a hand. "I need to go bigger, you know? Bigger things, bigger money."

"They call that the American disease."

Clyde frowned. "Money?"

"Ambition."

"I don't really know any other way to be. I spent the first years of my life in Korea."

"North or South?" Slater said.

His eyebrows shot up. "Are you freaking kidding me? Do you even know what you're saying?"

"I've never met a North Korean, but saying that always gets a rise out of South Koreans."

"Well, lucky for me, I was born in the south. Even there it was all about scarcity. Life was hard. Over here it's tough too, but at least you can get a piece. It's like a banquet with great food, but nobody saved you a place. You have to elbow your way to the table."

"Interesting analogy."

"You don't see yourself as a striver?"

"Mostly I'm just trying to keep my head above water," Slater said.

Clyde nodded. "You think like a gardener. My father called that the peasant mentality."

"I'm not sure I need a label for it. It feels like I spend most of my time helping chumps like you keep all this going." He waved at the room. "At least until somebody bigger than me comes to take what I've got."

"That's a dark view."

"I'd call it a realistic view, babe."

"I like the banquet better."

"Do you know a guy named Roscoe?" Slater said. "He works for the Treasury Department."

"Why would I?"

"I saw him hanging around Greenleaf."

"How do you know he's a fed?"

"I talked to him, and he flashed his badge."

"Seriously." Clyde sat up. "What did he tell you?"

"Those people don't tell. They only ask. Information goes in and nothing comes out."

"Maybe it's about Les. What did you tell him?"

"To get a subpoena if he wanted me to squawk."

"What about Les?" Clyde said. "Have you even seen her yet?"

"Several times. She seems pretty focused on the nightclub. I know she uses the back hallways. It would help a lot if I knew exactly what I was looking for."

He lowered his voice and held his gaze. "To spell it out, Slater, I think Les is stealing from my other tenants. The jewelers. She's stashing the spoils somewhere in one of my buildings. I need to know what she's hiding and where."

"Did someone tell you that's what was happening?"

Clyde rose and stepped around the desk, then dropped to one knee in front of him. It was an odd stance. He ran a hand along Slater's thigh and looked up at him.

"I trust you, Slater. I don't know what I'd do without you."

Taking hold of his arm, he pulled him up and met his mouth. Clyde sat in his lap, and put his arms around his neck, and mouthed his jaw.

"Hold me," Clyde said under his breath. "Keep me safe."

Slater ran a hand slowly up and down his back and nuzzled his neck. This wasn't real. He knew that. But it felt really good.

Eventually Clyde pulled back. "You're getting me turned on. Can I smoke you?"

"When a man is tired of blow jobs, he's tired of life."

Rising, Clyde bolted the door, then knelt and shoved Slater's knees apart. Slater unbuckled his belt, and Clyde grabbed his fly, pulling it open, and took him into his mouth. He quickly got hard. The guy knew what he was doing, and Slater guided him with a hand on his head.

Clyde looked up at him as he worked him, eyes wide. That sent him over, and he climaxed, straining into him.

"You're so damn good at that," Slater said, and pulled him up, meeting his mouth.

"Come here." Clyde stood up, and pulled him out of the chair. "Stand behind me."

Slater sat on the edge of the desk, and pulled him close, one hand around his chest, and groped his crotch. Unzipping his pants, Clyde pulled out his cock, already hard. Slater took hold of it and stroked him, squeezing him tightly around the chest, and mouthed his neck and his ear.

Grunting, Clyde shuddered and jerked as he came. Slater held him close for a minute, until his breathing slowed. Eventually he pulled back.

"That was really nice," Clyde said, and gave him that big-eyed look again. "What do we do now?"

"I've got work to do. I'm thinking you do too."

Stepping toward the door, he flipped the bolt, and went into the hall. He adjusted his belt as he trotted down the stairs and out to the street. When he went into Milena's shop, Erik was behind the counter, and called out a greeting.

"Is Milena not around?" Slater said.

"What do you want with her?"

"Why would the feds be sniffing around here? What are they after?"

"What feds?"

"I saw a Treasury guy in your shop yesterday."

Erik's expression darkened. "Roscoe. That guy has a hard-on for anybody who says anything about Armenia."

"They're policing your speech? You should sue the fuck out of them. You've got your Third Amendment rights."

"You're thinking of the First Amendment. The Third says the military can't take over your house."

"Don't let them do that either." Slater narrowed his eyes. "Someone was paying attention in civics class. Why are they messing with you about Armenia?"

"They think we're interfering in a foreign conflict."

"I've heard that's illegal."

"So is speeding, and giving an undocumented person a job, and buying your medications in Mexicali. It doesn't mean it's also immoral or unjust." He raised his eyebrows. "All we're doing is sending them humanitarian aid. Clothes and blankets and stuff like that."

The sound of the door opening came from the back room, and Milena stepped out, and flashed a smile.

"Have you found your way into the tunnels?" she said.

Erik threw up a hand. "I can't believe you showed him that."

"Nobody's using them, but it's no secret. Besides, what's he going to do with that information?"

He furrowed his brow and eyed Slater. "It's hard to say."

"I get it," Slater said. "You have no reason to trust me."

"But you're here to check on the fire exits."

Milena had told him that, he realized. She was the only person he'd said that to.

"I need to inspect all the hallways and connecting doors," Slater said. "Maybe you can show me around. Share your knowledge."

"I don't know anything about this place."

"You might remember stuff if you come and poke around with me. It'll give us a chance to catch up."

Erik stared at him for a moment. "I'm in."

"Don't be gone all afternoon," Milena said. "I've got things to do."

"Come through the back." Erik waved him behind the counter, and he followed him into the back office, and they stepped out into the hallway. He locked the back door. "Which way? I know there are connecting doors between the buildings, but they're usually locked."

"I have keys for some of them." Slater led the way to the end of the hallway and unlocked the door.

"This has to be the next building," Erik said as they stepped through.

"That sounds right."

They mounted the stairs and walked to the far end. Slater unlocked the door, and they stepped into the dining room. Sitting at a table nearby, a dark-haired guy had both hands wrapped around a sandwich, and briefly looked up at them.

"Upstairs at Sackett's," Erik said. "I didn't know there was another way in."

"Somebody told me Les James has a key to this door."

"I guess that's not surprising. Her business is right upstairs. Have you checked on that level?"

"I don't think there's direct access to Greenleaf."

"Let's have a look." He stepped back through the doorway and waited while Slater locked it.

Walking down the hall, they stepped into the stairwell, and ascended a flight, then walked back toward Greenleaf. The hallway ended in a blank wall, but as they approached it, he saw that it continued to one side. There was a door in the wall, offset a few feet from the main hallway and painted to blend in. He hadn't walked this far before. Why hadn't he noticed this? That was sloppy.

"This has to go into Greenleaf, doesn't it?" Erik said.

"It's on the right level." Digging out the keys, Slater found one that fit. It was the same key as the connecting door one floor down. That meant Les could get through this one too. He pulled it open. Inside was a few inches of dead space and another door handle with a keyhole. He tried it, but it was locked.

"That door looks new compared to the one on this side," Erik said.

Slater spent a minute trying Clyde's keys. "None of these fit."

"I bet Les put this in when she did the restoration. So that she'd be the only one with a key."

He closed the door and locked it. "Let's go below street level."

They trotted down the stairs, and on the ground floor walked around to the stairwell that led down.

"I know some of the people with offices down here," Erik said. "They manufacture jewelry and do repairs for the local retailers."

"Do you know about the incinerator room?"

"What about it?"

"Can you show me?"

"I guess I know where it is." He stopped for a moment and absently scratched at his beard. "This way." As they walked, Erik eyed him sidelong. "So what did you do after you were on the middle school wrestling team?"

"I didn't stick with wrestling. High school was a bumpy ride. I went to community college after and studied horticulture."

"How did that lead to being an insurance investigator and a fire inspector?"

"It's not super skilled work. A couple days' training. What about you? What was your life about after you handed out all those oil checks?"

Erik chuckled. "I never did that either." He

pointed the way into a side corridor, leading farther from the street. "I've been working in the family business. Sometimes I think I should be looking beyond that. It seems like a limited life. Like I'm in a box."

"I'm sure you've got other options. What about the Artsakh cause?"

"That's like going to church. You just do it, and you know it's right. It's not really a career opportunity." He stopped at a door that had a window in it, with wire mesh in the glass, and tried the handle. "It's locked."

Slater tried Clyde's keys, and found one that turned the bolt. Pulling open the door, he stepped inside. The walls were unfinished concrete, and the long room was divided into storage spaces, separated by wood framing with wire mesh. Each of the half dozen units had a rudimentary door made of one-by-fours and the mesh, and each bore a different brand of padlock. Inside he could see plastic storage tubs and cardboard boxes, some of them on metro shelving, and some boxy stuff covered in blue plastic tarps. There was a wooden desk in one, and a floor lamp, and a bicycle.

Stepping over to one of the doors, he prodded the mesh. It was the lightweight stuff they used for landscaping to keep rodents out of new plantings. Whoever was storing stuff here, it wasn't the jewelers. Or at least it wasn't storage for their high-value inputs or their stock. This was a minimal security measure, like that chain across the stairs at Greenleaf. You could break into any of these spaces with a pair of pliers.

"I'm pretty sure this was the incinerator room," Erik said. "I bet it was right over there." He gestured to a dark corner of the room. "Back in the old days people would bring their trash down. Chuck it in, burn it on up."

The guy wasn't a very good liar, Slater thought, watching him talk. He was trying too hard. Looking around, it didn't wash. There had never been an incinerator here. It would need ventilation, and there was no sign there'd ever been a chimney. Talisha had said the room she'd seen still had the machinery in it.

"Well, you've seen it," Erik said. "We should go. I need to be in the shop."

Slater followed him out, and they went up to street level. Slater walked toward the stairwell that led up.

"Where are you going?" Erik said.

"What's it to you? I've got stuff to do too."

He raised a hand. "Later, man."

FIFTEEN

᠌᠌ᘈᘈᘈᘈᘈᘈᘈᘈᘈ

CLIMBING TO THE TOP floor, Slater stepped into the hallway, and found the door marked 604. When he knocked, Talisha pulled it open. She was dressed casually today, in jeans and a blue sweater.

"If it isn't the dick hound," she said.

"Have you got a minute? You need to show me the incinerator room."

"I'm kind of working."

"I can pay you."

She frowned. "I'm not going to take money for that."

Digging deep, Slater tried to recall a tactic from one of the shrinks Doris had sent him to in his youth. The idea was that people liked to be asked for help, as long as it was something easy to achieve. For the shrink it was intended to build bridges and make him compliant, but it was way more useful as a technique to manipulate people.

"I could really use your help." He held her gaze. "I don't have anyone else to ask."

Pursing her lips for a moment, she looked him up and down. "I guess I have time. Let me get my keys."

Closing the door, she returned a minute later, and stepped out, and locked it behind her.

"So how's it going with the blond?" Slater said, following her to the stairs.

"She's not really a blond."

"I figured."

"She slept over, so that's progress."

"Right on."

When they got to the ground floor, Talisha led him out to the sidewalk, then into the next building. He could have opened an interior door for them if he'd known this was where she was headed. Talisha went into the stairwell down. This was a completely different building from the storeroom Erik had taken him to.

Stopping in front of a heavy door, Talisha pulled out her keys, and unlocked it, and pushed it open.

"Why do you have a key to this?" Slater said.

"It's the same one for the main entrance. I tried it, and it worked."

It was a trade-off, he knew, security versus convenience. Clyde or his predecessor had keyed all these doors the same so they'd only need a few of them, and finding the right key would be quick. But the downside was that anyone with one of those keys could run wild.

Stepping inside, he saw that this actually looked like an incinerator room. Against the wall was a tapered structure, built of concrete blocks, and above it a blackened block column. That had to be the chimney. On the front of the bulky unit were two rusty metal doors, one at chest height and one near the floor. Stepping over to it, he pulled on the handle, but it wouldn't budge. He looked closer.

"It's welded shut."

"That's a great way to stop people from using it," Talisha said.

He looked around the space. There were doors at either end of the room. The far one, near the chimney, probably gave access to the alley. In the side wall was a third door. That might lead into a neighboring building, he decided, unless his reckoning was off.

The door was narrow, and made of steel, old and rusty and battered. But there was a lone bright spot. He stepped over to it, and gave it a tentative tug, but it was solidly locked. The little circle of new metal was a keyhole. The lock hardware was completely hidden inside the door, and the plate extending over the jamb covered any view of the bolt. The only sign of anything from this century was that shiny little disk around the keyhole.

He knew that shape. There was nothing else like it: a Masamune lock. Those cost a fortune and were impossible to defeat. It was easier to go through the door with a ram or a chainsaw than to try to pick one of those. Somebody was protecting something here. It could be inadvertent, but it felt like the lock was hidden. Were they intentionally trying to keep it on the down-low?

"What are you looking at?" Talisha said.

"Nothing. I was just wondering how old the building is."

"It was built around 1910," she said. "Why did you need to see this room specifically?"

"Research. What else have you found when you're poking around?"

"Have you heard about the hotel wing that's been sealed off since 1938?"

"Clyde just busted into it on the fourth floor."

Her eyebrows shot up. "I didn't know that."

"He says the new owner agreed to reconnect it to the main part of the hotel. They're going to renovate the whole thing."

"I read about it on a history blog that talked about why it had been bricked up," Talisha said. "Then I found a way in."

"Seriously? Where?"

She grinned. "I can show you, if you promise to keep it quiet. It's extremely cool."

Slater followed her up the stairs and out to the sidewalk. They walked up the block, and Talisha went into one of the stores at the bottom of the sealed wing. It was a narrow space, lined on both sides with spreading quinceañera dresses in airy pastels and shades of white.

Leaning toward him, Talisha spoke under her breath. "No smoking."

They did look a little flammable, he realized.

At the counter at the back, a woman greeted them in Spanish. Wearing a skirt and jacket, she had her dark hair pulled back. Talisha talked to her in Spanish for a while, and at one point the woman touched her shoulder. They clearly knew each other.

Eventually Talisha waved for him to follow, and they stepped through the open doorway into the back. It looked bigger than the actual shop. Corrugated boxes were stacked along the wall, with dresses draped on some of them, and a rolling rack that held more clothes. A trio of naked mannequins stood nearby, one missing its head, and one with only one arm.

Talisha walked to the end of the room. A wooden ladder was propped at an angle, leading into an open hatch in the ceiling. It had to be twelve feet up. She gestured to it.

"You first. I don't need you ogling my ass."

As he grasped the sides of the ladder and started to climb, he eyed her. "You should lean into it. Profit from your assets. If people want to ogle, let them ogle."

"Spoken like a man."

When he got to the top, he stepped onto the floor. These were the same blackened boards as where Clyde had taken him. That had to be a level or two higher. This was an open space, as wide as what he'd seen upstairs but without interior walls, just a few columns that broke it up. The hanging light fixtures were thick with dust. They looked period, and ornate, like the bar and the ballrooms at the Baltimore. That hotel dated to the same era as these buildings, the first decade or so of the last century. These would have been dramatic when they were new and turned on.

The room was well lit from the row of filmy arched windows. He could see the buildings across the street, the parking structure at the end of the block. In the middle three windows the glass was still painted in reverse gold lettering: HOTEL and

REASONABLE RATES and PRIVATE BATHS.

"Can you believe this hasn't been touched for all those decades?" Talisha said, stepping off the ladder.

"How did the shopkeeper know about it?"

"I'm not sure. I came in to ask and she showed it to me. She wanted to use it for storage, but it's just too awkward without stairs."

"I don't think Clyde knows about this."

"You realize that if you tell him," Talisha said, "he'll make this woman's life miserable."

"Why would I tell him anything?"

"Aren't you working for him?"

"Sure, but it's not anything to do with this. What do you think this was?"

"A ballroom, maybe, or a lounge? It gets great light." She pointed to the edge of the ceiling. "Check that out."

Elaborate crown molding ran the length of the wall. Stylized grape leaves, maybe, the scrolling curves still showed some gold paint.

"I hope they preserve this," Talisha said, "rather than turning it into yet another slate-gray dystopian hellscape."

"There's not much to stop them." He gestured to the far end. "That's where they bricked it off. Clyde is going to bust in here from the other part of the hotel any day now."

"At least I got to see it before they ruined it."

"Have you put a bunch of pictures of it online?"

She chuckled. "If I did that, the place would be crawling with urban explorers. I took photos, but I won't post any until they do their stupid renovation."

Stepping over to the ladder, she started down.

Slater followed, taking his time. It took more focus than on the way up. When he got to the bottom, Talisha met his gaze.

"You should excuse yourself and thank the shopkeeper."

He frowned. "Why?"

"We're tramping through her business. You can just say it in English."

Slater followed her out through the shop, and on the way met the shopkeeper's eye, and mumbled *"Discúlpeme"* and *"Gracias."* He wasn't even sure that made sense, but she smiled and said something back.

Out on the sidewalk, Slater paused at the door into her building. "I appreciate the tour."

"I'm actually headed over to the parking lot."

"That's where my rig is too. I'll walk over with you. And I'll try not to look at your ass."

In the structure he trudged up the stairs behind her, and they stepped out on the same floor. They walked the row of cars, and Talisha stopped at a dark-red Trans Am, parked nose out.

"Such a sweet ride," Slater said. "I did not know you were a car whack." He stepped to the passenger side to look at the interior. "I get it now. It's like the gilded crown molding. You like beautiful things."

She laughed. "That's true. Although this isn't the best year for this model."

"It's not gilded either, but it's still beautiful."

"Driving an old car is a grind."

"It's a classic." Slater walked around behind it. "What years did they do the notch back?"

"I'm not sure. This is an '88."

"When cars looked like cars, not amusement

park rides."

"I'm with you on that. I wish it was a little more reliable. It doesn't always start."

"It has that small-block 305 engine, doesn't it?" Slater said. "Do you know the trick to starting it?"

She frowned. "What trick?"

"You crank it once, and wait a few seconds, then crank it for real. It'll start every time. No messing around."

"How do you know that?"

"I drove a rig with the same engine for a while. I'm in the thrall of a classic beauty myself." He gestured up the row to the Continental.

"The Mark IV? I was admiring it the other day. You maintain it yourself?"

"I'm not smart enough to do that," Slater said. "I've got a guy."

"I should get his number. I spend way too much time out at the auto wreckers."

"Where do you work on it?"

"My parents' driveway," Talisha said. "This was actually their baby before I was born."

"Take that bottle blond for a spin in it. You'll totally lock it down."

He walked over to the Continental, and backed out, and followed the Trans Am out of the structure. Up the block, as he braked for the stoplight, Talisha punched it to bust the yellow. That had probably been for his benefit, and it made him smile.

———•———

SLATER DROVE DOWN TO Olympic and headed west. Tapping at his phone, he checked Andy's text. The owner of the bar was named Madwen.

He drove past the Blue Finch, stretched between a cigar lounge and a clothing store, its name in rusted steel letters mounted on a weathered-board facade, and found an open meter around the corner. The bouncer at the door was a burly guy, dressed in black, with a big nose and a scraggly brown beard. He always felt a twinge of culture shock coming to the Westside, where white folks were in the vast majority and had jobs like this, unlike in most of the metropolis. The guy carded him, and once he had his ID again, Slater stepped inside.

Even in the late afternoon the bar was busy, with all the stools occupied. A couple of people were playing pool at the far side. There was lots of rustic wood, and a ratty old wagon wheel mounted on the wall by the pool tables, and the obligatory wall of fame, an array of headshots of celebrities both ersatz and genuine. Two women were working the bar, both wearing plaid shirts to go with the western vibe. The music wasn't up loud. It sounded like roots music, an Appalachian sound rather than Nashville pop.

At the service area one of the women stepped over and tucked her hair behind her ear as she flashed a perfunctory smile. "What can I get you?"

"I have a meeting with Madwen."

She pointed to the arched doorway into the back, and Slater went over. A short hallway led to the restrooms, and at the end a crash door with an exit sign, and before that a couple of unmarked doors. One of them was open, and he stepped into the doorway. It was a little office with a desk, and a couple of file cabinets, and heavy black bars on the outside of the window.

Sitting at the desk was a guy with his black hair in a trendy cut. In his forties, maybe, he looked buff. Essentially fuckable, Slater decided.

The guy looked up, his eyes flicking over Slater's form. "Can I help you?"

"You're Madwen, I'm thinking? I'm an insurance investigator." Slater dug out his business card, and handed it across the desk. "Is that an Irish name?"

Madwen scanned the card and then sat back. "Do I look Irish? It's Tagalog."

He gestured to the chair in front of the desk, and Slater dropped into it.

"So what insurance drama are you investigating?" Madwen said. "Is some slip-and-fall artist temporarily paralyzed from my wet floor? Or is it some ADA scam? It won't work. The place is totally compliant."

"Nothing like that. When you bought this place from Les James, she opened a nightclub called Greenleaf."

He nodded. "I've been. It's swank."

"Who were her other investors?"

"Why are you asking?"

"It's been suggested that she's in bed with the syndicate," Slater said. "I'm trying to determine whether she has gangland partners in her business."

"I wouldn't know anything about that. But I will say it sounds unlikely. When I bought this place there was no talk of other investors or financial obligations. She was the sole owner."

"Setting up Greenleaf would have cost a lot more than what she got from you. She did a whole restoration job over there."

Madwen shrugged. "I don't really know her, or what her resources are."

"What about you?" Slater said. "Do you have gangsters for partners?"

"All right." Madwen rose, his brow furrowing. "Time for you to leave."

One of the bartenders appeared in the doorway, her eyes wide. "Boss—there's trouble."

She left again, and Madwen strode after her. Slater walked out behind him. In the middle of the barroom a guy was waving his arms, holding an empty beer bottle by the neck.

"You're all in on it," he shouted, shaking the bottle. "I know you are. I can smell it."

The patrons had cleared the barstools, standing at the sides of the room, moving as far away from the guy as possible. Several people on the side where the entrance was pushed their way outside, one after another.

"He came in off the street," the bartender said to Madwen. "I think he's homeless."

The bouncer was the only person standing near the guy, but he was hanging back. As they watched, he took a step toward him, but the guy swung the bottle at him and screamed, and the bouncer retreated.

"They're fricking everywhere now," Madwen said. "Why are they always psychotic and on drugs?"

Slater watched as the guy continued his rant.

"Who set this up?" he shouted. "Who's after me? That's all I want to know."

Madwen snapped his fingers, and the bouncer looked over at him. Madwen threw up his hands, a tacit *Do something*, but the bouncer just shrugged. It made sense—you didn't tangle with a crazy person unless you had a weapon, and this guy was armed with that bottle.

But something was off. Looking at the guy, he didn't seem homeless. He was wearing grubby clothes, but his hair was cut, and he didn't have much of a beard. He had none of the mannerisms or physical damage of a drug user. Like that guy he'd had to educate outside city hall. Fetty and tranq made them scabby and hunched over. This guy could be recently homeless, but no way was he drugged out and unmedicated and on the skids, even though he was acting like that. This was performative.

He leaned toward Madwen. "Do you have anything valuable here? Maybe in a back room?"

He glanced at him and scowled. "Why?"

"This guy isn't homeless," Slater said. "He's playing you. It's a distraction. Somebody wants you to be focused on this while they're doing something else."

"Fuck," he snapped, and turned on his heel, and hustled into the back.

Slater followed him, and saw the exit at the end of the hall was hanging open now, with daylight streaming in. The crash bar was hanging from it at an angle.

Madwen yanked open his office door. Two guys were inside, wearing jeans and dark jackets. They were standing at the file cabinet next to the desk, and one of them had a jimmy shoved in the back of his jeans. They could be Filipino too, Slater decided, following Madwen inside. Both were wearing blue latex gloves, and there was a messy pile of paper on top of the cabinet, and spilled on the floor in front of it. Neither of them looked especially worried to see them come in.

Shouting something unintelligible, Madwen lunged at the closest one, and the other guy came at Slater, his face contorted with that unmistakable rage that said a dustup was imminent. He managed to duck the guy's fist, swinging at the same time with a right hook. It landed on his jaw, and his head snapped, but the guy was still punching, and hit Slater in the chest, and a glancing blow to the side of his head, above his ear. That one hurt like hell, and Slater yelped. Leaning in, he landed a solid dick punch, and the guy yowled, and doubled over, his hands on his crotch.

He hadn't seen what Madwen had done, but as Slater stepped back, the other guy darted out of the office. The one Slater had punched hustled after him, groaning and bent over.

Following them to the doorway, Madwen shouted something after them that he couldn't understand.

"Is that Tagalog?" Slater said, still breathing hard.

Madwen was panting too, and his face was red. He went over to the cabinet and riffled through the mess of paper. The front of the top drawer was bowed outward, the lock broken. They'd used that jimmy to get into it.

"Did they find what they were looking for?" Slater said.

"I don't think so."

The bouncer stepped into the office doorway, his brow furrowed. "What happened in here?"

"A break-in," Madwen said.

"Oh, man. At least the crazy guy is gone."

"That figures. Check on the back door. It looks broken."

The guy left, and Slater raised his eyebrows.

"Are you sure you don't have any gangster investors?"

Madwen met his gaze. "Thank you for alerting me to the diversion, and for dick-punching that goon. Have a drink in the bar if you'd like." He waved a hand. "On me."

"You should get a safe," Slater said. "One that bolts to the floor."

He walked out through the bar. The pair who'd been playing pool were back at it, and the barstools were occupied again, with a twangy banjo song on the sound system. Walking to his car, he took deep breaths to dispel the residual adrenaline.

Why did people insist on jumping him like that? It wasn't even his beef. Svetlana would say, "Not my circus, not my monkeys." Pike and Doris thought he was the belligerent, but it wasn't like he was out looking for it. They came at him.

SIXTEEN

DAYLIGHT HAD FADED TO dark by the time Slater got to his house. When he trudged up the stairs, he found Pike on the sofa, still dressed for work, stretched out and dozing. He knelt on the faux grass next to him and leaned in to savage his neck, and his jaw, and his mouth.

When he pulled away, Pike grinned. "Nice to see you too."

"You're so damn beautiful. Why do you do this to me?" He raised his voice. "I can't stand it."

"Suck it up."

Slater buried his face in his belly for a moment, inhaling his scent.

"So why was Agent Roscoe looking for you?" Pike said.

"Fuck that guy. Whenever somebody recites your

full name, I know they've never actually met you. Did you tell him where to find me?"

"I did not. He called me and asked what your angle was with the nightclub and the jewelers in that neighborhood. I told him I had no idea, but that you probably weren't plotting an insurrection, or aiding and abetting foreign combatants."

"'Probably'? Thanks for that ringing endorsement."

Pike chuckled. "They're just fishing."

"For what? What is he investigating?"

"He didn't lay it out for me, but I know they look for patterns in banking activity, and try to link it to other data sources. Then they start digging. I wouldn't worry too much about it. If they had hard evidence, they'd be making arrests, not asking questions. But it's good to be aware that he's around."

Slater caressed his belly. "How did he ID me?"

"Most likely he just asked somebody your name. Remind me who hired you over there?"

"A guy named Clyde. He says he's the landlord but he's really the property manager. He's thin-built but buff. Great hair, and a sweet little caboose."

Pike's brow furrowed. "Now that we've established how attractive he is, why did he hire you?"

He told him a little about Clyde's ask, and Les, and the hotel renovation. "I'm not sure what's going on with Les James. Clyde is a cake-eater, but I think he wants to be a *macher*."

"So Lars left a bunch of change in the back bedroom last night. There were coins all over the place. On the desk and on the floor. Like he'd thrown a handful up in the air." He mimed the gesture, spreading his fingers. "I wondered if he was shaking out his pants or something."

"The guy is a little odd. Like the thing about writing on his hand to look for it in a dream. How the hell is that supposed to work?"

"I wonder what's on that videotape."

Slater scoffed. "I'd bet money on absolutely nothing. I guess you have to cut him some slack. He's a sick person trying to get well, not a bad person trying to be good."

"Is that from twelve-step?"

"One of the rum-dumbs in Lars's meeting talked about that."

Pike put a hand on his jaw, and caressed his cheek with his thumb. "I love that you're absorbing it. You should totally go to more of those."

"Thing is, I don't need it."

Pike pulled him up, and he stretched out on top of him, a hand on his shoulder, his knee between his legs.

"Because there's nothing wrong with you?" Pike ruffled his hair.

"I didn't say that. I'm actually one of those bad people they were talking about."

He mouthed his jaw. "A bad boy."

"I'm a wrong guy, son. You know that firsthand by now."

"Trouble in button-fly jeans," Pike said. "Like the raccoons rummaging in the trash."

"I'm not the raccoon. I'm the trash. You know this." He sighed at the feeling of his hands in his hair.

He pressed their mouths together, and he got lost in it. Eventually Pike pulled back.

"So I had an idea for tonight. There's an opportunity to learn the *froog*."

"What the hell is that?"

"It's a dance," Pike said. "From the sixties. It's spelled f-r-u-g. There's a class."

"Dancing. I'm just so bad at it, and you're so good at it. It's way outside my comfort zone."

"When you're habitually aggressive, doing something low-key feels like weakness. Your comfort zone isn't a very good way to measure the potential value in something."

"Do not go all shrink on me," Slater said. "I had enough of that from all the nutjobs Doris sent me to."

"I'm not being shrinky." He furrowed his brow. "But seriously, how does that make you feel?"

Slater mouthed his neck. "I am going to mess you up so bad."

"Bring it," Pike said. "You're totally getting me revved up."

He pulled back and climbed off him. "So where's this class?"

"Hollywood Boulevard."

"I need to eat first."

Downstairs he changed into chinos and a pair of dress shoes. He knew from experience it was hard to dance in boots. Pike put on different shoes too, and they drove to Hollywood, and ate at a vegan Thai joint. Between mouthfuls, Slater gestured with his spoon.

"I forgot to tell you—I finalized buying Lenny's land today. He should be able to hire a lawyer."

"That didn't take long. What are you going to do with it?"

"Pay the property taxes, and let it sit there, and worry about it."

Pike laughed. "Maybe you can put up a shack. We

can go out there on weekends."

"There's no power and no water. It'd be pretty damn rustic."

After they'd paid, they walked the few blocks to the address for the class. It was up a flight, above a row of shops on the boulevard, in a long studio space with a blond wooden floor and big windows looking toward the hills. There were nine of them besides the instructor, mostly straight couples, plus a woman on her own.

The instructor had her dark hair tied up, wearing leggings and a sports top, and orange shoes with thin soles. She stepped to the middle of the room.

"Gather round." She waited for them all to approach. "My name is Fabiana. I assume we're all here to learn the frug."

Her accent was Spanish, but her vibe wasn't typical Angeleno, the people with roots on the ranchos of Durango and Zacatecas. She looked more Mexico City or Buenos Aires.

Fabiana raised her eyebrows. "Any questions?"

No one spoke, and then Pike said, "I love those shoes."

"Thank you. They're bright, so it's easier to see the step work."

She tapped at her phone, and peppy instrumental music came from the sound system, the volume low enough that she could talk over it. First she demonstrated the dance, then talked it through, explaining the moves as she did them in slow motion.

"The key to the frug is to remember it's about your lower body. We have to add other elements up top."

Fabiana had them all practice, and walked around

to give them pointers. It wasn't just about footwork, and she got them to use their hips, bouncing on one side and then the other. It wouldn't work without the fast music, and soon everybody was sweating and breathing hard.

"You're all getting so good at it," Fabiana said. "Let's add some upper-body action from the same era. The first one is called the jerk."

Soon she had them all doing it. The jerk was about throwing your arm up past your head and thrusting your chest out while the other arm was down, then switching arms, one after the other. It actually felt like good exercise, Slater decided. He could feel his spine flexing, the muscles getting a workout.

Next Fabiana showed them the monkey. The arm movements felt similar to the jerk, but a little more controlled. Once she'd approved of everyone's technique, she demonstrated the hitchhiker. It had the same up-and-down thing happening but it was smoother again, and from the name, predictably, it involved bent elbows and extended thumbs.

Fabiana had them mix it up, combining the frug and the upper-body styles, walking around and giving advice. Once she wrapped it up, they all clapped for her.

Out on the boulevard, walking back to the Continental, the cool night air felt great. Pike looked sweaty but content, and put his arm around his shoulder.

"That was fun, wasn't it?"

"Totally," Slater said. "But my arms are fricking tired."

Back at the house, they climbed the stairs, and in

the bedroom he ditched his shirt and the chinos.

"I need to shower."

Pike pulled his shirt off. "Not yet." He stepped close. Putting his hands on his neck, he met his mouth, and pressed his woody into his leg.

Grabbing the sides of his belt, Slater pulled him close, and mouthed his neck, and his clavicle.

Pike squeezed his cock. "You're hard. You need to fuck me."

Once Pike had ditched his trousers, Slater pushed him toward the bed and climbed on top of him, kneading his chest.

"You built up your pecs from all that monkey and hitchhiker action."

He chuckled and pulled him into a kiss. Working a thumb into him, Slater held his gaze, and pressed deeper, then shifted position and pushed into him. Pike winced as he started to pound him, and Slater leaned in, squeezing his arms and his shoulders, then burrowing his nose into his hair to inhale the heady scent of his sweat. Thrusting deeper, he came, and lowered his weight onto him.

When he pulled back, he grabbed Pike's cock, shifting down and taking him into his mouth. He worked him for a minute, and Pike soon climaxed, with a spasm racking his body.

Rolling onto his back, Slater stretched out next to him.

"That was so freaking hot," Pike said, breathing hard.

He needed to shower, and claim his ration, but sleep was already encroaching. "That's you," he mumbled. "You're so freaking hot."

Pike was gone when Slater woke, with bright daylight in the windows, and he grabbed his phone. Della had left a voice message: "I have some paperwork for you. I'm in the office today."

Pushing himself out of bed, he took the shower he'd missed last night, then got dressed, and went upstairs. There was lukewarm java still in the pot, and he poured a mug, and took it with some fruit out onto the deck. It was cold out but the sun felt good.

On his phone he checked the tracker on the Pacer. Clyde had driven to Koreatown not long after office hours last night, then drove back to Downtown this morning. He zoomed in on the place he'd parked. The location was imprecise, because Svetlana's trackers didn't used GPS, instead sniffing out the cell network and Wi-Fi signals to calculate their position. The estimated circle on the map overlapped a couple of bungalows on a backstreet. It was a crowded old neighborhood, and some of those houses had likely been subdivided, and many had garden ADUs. It wasn't especially informative, but now he knew generally where the guy slept.

There were new recordings from the bug in Les's office, and he listened through them as he munched on his fruit. Several of them were one-sided phone calls, all in English, about mundane business stuff, supplies and staffers and performers. The last one was time-stamped early evening yesterday, and started with the sound of a door opening, and then two voices. They'd stepped into the room in the middle of their conversation. The sound was tinny through the phone's little speakers, but he knew both voices—Les and Lars.

"You slept with him," Les said. "I can't believe you didn't learn anything else."

"He's not really chatty. Maybe I can get him talking about twelve-step. I saw him at a meeting."

"Are you kidding me?" she demanded. "He sat here and drank my bourbon."

They were talking about Slater, he realized.

"That's terrible," Lars said. "He must have had a relapse."

"Or maybe he's lying to you."

"I didn't actually ask what his main substance was. There's a whole spectrum of what people count as dry. Maybe he's California sober."

"What does that imply?"

"You lay off the smack or the meth," Lars said, "and you can still drink and smoke weed."

"Shouldn't you be warming up?"

With that, the clip ended, and he sat for a minute, thinking about it, and slurped his joe. They were suspicious of him. He was going to have to watch his back.

Trotting down to the garage, he backed the Continental into the street, and drove to the Financial District. Once he'd parked in the garage under Della's office tower, he rode up to her floor.

Jacob scowled in recognition as he walked in. He was wearing a tan linen shirt with a yellow patterned necktie. Despite his attitude problem the guy actually dressed well. Slater stood in front of his desk.

"Is she available?"

Picking up the receiver of the desk phone, Jacob

tapped a button and spoke into it. "One of your grubby button men is here." Hanging up, he eyed Slater. "Go on back."

"Fuck you very much, Jake."

"The name is Jacob."

Ignoring that, Slater walked back to Della's office. She was standing next to a file cabinet, wearing a dark skirt and a blouse that showed a bit of cleavage. Stepping toward him, she handed him a stack of paper bound with a spring clip.

"You didn't get all this from me."

"I knew you'd find something," Slater said. "This looks like a lot."

"With a big project, the insurer needs to look through every part of the plan."

"Is Cudahy Mutual their insurer?"

"We compare notes on clients with other insurers. It's a way to prevent fraud. There's a whole system."

"That makes it sound like a racket," he said, and flipped through the pages.

Della waved a hand. "I can't really tell you much about the content. That's for the lawyers and the accountants."

"I get it. I'm going to need an interpreter." He gestured with the stack. "I appreciate you making time for this."

"I'm never going to complain about an opportunity to see those jeans walk into my office."

Slater jabbed two fingers at his face. "Hey—my eyes are up here."

She laughed. "When you wear those pants, sweetie, nobody's going to be looking at your eyes."

When he walked out, Jacob was away from his

desk. It seemed like a waste of the glare he'd prepared. In the Continental, cruising up the ramp and onto the street, he called O'Dowd, glad that she answered.

"Do you work Fridays?" he said.

"I work every damn day, Slater. I've got bills to pay."

"I hear you, sister. Can I bring you some paperwork to explain to me? I need to do it today."

"As long as you settle your lawyer's bills."

"Do you accept payment in euros?"

"No," O'Dowd said flatly. "I'm in my office now."

He got on the 10 and headed west, the Continental humming contentedly at the speed of the traffic. Soon he was nosing into the garage under her building. Upstairs, he knocked on O'Dowd's office door and stepped in.

Dressed down today, O'Dowd was wearing a green sweater, and her hair was loose. There seemed to be a lot of it, like she was letting it grow out. She sat back and greeted him. When he handed over the sheaf of paper, she leafed through it.

"More real estate stuff."

"Can you look at it now," Slater said, "and just tell me what's going on?"

"What do you need to know specifically?"

"My client is a guy named Clyde Park. I saw his name in there. What's his role in this? How invested is he? And who are the other players?"

"It shouldn't take long. You can sit there," she said, raising her eyebrows, "as long as you don't watch me work."

He dug out his phone and waggled it as he sat down. "I'll stay focused on other stuff."

In the periphery he could see her get into it,

methodically flipping through the pages. Eventually O'Dowd spoke.

"So this project is a hotel renovation. There's two separate properties that are both part of the hotel."

"I know that part."

"It's a little hard to parse, because each of the parcels is in a trust, and when it changed hands they just named new trustees." She met his gaze. "They do that so the property taxes won't reset. They're paying the same rate as they did in 1978."

"I'm sure corporate America loves that particular loophole."

"One of these documents names your man Clyde as the rep for one of the parcels. The smaller one." She glanced at the paper and recited the street address. That was the sealed wing.

"Clyde is a property manager," Slater said. "He told me he's repping the landowners. They're in Red China."

"There's a disclosure here that says one of the trustees is foreign. Based in Shanghai." She looked up. "Clyde's not a lawyer?"

"No way. He would have mentioned that. His work isn't lawyer type stuff."

"That makes it a little odd. Usually you'd get a lawyer to be your agent or your trustee. Somebody who knows how to write up contracts, navigate the bureaucracy, things like that."

"The landowner signed off on Clyde being a representative, or an actual trustee?"

"If he'd been assigned that role," O'Dowd said, "that piece of paper should be part of this. But it's not."

"So he's a fraudster."

"From these documents alone, a non-lawyer might make the assumption that Clyde is part of the company that owns the land. The one in Shanghai. But it's not documented here. For me, looking at it as a lawyer, what is laid out clearly is that he's entitled to handle transactions and contracts."

"Is there anything that says he put the bite on somebody else?" Slater said. "Like he's taken their money for some reason? Maybe to start the renovations."

"Not in this documentation, but it's possible. I can't imagine they'll be starting work anytime soon. It's still under CEQA review."

"That's the environmental thing?"

"They applied for a CEQA exemption," O'Dowd said. "That was denied in November. It means they have to go through the full review process. It takes months. I'm not sure if they've even started that. There's nothing about that step in this material." She put the binder clip on and handed him the stack. "If your guy's not part of the company that owns the land, I'd say something hinky is going on."

"Those are valuable insights." Slater rose. "Clyde implied that he was frustrated about the project. If it's stalled in environmental review, it sounds like he's rolling boxcars."

"Is that from craps?" She frowned. "I thought snake eyes was the losing throw."

"There's lots of ways to lose. You don't want snake eyes or boxcars. It sounds like Clyde's got both."

SEVENTEEN

ON THE DRIVE BACK to civilization, Slater thought it through. If Clyde was running bunco on his hotel partners, that said a lot about who he was. But it didn't feel like it was connected to Les James, or the jewelers, or their politics.

Exiting the freeway into Downtown, he parked in the structure across from Greenleaf and walked over. Les might not even be here, he realized, as it was barely lunchtime. Upstairs a couple of people were on the bandstand, and the chairs and music stands had been moved to the sides. They ignored him as he walked through toward Les's office. Her door was open, and he rapped on it with a knuckle as he stepped in.

Looking up, Les smirked and sat back. "Thanks for bringing your friend Celeste around. I'm happy to know more about this painting."

"That's quite the mountain."

"It's the symbol of a nation. Unfortunately it's in someone else's nation."

"I get it," Slater said. "Europe is a quagmire."

"It's not actually in Europe. I'd think you'd be more precise, considering your work is inspecting fire doors."

He'd never actually told her that—it had to have come from Milena, or Erik, or someone in their network. They were obviously comparing notes, the way she had been with Lars.

"What's your connection to Madwen at the Blue Finch?" he said.

Les frowned. "I know who he is. He bought the place from me."

"You don't do business with him?"

"I don't. Why are you asking?"

Before he could respond, Lars stepped in the door.

"Hey, Slater."

As he turned to greet him, he heard something fall on the carpet in front of him. Slater stooped to pick it up. "You're shedding cash."

"Heads or tails?"

"It was heads."

Lars stood at the side of Les's desk. "That's been happening since I slept at your house."

"Oh, dear, sweetie," Les said. "I think you spilled your tea."

"It's no secret." Lars waved a hand. "My roommate was painting the walls. I needed a place to do some research. Slater has a guest room."

"Sleepovers are my favorite kind of research."

She was obfuscating for Slater, he knew. He'd overheard them discuss this yesterday.

"What do you mean it's been happening?" he said. "I thought you launched it from your shirt pocket or something."

"It's called apporting. Stuff materializes out of nothing. In my case it's always coins. I think my dream research poked a hole in something supernatural. Now the coins are spilling out."

Slater frowned. "Apported from where?"

"The universe. Other dimensions." Lars raised his eyebrows. "Who knows?"

Slater looked at the coin in his hand and squinted to read the date. It looked ordinary, and it was just a couple of years old. He tossed it to Lars.

"It looks like an earthly quarter to me."

Lars awkwardly snagged it out of the air. "I think they all are."

"Why would other dimensions be throwing coins at you?" Les said.

"I think the why isn't the main issue. I have to figure out what it means."

She raised her eyebrows. "What was on the video-tape?"

Already she was contradicting herself. A minute ago she'd implied she was just hearing about Lars's sleepover, and now she knew what he'd been doing. They definitely had more going on than a work relationship, if she knew the crazy stuff he did in his spare time, taping wires to his head to record his dreams.

"I've watched some of it," Lars said, "but it's slow. I can only stare at the snow for so long."

"So there's only static?" Slater said.

"It's not supposed to be like watching a TV broadcast. You look for patterns in the static. Images or messages. I saw some stuff that might be meaningful. I definitely need to watch more of it."

Another coin dropped on the carpet next to Slater. "Damn it," he said, and stooped to pick it up. If Lars was tossing them, the mechanism was silent, and well hidden. He'd been looking right at the guy, and he hadn't moved.

"Was it heads?" Lars said.

"Affirmative."

"They always are."

"This one's hot. Like it's been sitting in the sun." Slater eyed him. "Son, you need to check yourself before you wreck yourself."

Lars laughed. "If I had a nickel for every time I heard that in a meeting."

"You do have a nickel." He waved it in the air. "And dimes and quarters and pennies. You could turn it into a paranormal income stream. Tell the universe ixnay on the chump change, and start manifesting those double-eagle gold coins."

Les stood up. "All right. Out, both of you. I've got work to do."

She followed them out into the club, and Lars headed over to the stairs. Several people were on stage now, with the chairs and music stands still disarranged. A woman sat plinking at the piano.

Standing on the parquet, Les gazed at her phone screen, then looked to the people on stage. "Is Bill Benson here?" she called.

Slater paused nearby to watch. A beefy guy with

his mousy brown hair slicked back stepped to the front of the stage.

"That's me."

The guy looked a little soft, but he had broad shoulders. Fuckable, Slater decided.

"Let's see what you've got," Les said.

Bill stepped over to the mike stand and tapped it with a finger, causing a *thunk* that echoed through the sound system. "I don't normally work a cappella, but here goes." Taking a deep breath, he leaned into the mike and launched into a slow song:

> Parlez-moi d'amour
> Redites-moi des choses tendres.

As he started into the second verse, Bill spread his arms wide as he sang. Les eyed Slater and nodded for him to step over.

"What do you think?" she said, still watching the stage.

"I don't know what he's singing about, but he sounds great."

Once he was through the song, Les raised her voice. "Thanks, Bill Benson. Don't go anywhere for a minute." She glanced at her phone. "Next, I'm looking for Mr. Squeezebox."

A guy dressed in black, with a red scarf at his neck and holding a concertina, stepped up to the mike.

"I might look like I speak French," he said, "but I don't. I'll leave that to the vocalist." He started into a song with the concertina. It was fast, and sounded like norteño music.

Les folded her arms and leaned toward him. "I hate the accordion. It's the absolute worst instrument ever invented."

"Is that actually an accordion?" Slater said.

"It's kind of like you saying Armenia is in Europe: close enough. I never hire accordion acts unless they're really good. The problem is, I need at least one of these birds for the floor show tonight. I had an act cancel on me."

"Well, I know you know what you're doing."

She chuckled. "I'm glad somebody thinks so."

He walked over to the stairs and headed down. The dining room was busier than he'd seen it earlier in the week, with most of the tables occupied. Stepping over to the subtle connecting door, he let himself through it, then climbed the stairs to Clyde's office.

The door with the MANAGEMENT sign hung open, but Clyde wasn't here. The only occupant was a guy wearing a ball cap backward and a heavy work shirt and pants. He was standing at a file cabinet with a drawer rolled open. This guy was dressed for manual labor, not for office work.

"What are you doing in here?" Slater said.

He scowled at him. "*No contratando.*"

"I don't speak Spanish, fool."

"We're not hiring anybody, *pendejo.*" Stepping toward him, he grabbed Slater's arm to steer him out.

Slater rolled his shoulder to yank away from his grip. "You don't get to put your hands on me, you rat fuck."

"I said move it."

Lightning fast, Slater slapped him hard, left and right. "Why do you make me do this to you?" He shoved him back against the cabinets. "You're going to make me crack you, aren't you. Why do you do it?"

It took a second for the guy to regroup, the surprise on his face contorting into anger. He lunged at Slater, arms flailing. Ducking his fists, Slater landed a hard right to his jaw. The guy stumbled back and bumped into the edge of the desk, budging it a few inches with a loud scraping noise.

"Knock it off," Clyde shouted. He was standing in the doorway, then stepped inside. "Both of you."

Ball Cap paused and eyed him, breathing hard.

"What's going on?" Clyde demanded.

"I caught this lowlife rifling your office," Slater said.

"Fuck you," the guy snapped.

"He works for me." Clyde looked to Ball Cap. "I'll get the paperwork for you later. Why don't you go on back upstairs?"

His face red, the guy glared at Slater as he walked out.

"Why would you come in here and rough him up?" Clyde demanded.

"He started it. My actions were purely self-defense. Why would you hire someone with a temper like that?"

"Great question." He waved a hand. "What have you learned about Les?"

"She hates the accordion."

"That seems harsh, from someone running a music venue. You should tell her the accordion is like the voices of a thousand angels. That means it's the best instrument of all."

"I can mention it," Slater said. "So why is there a high-security lock on a door in the incinerator room? None of the keys you gave me fit."

Clyde frowned. "What kind of lock?"

"One that costs a grand and has keys you can't copy."

"Can you show me?" He held up a hand. "No, I can't right now. I've got a meeting. Not tomorrow either. I'm in meetings in Beverly Hills with these hotel dummies. They own the place but it's like they're afraid to come to Downtown."

"Hotel dummies don't take the weekend off?"

"One of them said he has to go to temple tonight. He's Orthodox or something."

"He's not Orthodox if he's meeting with you on shabbat," Slater said. "If he only does Friday night he's Conservative or Reform."

"Whatever he is, it means I'm working Saturday."

"You poor thing."

Clyde stepped up and embraced him for a minute, arms tight around his back, his chin on his shoulder. The heat of his body felt good. Pulling back, Clyde met his mouth, lingering in it. Slater could feel his dick tightening in his jeans, and ground it into him.

"Can you push your meeting back? We could do something quick."

"I don't have time." Clyde pulled away, and stepped behind his desk, and grabbed a briefcase.

Slater stepped into the hall, and Clyde followed him and locked the door, calling good-bye as he stepped into the stairwell.

Walking farther down the hall, he climbed the stairs, and went to 604, and knocked. When Talisha pulled open the door, she was dressed in a sweatshirt and jeans.

"You're like a bad penny."

"Come with me," Slater said. "I want to show you something."

She frowned. "Like what?"

"The underground labyrinth."

Her eyebrows shot up. "You found it. How did you manage that?"

"You just have to know where to look."

"Let me get my keys."

She stepped back from the door but left it open. Inside Slater could see daylight filtering in from overhead, reflecting on the dark polished wood of the floor. That was one of the skylights he'd seen on the roof. A sofa and lounge chairs were parked in front of the windows. Those looked out at Broadway, but this floor was high enough to get good light. On the table by the door was a black wallet, splayed open, with a shiny piece of metal inside. He couldn't read it from here, but from the shape, it was undeniably a badge.

Talisha returned a moment later, and he gestured to it. "What's with the badge?"

"It's for my job." She stepped out and locked the door.

"You're a cop?"

"I'm a financial inspector for the county. I go around to public facilities and dig through their spreadsheets and receipts."

"They give you a badge for that?" Slater led the way to the stairwell.

"I can carry a firearm too, but I don't."

"Accountants packing heaters. That seems like a lot."

"The badge is useful," she said. "I get plenty of pushback. Especially from people who actually are scamming the taxpayers."

They went down the stairs, and around to the flight that led below street level, and into the side hallway. At the double doors into the tunnels, Slater handed her the brass key that he'd copied. Talisha took a moment to get the door open, then stepped into the tunnel.

"This is totally it." She looked up. "Is that the side-walk?"

"Did you ever notice the glass blocks in the con-crete?"

"Of course. They're all over Downtown."

"Some of the tunnels have the blocks," Slater said, "and some have functioning electric lights, but some don't. You should bring a flashlight."

She took a few steps, looking over the walls and up the tunnel. "This space is old. You can feel it."

"If you go that way and left, there's a sign for Spring Street. If you follow it all the way down, there's a set of one-way crash doors into city hall."

"No kidding."

"They copped an attitude when I went through, so I wouldn't go after hours. You'll set off an alarm and wind up in a jail cell. That place is crawling with cops." He waved a hand. "Nothing personal."

She laughed. "I'm not a cop. I love the smell in here. It's like the earth, but clean. Not like up top."

"Because there's nobody sleeping rough down here to piss on the walls."

"I wish I had time to check it out right now." Talisha held up the key. "Maybe I can borrow this sometime."

"You can keep that. Explore at your leisure."

"You got it from Park?"

"Don't ask. I know you can keep your mouth shut. Otherwise the selfie brigade would be lined up in that quinceañera joint, trying to get into the sealed-off hotel mezzanine."

"That's not who I am," she said.

"There might be other people around with access to this door," Slater said. "You already know Clyde keyed a bunch of them the same."

"Like how the front door key fits the incinerator room." She gestured with the key. "I don't know how to thank you for this."

Slater shrugged. "It's transactional. You gave me good dope about the building, and showed me the mezzanine. This is payback."

"I'm going to call bullshit on that one. It's not that you owe me anything. You did it to be nice. You just don't want to admit that you're connected to other people. Remember how you told me you didn't have anyone else to ask? We all rely on one another." She raised her eyebrows. "Like the man said, lean into it."

"That doesn't really sound like me."

He stepped inside, and Talisha followed. She pulled the door closed and locked it with the brass key.

"I guess I'll see you at Greenleaf," she said.

"More likely I'll see your taillights rapidly fading in the distance, the way you drive that TA."

EIGHTEEN

T HE SHADOWS GREW LONG in the golden light of the end of the day as Slater drove to his house. He thought about what Talisha had said, that he was getting soft. He'd felt it too since Pike had been around. Their narrative complex was an upgrade in his emotional life, but the whole thing had upended his world. The last thing he needed was to become a goddamn square.

He rolled into his neighborhood and pulled into his garage. Upstairs he found Pike out on the deck, stretched out on a lounger. He sat facing him, between his knees.

"You must be freezing out here," Slater said. "Nyx is about to begin her nightly journey."

"I love the light right now." Pike gestured to the planter boxes that lined the low wall surrounding the deck. "What did you do to those? There's nothing left but little stubs in the dirt."

"You have to cut them down in winter. They'll be back in spring."

"They don't flower for very long."

"They're natives. The pollinators love them." He raised his voice. "It's worth it."

Pike chuckled. "What's the name of it again?"

"California fuchsia." He leaned in and mouthed his neck.

"A native, like my California boy."

"You're a local now too."

"Already?"

Slater pulled back. "LA has never been about your pedigree or your bloodline or the depth of your roots. That's for the suckers east of Saint Louis."

"Your analysis is so specific." He massaged his biceps. "I should have you draw me a map."

"I can do it in Sharpie on the back of your hand. Like Lars."

"So what's your plan for the evening?" Pike said.

"I need to go back to Downtown."

"Will you be able to squeeze in a twelve-step meeting?"

"That's such a great idea," Slater said, "but I can't. Lo, it's shabbat."

"I'm surprised you even know when shabbat is. You remember we're doing Hannukah at Doris's tomorrow."

"Now I do. My brain flagged it as traumatic information and blocked it."

"It means something to her," Pike said.

"I'll be there. Tonight I'm doing low-key surveillance at Greenleaf. You want to come with?"

"I love that place, but can we eat first?"

Pike put on a fun collared shirt with tiny red and blue flowers all over it, and black dress pants, and Slater wore the green-and-brown houndstooth suit. They drove to Greenleaf and ate downstairs at Sackett's. Despite the renovation the food wasn't a substantial improvement over the steam tables of yore.

When they climbed the stairs to Greenleaf, the bouncer carded them, and when Pike had his ID back, he stepped over to the arched windows nearby. He looked over the neon sign mounted in one of them. It faced out to Broadway and was lit up in orangey-red. From the back it was possible to parse the lettering.

"Dancing," Pike read. "It looks old. When you're this close to it you can hear the buzz of the transformer."

"Les told me about it when I first came in here," Slater said. "When she pulled down the wallboard to renovate, she found it right where it is now, still plugged in, still lit up. Sometime in the 1940s they boarded over the windows and completely obscured it."

"I guess it was built to last."

From the direction of the bar Les stepped over, fully glammed out now, in a dark-red crushed-velvet dress that hung off her shoulders. Her hair was down, and she was wearing evening makeup.

"People come in here just to admire the neon," she said. "The historical society wrote a piece about it."

Slater waved a hand. "I was telling him how you found it behind the wallboard."

"It's a great story," Pike said.

"It's a true story. For eighty years that sign was switched on and inside the wall." She eyed Slater and tilted her head toward Pike. "So who's this long drink of water?"

Pike laughed and introduced himself.

"Are you two together," Les said, "or can I flirt?"

"Those things aren't mutually exclusive." Pike raised his eyebrows. "And in that dress, you don't have to flirt. The flirting will come to you."

"Oh, I like this one."

"How long does it take you to get ready for the evening anyway?" Slater said. "The makeup, and the hair alone. The transformation is remarkable."

Her eyes narrowed. "I'll take that as a compliment. You look good in a suit too."

"It's vintage. 1970s dead stock."

Nearby a guy in a band jacket was keeping a respectful distance but was clearly aiming to get her attention. When she noticed him, Les briefly touched Pike's arm before she walked away.

"Have fun tonight."

They found a table and sat on the same side. The server came over and took their drink orders, and they focused on the act on stage. At the mike stood two women, with the same glammy blond hair, swept up in the same beehive, and wearing the same black cocktail dress. They started into a song, the lyrics romantic, and sang parts of it in harmony. There was no sign of the band, but it worked even without accompaniment.

Their drinks arrived, a highball for Pike and Slater's OJ and grenadine, and the doppelgängers on the stage started into another song with a torchy vibe. From the doors into the back, Lars walked out, wearing the green velour band jacket. The fact that he made a beeline for their table meant he hadn't just noticed them. Les had tipped him off.

Stopping beside their table, Lars grinned at them like a goon. "You like the sister act?"

"They sound great," Pike said.

"They really are sisters. Up close they look identical. It's actually a little freaky."

"I believe that."

"They're not headliners. Just part of the floor show," Lars said. "The band is up next, but there's a fan dancer on later. She's amazing."

"You mean a sizzler," Slater said, "or she actually dances with fans?"

"There's totally fans involved. It's more tasteful than in a strip club. She doesn't really get naked." He raised his eyebrows. "You should tell your server you're the designated driver. They'll comp your soft drinks."

"Good to know," Slater said.

As Lars walked away, Pike said, "He thinks you're on the wagon."

"Tonight I kind of am. I need to stay sharp."

Reaching for the crook of his arm, he held up a quarter. "This was on my sleeve."

"Heads or tails?"

"I think it was heads. What's his damage with the coins?" Pike said. "Do you think he dropped it on me deliberately?"

"He says it's paranormal. They materialize out of nothing. The technical term is that they apport. It's been following him around since he did the psycho-electroid dreaming."

"They apport from where?"

"Who knows?" Slater said. "That's why it needs its own word. It's unexplained."

He set the coin on the table. "That boy is a handful."

After the sister act, the house band set up, with Lars at the drums. The musicians quietly futzed around for a minute, then the lights went up, and they started into a song. It was slow but they sounded great.

As the band played, they drank, and Slater watched Les James work the room. She talked to people at the tables, and at the bar, then conferred with a server for a minute. On stage one of the trombone players had a solo, and then Lars did, wildly flaying the drum kit. It was entertaining to watch him.

Slater had to be here, he knew that, even though it didn't feel especially informative to watch Les or the band. He had the gnawing feeling that he was missing something. Like he hadn't put the pieces together, even though they were all scattered right in front of him.

When the song ended, with a smattering of applause, the woman with the sax stepped up to the mike. "Let's hear a warm welcome for the inimitable Bill Benson."

This guy had auditioned for Les earlier today. He was dressed better now, in a midnight-blue silk suit and a bow tie. The band started up again, and Bill sang, his voice filling the room to the point that he didn't really need amplification:

My heart and my soul are true
Can't you feel it in my kisses
Every part of me, it's all for you
It's just for you.

Pike folded his arms. "This freaking guy."

"What's wrong with Bill?"

"Listen to him. He's going to break your heart with that baritone."

"You big softie. You can take down a biker gang headed by a psycho who murdertized four people, but then you get crushed out on Bill Benson." Slater punched his shoulder.

Pike gestured to the stage. "Tell me I'm wrong."

The guy did have a great voice, even though his delivery might be a little rote. They listened and sipped their drinks as Bill got into another song, the one he'd auditioned with.

"Great," Pike said. "Now he speaks French."

Slater had to laugh.

"Why are you not jealous of Bill Benson the way you are with Davis?"

"I'm not jealous of anybody. I just need to keep apprised of threats. This guy is not trying to get with you the way Davis is. Plus Davis has an extremely punchable face."

"I wouldn't do that," Pike said. "He could take you."

"Him and what army?"

He leaned over to kiss him, and mouthed his jaw.

After Bill did another torch song, the band heated up. More people were arriving, and with the hard music, several were dancing. When the band started a song with a fast beat, Pike stood up.

"We have to dance."

Slater rose with him, and left his suit jacket on the back of his chair. "Are you going to make me frug?"

"The song has the right beat, so you have to." When they got onto the parquet, Pike jabbed a finger at him and raised his eyebrows. "Have to."

He chuckled as they got into it. It took a second, but his body remembered the movements, with the hip and the knee. Of course it looked better when Pike did it. The guy made it seem effortless. He added the monkey, and then the jerk, and Slater followed his lead with the upper-body movements. Pike was so earnest with the rhythm, his arms practically flailing, his brow furrowed in concentration. Just watching him made Slater laugh.

Nearby on the parquet, a pair of women moved closer. They looked to be in their twenties, and were dressed for a night out, one in a skirt and one in a linen suit.

"I like your moves," the one in the skirt said, talking loud to be heard over the music.

"It's called the frug," Pike said, "and the jerk. You move your hip like this."

He showed them how to do it, and they both picked it up instantly. Soon the pair of them were doing it with them. What was it about dancing? People looked silly and hot at the same time.

They did the frug through another song, and the women drifted away. The next song was slower, and Pike put his arm on his back, and grasped his hand. Slater put his other arm on his shoulder and followed his lead. His muscles remembered the steps, mimicking Pike's, from a different dance class they'd taken. The pace made it easier than the frug.

"I've worked up a sweat," he said when the song ended, and they went back to their table, and ordered another round.

"I haven't seen you laugh like that in a while," Pike said.

"It's so frivolous, but I have to admit it's fun. And watching you doing anything makes me happy. You're so damn beautiful."

He grinned and squeezed the back of his neck. The place was getting crowded, and more people were up dancing. He couldn't see Les anymore. Eventually Slater gestured with his chin toward the stairs. Pike nodded and rose.

When they got to the top of the stairs, Les was standing nearby, and turned to them, raising her voice over the music. "I love to watch you two dance. That was so mid-century."

"It's the frug," Slater said. "We took a class."

"You got other people doing it too. I'll have to put you on the payroll."

"It feels like the music is for a different style though," Pike said. "The big band."

"You can frug to anything if it's fast enough," Slater said.

"I saw proof of that." Les raised her eyebrows. "And I'm completely comfortable with you fruging to the house band."

NINETEEN

I N THE MORNING SLATER slept late, waking when his phone buzzed. He scrabbled for it on the bedside table and peered at the screen. No name was displayed but it was a 213 number. When he picked up, he recognized the voice.

"You sound like you're asleep," Erik said. "Where are you?"

"What do you care?"

"Something went down at the store. My mother is freaking out. Were you here today?"

"I was at Greenleaf last night. I haven't been over there since. What went down?"

"It's not really any of your business."

"You made it my business by calling me," Slater said, and louder, "Sing, brother."

"I can't talk right now."

He looked at the screen. Erik had hung up on him. "Idiot," he muttered, then got up and got dressed.

Not taking the time to go upstairs, he hustled down to the garage. He knew Pike had left early, headed to the gun range with some of his work cronies. It made no sense why they'd do that for fun when they had to do it for work.

On the drive to Downtown he opened Svetlana's software to check the tracker on the Pacer. Clyde had gone to the same place in K-town last night. That had to be his crib. But then he'd gone into Downtown. The location circle showed the vehicle was parked between Hill and Olive, and it had been there since 3:22 a.m.

Maybe he'd had a late-night hookup. But that was so close to his office. Why wouldn't Clyde park there and walk? It was only a block or two away, and he already had a parking pass for that structure.

There were no new recordings from the bug in Les's office. It had been more than a day. It wasn't likely she'd made no phone calls or had any conversations in there. Les or a cleaner must have found the calculator and put it somewhere out of audio range.

He parked in the structure on Broadway, then walked across to Milena's shop. The interior was dark, and the sign in the glass said CLOSED. He tried the door. It was locked. That was a little surprising, as Saturday was a primo shopping day.

Erik had acted a little squirrely about the incinerator room, ham-handedly trying to mislead him about it. And then there was that Masamune lock, almost unnoticeable in the grimy ancient space, but bright like a laser beam once you spotted it. That was his next stop.

Slater let himself into the building, and walked the hall to the stairs leading down. He didn't need to use a key to get into the incinerator room as the door was wide open. Inside, two guys were standing next to the small door with the Masamune lock. It was open now too. Slater knew one of the guys, the baldy. They'd talked this week in one of the offices upstairs. He'd called himself a bookkeeper. He might have met the other guy too, with Vahan, working on jewelry in one of the basement suites.

As he stepped toward them, the bookkeeper jutted his chin. "What are you doing here?"

"I work for the property manager," Slater said. "What's going on?"

"I don't know." He turned away and stepped through the doorway.

Slater followed him in. Milena was here, with three other people, standing near the door and engrossed in intent conversation. They had to be speaking Armenian. Even though he couldn't understand them, the grim vibe was palpable, with sober expressions all around. He recognized one of the men from the offices upstairs. He gave Slater the once-over as he walked in.

Looking over the room, he saw that one wall bore ancient wooden storage shelves with nothing on them. Jewelers had valuable stuff, but they'd never use this space for that. He'd seen safes in their shops and offices. But then why were they acting like something serious had gone down? What had they been keeping in here?

Watching them talk, one of the guys gestured to the door with the Masamune lock. Milena briefly switched to English—just a phrase, spoken intently: "You had the only other key."

That was the only way in, he saw, looking around the room. He took a few steps and studied the walls. One was unfinished concrete, and the others were wood, painted dark gray a long time ago. The shelves weren't built in but they looked old, with unfinished posts and boards.

Walking over to the far wall, he looked back toward the door. He could corner Milena, if she ever took a break from that conversation, and ask her what had happened. For now she hadn't noticed him, and the others were ignoring him, engrossed in whatever drama this was.

As he watched them, he shifted his weight on his feet. A mark on the gritty concrete floor caught his eye. It stood out because it was different than the other random scuffs and scrapes, forming a perfect arc. He stepped toward it to look closer, but it disappeared. When he stepped back, he found that he could only see it in a specific position, when it caught the light from the overhead fixture near the door.

When he walked over to it, he couldn't make it out even when he was standing right over it. He went back to the wall to look again. It was a scuff mark, he decided. Something anchored to a point had scraped the floor to make the arc. The most logical explanation for that was a door anchored to a hinge. But there was no door there.

In his mind's eye he projected the arc to where it would meet the wall. That's where the jamb would be.

There were studs spaced the usual way, sixteen inches apart, with ancient boards backing them, the same as the rest of that wall. He stepped over to examine that part of it. There was no sign of a handle or hardware, no hinges or door frame. Looking up at the top of the wall, where it met the concrete of the floor above, there was nothing to say it was a door. But something had made that mark on the floor.

What was on the other side of this wall? Thinking about it, he tried to get his bearings, remembering the route down to the incinerator room. This wall had to be perpendicular to the street. It felt like it should be between adjoining buildings, but it was hard to be sure. The whole block was a labyrinth. If there was something unseen here, an alternate way into this room, no one else had noticed it.

Finally Milena spotted him, and stepped over, concern in her eyes. "Slater, please tell me you weren't involved in this."

"Involved in what?"

"We never should have left it here," the baldy said. "It could have been anyone."

Slater waved at the space. "This looks like a storeroom. What went missing, exactly? I know it wasn't used clothes or blankets. You wouldn't all be so freaked out."

From the incinerator room, Erik stepped in, and looked around, and scowled at him. "Ibáñez. What do you know about this?"

"I don't even know what this is."

Stepping close, Erik jutted his chin. "Nothing changes. You were trouble back in middle school, and you're trouble now."

He knew he should resist the instinct, and take the high road, and do something to defuse the aggression. It's what all the shrinks had told him. But he just couldn't do it. He took a swing at Erik, but the guy reacted fast, grabbing his forearm. Drawing him in, Slater wrapped his other arm around his neck. The guy hadn't forgotten his wrestling maneuvers, Slater realized, as he deftly twisted sideways out of his grip. Hooking Slater's leg, he tried to throw him off balance, but Slater managed to stand his ground and shove him off. Still, Erik landed a couple of solid punches, to his mouth and his nose. Slater threw a dick punch, but he missed his target and hit him in the gut. Erik groaned and folded in on himself.

At that point it was over, but the baldy and one of the jewelers were on them anyway, and pulled them apart.

Milena raised her voice. "Both of you, calm down. There's no need for fisticuffs."

Catching his breath, Slater checked his nose. It wasn't broken but it hurt like hell. When he tapped his lip with a finger, there was a trace of blood, but when he tongued it he could tell it wasn't split open.

Erik was standing erect again, and wiped his mouth. "You've still got it. The red mist."

He jutted his chin. "You started it, toots."

"You've got blood on your lip." Milena handed Slater a tissue, then looked him up and down. "Have you eaten?"

From the door, one of the guys called to her. "Milena, you're wrong." He switched to Armenian, gesturing at the half-open door.

Milena stepped over to him, and Slater and Erik

stood watching them.

"The guy who led my mindfulness class said the same thing to me." Slater imitated his breathy voice. "'I think you need to go nourish yourself.' It was the New Age equivalent of 'Go fuck yourself.'"

"You took a mindfulness class?"

"Court ordered."

Erik nodded. "OK, that, I believe."

"Still, I'd rather take the tombé or the punch in the face. It's a lot more honest."

"I hear you."

"Can you understand them?" Slater said.

"Mostly. They're arguing about how the door got opened without a key."

"Did anybody call the cops?"

"Don't do that." Erik met his gaze. "This isn't your problem."

There was no point in asking exactly what the problem was. None of them were in a talking mood. But he could put most of it together. He wanted to ask Erik about Les James, but if she's the one who stole from them, mentioning her name would put a target on her back. This crowd was already amped up.

Maybe it was like that hotel wing, Slater thought, looking at the wall where the arcing scuff was. It had been sealed off for decades, but the quinceañera vendor and Talisha had found a way in. This stretch of wall didn't look like it had a door in it, but there was definitely another way to get into this room. That scenario was way more probable than someone defeating a Masamune lock.

There was no reason to hang around here, and they were already suspicious of him. It wouldn't take a big leap for somebody to try to make him the patsy. He walked toward the doorway to the incinerator room.

"Where are you going?" Erik called after him.

"Why do you care? I've got no idea what's going on here, and nobody's willing to tell me."

Walking up the stairs, he gently massaged his nose. It was already swelling. Erik was a damn hothead.

Stepping into the hallway at ground level, he found that the connecting door into the next building was right here. That meant the little storeroom was definitely in proximity to the adjoining wall. He let himself into the next building with the ring of keys, then headed down the nearest stairwell in this building. Below street level again, it felt like this sublevel wasn't as deep as the one with the incinerator room. Back in that direction there was no connecting door.

He walked the hall, painted that industrial brown-tan color and studded with doorways. The door closest to the end of the hall was unmarked, he saw. If it was somebody's office or workshop, it would be labeled with a suite number, like all the others. When he tried the handle, it was locked. Digging out Clyde's keys, he found one of them that fit, and pulled it open.

On the inside of the door was an emergency-exit crash bar, with a lighted exit sign overhead. That meant the way out was behind him. He hadn't been here before. It was another hallway, but it looked more like the delivery tunnels, with unpainted concrete towalls. Just inside the door was a few feet of landing, then four concrete steps down, and the hall continued. Old wire-covered light fixtures hung overhead.

Slater walked the length of it. The floor was gritty with neglect, like in the delivery tunnels. There were no doors here, until he got close to the far end. The lone doorway looked more like a hatch, just four feet tall with rounded corners. It had a rusty grab handle rather than a latch or a lock. The bottom was at least a foot above the floor. Maybe it had been meant for moving stuff, not for people.

Thinking about it, this wall was definitely where the buildings adjoined, and this was about as far from the street as that storeroom. The fact that the sill was so high here could be because the floor in the other building was higher. Maybe this had been some kind of garbage hatch, so the buildings could share the incinerator, the way Milena and Les James shared the dumpster out back.

But why did it not look like a door on the storeroom side? Celeste had shown him a speakeasy in the tunnels, and said the entrance was in a shop, hidden in a wall. Maybe the way out of the storeroom into this hallway was hidden because it was an escape route. If the cops couldn't see it, they couldn't follow the boozers when they raided the place.

Slater stood listening, but he couldn't hear anything, even though Milena and her cohort were likely still right there, just a few feet away. He couldn't open this door right now either. They'd think he was the one who'd jacked whatever they'd lost.

He stood staring at the hatch. Les James had keys to some of the connecting doors, which meant she could have gained access to this hallway. She definitely could have found this the same way he had. But this was also Clyde's domain, and Clyde definitely had all the keys. He just couldn't see Les as the lowlife who'd robbed these people. In his gut it felt wrong. With Clyde it felt more plausible, and he already knew Clyde was on the grift with his hotel project. But he couldn't rule anything out. Not without solid evidence.

Walking farther down the hall, he found it ended at a half flight of concrete steps up to a heavy door. It had been painted somber green long ago, mottled and peeling now, and two wooden planks were nailed across it to block access. He'd bet money the fire marshal hadn't signed off on that. But the planks looked as old as everything else, and this was a thoroughly disused space.

If this was the back of the building, it had to be a door into the alley. He'd noticed that some of them behind the dumpsters were set a few feet below street level. Maybe they'd closed this one off when they stopped using the incinerator and needed to park a dumpster in front of it.

Walking back to the emergency exit, he went into the hallway, and upstairs, and into the next building. He found Clyde's office with the MANAGEMENT sign on it. When he tried the handle, it was locked, and he knocked, but there was no sound inside, no light under the door.

Trotting back down in the stairwell, he walked through the next building to the end of the hall, and through the door into Sackett's dining room. He stepped across the chain and hustled up to Greenleaf. A woman was on the parquet maneuvering a heavy-looking machine. Polishing the wood, maybe.

Looking up as Slater appeared, she said, *"Está cerrado."*

"I need to talk to Les James," he said, and kept walking.

She raised her voice. "Her office is closed too. She said she'll come in at 5."

Slater paused. "No one's back there?"

"Nobody. You have to leave."

As he went back down to the dining room, he dug out his phone, and found Lars in his contact list, and dialed.

"Have you seen Les today?" Slater said when he picked up.

"On Saturdays she deals with suppliers," Lars said, "so she's probably down on Alameda somewhere. She'll be in her office before Greenleaf opens. Why are you looking for Les?"

"No reason."

He ended the call and stood there thinking about it. He'd never talked to Les about the incinerator room, but he'd talked to Clyde about the Masamune lock. He'd made the stupid assumption that Clyde was the one who'd put it there. If Clyde had robbed that storeroom, the guy had been playing him all along. He stared absently at a woman with dark hair as she topped the stairs, carrying a tray, followed by a couple of little kids. He felt nauseous now as the realization sank in. This was his fault. He'd told Clyde where to look. Slater had directed him right to that storeroom.

The woman sat at a table, and the kids climbed on the chairs. She glanced at Slater sidelong, and he turned away. He didn't need to be scaring people. Dropping into a chair at an empty table near the stairs, he could feel his heart pounding. He hadn't robbed Milena and her posse, but it was still his fault.

TWENTY

S LATER NEEDED TO THINK clearly right now, and he took a couple of slow breaths. Pike had once talked about a technique the military used: slow down, because slow is smooth, and smooth is fast. He meant that if you did things methodically, it would get better results than if you reacted with the hair trigger. Tracking down Clyde and punching him in the face was the wrong approach right now. He needed to slow down.

Clyde said he was in Beverly today, but the Pacer was here, or near here. And why hadn't he parked it where he usually parked? Looking at his phone, he texted Clyde:

Are you around?

Whatever had been in that storeroom was valuable, and confidential, as none of them would say anything about it. It also had to be bulky. Something that was bigger than their small businesses could keep in their jewelry safes. How would you jack something bulky? Les could have carried it back to Greenleaf, and she wouldn't have had to go out to the street. She had the keys to move around unseen. Similarly, Clyde might have taken it to his office. But that was risky. Other people seemed to come and go. Greenleaf had the same issue. There were lots of people around day and night. Any sensible thief would want to get it away from here.

His phone buzzed with a text from Clyde:

> I'm in BH for a meeting today. I thought I told you that?

Maybe Clyde had another set of wheels. Lots of classic car people had a square ride for routine use or long trips. But why was the Pacer over on Olive? He pulled up Svetlana's software. The tracker was still in the same place. Zooming in, he saw that it was a residential conversion, a huge building fronting Olive. But the circle also covered part of the multistory parking structure behind it on Hill.

Thinking about it, if Slater were trying to move something big out of the building on the down-low, he'd use those tunnels. There was nobody down there to notice, especially at that hour of the morning.

He got up and unlocked the connecting door, then trotted down the stairs to the level below the street, and found the door into the tunnels. Stepping inside, he locked the door again, and took a deep breath. Down here most of the signs for the streets above had faded away, but he knew where Seventh was. He turned toward Hill and strode along it. With Celeste he'd gone the opposite direction, so this was new ground. The first cross tunnel wasn't marked, but it had to be Hill, and he headed toward where the tracker was.

The doorways on this whole stretch had been sealed up with cinderblock and mortar. Maybe whoever built the parking lot decided they didn't need access. Turning around, he walked back to Seventh, then turned down the tunnel under Olive. Here the doorways were still intact.

Pausing under a stretch of the glass blocks where daylight filtered in, he checked his phone. He had a signal down here, surprisingly. But he really wasn't that far from the street, just a dozen feet below it. He checked the number of the building where the tracker on the Pacer was, then continued walking. The number was painted on a door. He tried the handle, but of course it was locked.

If Clyde had used this route, maybe he had a crony in the building. Somebody to come and open it for him. If Slater could get into this building from street level, he could check it out from the inside.

Walking back toward Seventh, he noticed the next set of doors had a sliver of light between them as he passed. When he tried the handle, it was unlocked, and he pulled it open. Inside was a hallway running parallel to the tunnel.

Standing there was a guy with a little mustache, wearing blue work clothes and carrying a toolbox. A handyman or a plumber. He didn't look surprised to see him, but he'd stopped, and looked wary, and greeted Slater in Spanish. Behind him was a set of doors into the building, and in the opposite direction the hallway made a right turn away from the tunnel. He paused just long enough to make the decision.

"How you doing?" he said to the guy, then walked the other way, relieved that he didn't challenge him.

From the distance he'd walked, this had to be part of the same residential building. Likely there had been separate addresses when the tunnels were built, and the larger structure went up later, and had multiple access points from the tunnel.

The hallway was clean and well lighted. It would have been renovated whenever they turned the building into apartments. There were no cameras in here—Clyde would have been able to come in unnoticed.

He passed an exit sign over a crash door, and looked in through the narrow glass panel. There were stairs leading up. Farther along was another stairwell, this one marked with a sign that said OFFICES next to an official-looking seal. It was the county's, he saw. That probably meant the building was public housing. It also explained why the place looked maintained.

At the end of the hall was a third exit sign with a crash door. He must have walked the length of the building. The door wasn't alarmed. He wouldn't be able to get back in, but he pushed it open anyway, and climbed the stairs. As he stepped out the door at the top, he had to smile. He could see daylight in the distance beyond a sea of cars. This was the parking structure on Hill, and he was on the ground floor, halfway across the block, where the residential building adjoined the lot. The Pacer had to be right around here.

Walking to the middle of the space, he looked around for it, but there was no sign of the distinctive ride. There was a stairwell, and he climbed to the next level, and walked a circuit of the floor. Stepping into the stairs again, he went up another level. There were a lot fewer vehicles up here.

And there it was, parked nose-in, near the stairs at the back. This was about as close as you could get to a direct route from the tunnels. Clyde would have picked this floor because it was a lot quieter than the first couple. At that hour of the morning he would have been able to walk all the way here from his own buildings without seeing anyone.

As he approached the Pacer, he saw that it was riding low. It was a low-slung car anyway, but the suspension was sagging more than normal. There was something heavy in the back. Cupping his hands against the glass to look in through the rear window, he could only see a dark blanket covering something bulky.

"Milton, what the hell are you up to?"

He stood there for a second, thinking about it, then turned and trotted down the stairs. As he walked the length of the building to the street, he looked up, scanning for cameras. There were a couple that covered the vehicle entrance and the exit, but he hadn't spotted any inside, where people parked.

Walking back to Sackett's, it seemed much closer on the sidewalk than below it. Clyde's buildings were literally around the corner. He let himself in from the street and climbed the stairs to Clyde's office. It was still dark under the door. His workers used the office, and it had locking cabinets, so the office itself wasn't a high-security place. Was it keyed the same as the other doors? He tried the keys on Clyde's ring, one after another. Finally one of them opened the office door.

Stepping inside, he had to grin. It seemed inept that he'd given Slater the keys to his own office. Honest people were artless like that, but crooks usually weren't. Even when he'd planted the tracker on the Pacer, Clyde had basically caught him in the act, but the tracker was still there. A devious-minded person would have checked to see if he'd done something. It was like he wasn't cut out to be a lowlife.

The real-estate lockbox was still on the credenza. He tried the code 1908, and it popped open.

"Idiot," Slater said under his breath. This guy was way too trusting. He'd positioned himself in the world of grifters and fraudsters and con artists but he was definitely a tyro.

Digging out the keys to the Pacer, he closed the box again and put it where he'd found it. As he was pocketing them, he heard keys in the lock, and the office door swung open. It was the guy in the ball cap and the work clothes. He scowled in recognition.

"If it isn't the *payaso*. What are you up to?"

"I work here, dumbass. Where's Clyde?"

"How should I know?"

Slater scoffed, and walked past him into the hall, and took a deep breath to dispel the surge of adrenaline. It was a stroke of luck that the guy knew his face, since he'd given him a tune-up yesterday. Otherwise he'd have had a lot of explaining to do.

Once he'd hustled across the street, he got into the Continental, and drove to the structure on Hill.

He took a ticket from the machine, and the barrier swung up, and he drove up to the level where the Pacer was. There was an open stall next to it, and he nosed in. The bigger vehicle would block the view from most of the floor.

Using Clyde's keys, he opened the Pacer's hatchback and pulled off the blanket. Underneath were black bags, made of heavy nylon, with reinforced handles. Four of them were lined up against the back seat. Zipping one open, he knew at a glance what the contents were. The gleam of gold was unmistakable. These were gold bars. He took one out to look it over. It was about the size and shape of a cell phone, but it was so damn heavy. One side was stamped with 1,000 G and 999.9 FINE. The rest of the bag looked to contain more of them. Tucking it back inside, he zipped it closed. He didn't need to see any more. He knew now what had happened.

How many trips had Clyde had to make, carrying these on foot from that storeroom? Maybe he'd used a handcart to bring them all at once. He was smart to get all this away from those buildings, but it was brave to leave anything in this rolling fishbowl.

Opening the trunk of the Continental, he went back to the Pacer and lifted one of the nylon bags. It had two compartments, he saw, like a saddle bag, evenly weighted on either side of the handle. It was freaking heavy. He put the bag in his trunk, then transferred the others, heaving them out one at a time.

Once he'd rearranged the blanket, he locked the Pacer, then stood there for a minute, thinking about it. He knew he should bust the lock on the hatchback to make it look like a break-in. He could do it with the tire iron in his trunk. Clyde would have no clue who'd done it. But he just couldn't will himself to damage such a beautiful thing. Milton had made it through all those decades intact. Slater couldn't be the one to trash him.

Instead he unlocked the passenger-side door and left it closed but unlatched. Maybe Clyde would think he'd inadvertently left it unlocked himself, and someone had gotten in that way. Squatting next to the rear tire, he reached into the well and found his tracker, and pulled it off, and clicked off the power switch with a fingernail. Once he'd tucked it down next to the spare tire in his trunk, he slammed the lid, and stepped back to look it over. The Continental might be riding a little lower, but it was much less noticeable than the Pacer.

Once he'd driven back to Broadway, he pulled in at a meter in front of the quinceañera shop, and hustled back to the building where Clyde's office was, and climbed the stairs. It was dark under the door again, and he unlocked it and flipped on the lights. There was no sign of Ball Cap. Opening the real-estate box, he wiped his prints off the keys before he put them in, but he didn't bother with the box. Clyde had seen him handle it already.

Locking the office, he stepped into the stairwell and started down. Climbing toward him was a guy with his dark hair in a crew cut. Beefy and top-heavy like a weightlifter, with a busted nose, he was totally fuckable. The guy paused on the stairs and stared at him as he passed. Slater met his eye and scowled. The guy turned and called after him.

"You've been walking the halls all week."

He paused on the landing. "I work here, Butch."

"Did I see you last night? You were at Greenleaf."

"The fuck are you to be interrogating me? I don't know you."

"Did you steal from us?"

Slater scoffed and kept walking, but then heard heavy footfalls on the stairs behind him. No way was he going to get into a dustup with this ape. The guy would flatten him. He started moving faster.

"Hold up," the guy called. "I'm talking to you."

As he stepped out at the bottom of the stairwell, the guy was just seconds behind him. He held the door half open, and when the guy got to it, slammed it hard. He could feel it make contact with his face.

The guy yowled and then cursed. "Mother-fucker."

Slater was already running up the hall. He couldn't remember if there was a door to the street up this way. As he ducked into the stairs going down, he glanced back. The guy was hustling after him, arms pumping, rage in his eyes. There was a smear of bright red on his upper lip.

Busting out into the corridor, he realized that this was the level below the street. Why had he come down here? The way out was on the ground floor. That's why all the stairs started and ended there, so you wouldn't do something stupid, like flee into the basement, like he'd just done. He sprinted to the end of the building, and into another stairwell, and hustled up. There was no direct route to the street. He could hear the guy not far behind him on the stairs.

Running up the side hallway, he saw there was a crash door at the end, and he slammed it open. He was in the alley. Nobody was back here. He slammed the door closed and looked around. There was nothing to jam it shut with. But the dumpster next to it was on wheels, he saw, and he hustled around to the opposite side, planting his hands on the grimy steel, and shoved hard. It took effort, but the thing gradually moved, and he managed to roll it across the door.

The crash door snapped open, but only a few inches, slamming into the dumpster with a *bang*. Slater ran down the alley. This wasn't the end that had a gate to the street, he realized. Why had he come this way? At the other end he might have been able to scale the gate. Clyde said this was a dead end. Behind him he could hear the crash door slamming against the dumpster. The guy was trying to budge it, and eventually he would. It was just a matter of time.

Near the alley's dead end, a door was propped open with a plastic patio chair. This was the same side as Clyde's buildings. As he ducked inside, he glanced back down the alley. The dumpster had moved away from the wall, but the big guy wasn't outside yet.

Lifting the chair inside, he pulled the door closed, and made sure it was latched, and took a few deep breaths. This room looked familiar. The mangled mannequins and the big dresses. At the far side, a ladder was propped in an opening in the ceiling. This was the stock room at the quinceañera joint.

A woman stepped in from the shop, her brow furrowed, and said something in Spanish.

"I was in here a couple days ago," Slater said.

"With the woman from next door. I remember. What's going on?"

"I work for the property management company. I needed to get out of the alley."

"I leave the door open for the cross breeze," she said. "It gets warm in here. The alley is gated so I don't usually have trouble with people wandering in."

"Can you leave it closed for a few minutes? I'm going to walk out to the street."

She raised her eyebrows. "What's in the alley?"

"A very angry man. Don't worry about him. He'll fade when he can't find me."

Slater walked into the shop, through the rows of dresses, and out to the street. By chance the Continental was parked right here. For all his missteps, he couldn't have planned it better.

Looking down the block toward the corner, lots of people were walking around, but there was no sign of the ape. He climbed in and quickly pulled away from the curb, taking surface streets to his house. Negotiating the Saturday traffic gave him time to calm down and think.

Whatever was going on still wasn't completely clear. It felt like the gold belonged to Milena and her cohorts, since they were in control of the new lock to get into that storeroom, and they seemed to be in crisis mode. That ape could have been one of them. He'd implied as much, and he was angry enough to chase him. He definitely would have messed Slater up if he'd caught him.

Clyde had taken those nylon bags from the storeroom. There was no question about that part. Maybe he'd say he jacked that sunshine to prevent Les from stealing it. But he already knew Clyde was shady as fuck. It seemed much more likely that Clyde had played him, had used Slater as a bird dog to track down the hoard.

All that gold also explained what Agent Roscoe was worried about. The feds must have had some indication that Milena and the jewelers were amassing it. Roscoe obviously suspected the purpose was to influence political events overseas. If Milena and her crew were keeping it insulated from their businesses, in a storeroom that they thought was secure, that was pure subterfuge, and it fit with Roscoe's suspicions.

Rolling up on his place, he saw that Pike's janky old SUV was parked on the street. He'd seen it on the way out too, he remembered. One of Pike's buddies must have picked him up for their outing. He pulled into the garage, and waited for the door to roll down, then climbed the stairs.

His face was starting to ache, radiating outward from where Erik had punched him in the nose, and it made it hard to focus. Looking at himself in the bathroom mirror, his nose was definitely swollen, but his lip wasn't too bad. He popped some ibuprofen, then went up to the kitchen.

Pike hadn't been back, as there was still coffee in the pot from his breakfast. He grabbed a package of frozen peas from the icebox, and stretched out on the sofa, and put it on his face. The cold felt good, dulling the ache.

Milena wasn't sketchy, he knew that. Even Erik was a civilian. He could call one of them, and get them to pick up those heavy nylon bags, and tell them to put that stuff somewhere more secure than a storeroom with a hidden back door. But all the pieces didn't fit yet. Everybody involved was either lying to him or refusing to squawk. He needed to figure out for certain what was going on, to make sure of what he was doing. Move slowly and be smooth. No more fuckups, like telling Clyde where to steal from, or fleeing into the damn basement.

TWENTY-ONE

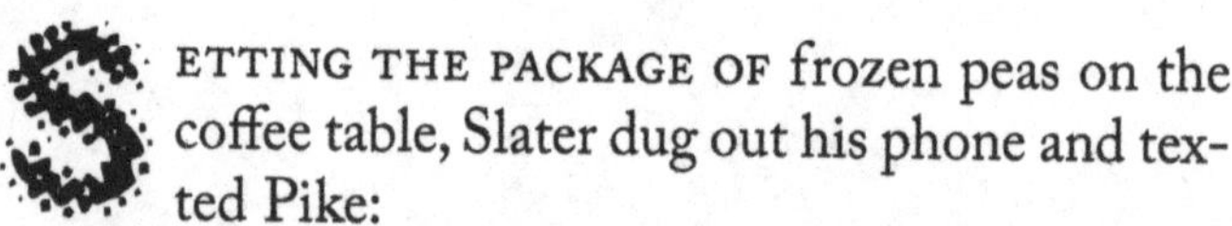

S ETTING THE PACKAGE OF frozen peas on the coffee table, Slater dug out his phone and texted Pike:

I'm borrowing your rig. Take the Continental if you need wheels.

Forcing himself to sit up, he threw the peas back in the Frigidaire, then went down to the back bedroom. He grabbed the spare key for Pike's SUV from a desk drawer, then went out to the street.

Pike had been driving this thing the day they'd met, at a backcountry crossroads out in the desert. It seemed like ages ago. It had had those sweet turquoise plates back then. Firing up the engine, he pulled it into the garage.

Climbing out, he hit the button to roll the door

236

down, then opened the trunk of the Continental. He zipped open one of the pouches to take a closer look. One of the gold bars just fit in his palm, but it was so much heavier than it looked. It was almost like his eyes were seeing it wrong, distorting the size of something that should be bigger. The pouch had eight of the bars in it, and the other side of the bag had eight more. Each of the bags had felt like it was about the same weight. If the bags were evenly loaded, it made them a lot easier to move around.

Tapping at his phone, he found that the 999.9 FINE meant it was close to pure gold, rather than an alloy for jewelry or some industrial use. The 1,000 G meant one kilogram. That was straightforward. In this country only the military and drug dealers used metric, but maybe jewelers used it too. A kilo was equivalent to just over two pounds, his phone said, and he tapped at the calculator. Four bags meant sixty-four bars total. That meant about 140 pounds.

He zipped it closed, and heaved the bag out, and loaded it into the back of Pike's SUV, then transferred the others. All the players in whatever racket this was knew he was hanging around those buildings. Any of them could easily track him down, the way Roscoe had, and find his office and his house. Nowhere was safe when the payload was so portable. But he could minimize the immediate risk by moving it away from here.

Climbing behind the wheel of the SUV, he tapped at his phone to call Conrad, his idiot ex, glad that he picked up.

"Are you at your place?" Slater said.

"I'm around," he said. "Why?"

"Can I leave my wheels in your garage for a day or two? It's nothing shady."

"When you have to say it, Slater, it makes it sound hella shady." He sighed audibly. "Sure, you can use my garage."

"I'm on my way."

He ended the call, and backed into the street, and got on the 101. As he drove north into the Valley, Pike's ride felt competent climbing through the Cahuenga Pass, and it had plenty of pickup. That didn't correspond to the scratched and dented body. From the outside this was definitely an A-to-B ride.

Slater had noticed that when he'd been out there. People in Albuquerque were way less concerned about cars than Angelenos were. Pike's mother had driven her Crown Vic for so long that it had inadvertently become a classic.

He thought about the hoard in the back. The fact that it was packed to be portable implied that Milena and her posse were getting ready to move it. Maybe they were keeping it in that storeroom temporarily because Agent Roscoe had been sniffing around. Maybe this was a mistake, absconding with it. But it would give him breathing room to sort things out.

Eventually he pulled onto Conrad's street. It was a decent stretch of bungalows, with front lawns that weren't fenced off like they were in rougher neighborhoods. It didn't feel crowded, with wide yards, but then most of the Valley felt roomy. Pulling into the driveway, he tapped the horn.

Conrad stepped out the side door of the house, wearing jeans and a black T-shirt, his dark hair brushed back. Barrel-chested, he was tall, and buff, and flashed that easy smile. Such a beautiful man. As he rolled down the window, Conrad waved at the vehicle.

"Who's rig is this?"

"It's Pike's. Can you roll up the door? If the second bay is still hoarded out, you need to move your flivver."

He frowned. "Cool your jets, cowboy."

He went to the side door of the garage, and stepped inside, and a moment later the door rolled up. Conrad backed his SUV out into the driveway, and Slater nosed in.

The garage wasn't really hoarded. The guy only had the one car, so it wasn't unreasonable that he was using half the space for storage. Climbing out, Slater locked it, then looked into the back. The windows had enough tint that it was impossible to see anything inside.

As he walked into the driveway, Conrad hit the remote to roll down the door, then climbed out of his rig and waved him inside. Slater followed him into the kitchen. Leaning back against the counter, Conrad folded his arms.

"So why are you stashing Pike's car? Did you run over somebody with it, or use it as a getaway car, or get into a pursuit with the highway patrol?"

"That's need-to-know type dope," Slater said.

"It's in my garage. I do need to know."

"It's too complicated to explain. There's no collision or car chase. Nothing illegal."

"But somebody might be looking for it."

"Not out here in the middle of nowhere. I'll get it out of your way in a day or two."

"What happened to your face, anyway?" Conrad said.

He gingerly touched his nose. It totally felt swollen. "I had a small disagreement earlier."

An unfamiliar guy appeared in the hallway and stepped into the kitchen. He was wearing boxer shorts and a tight T-shirt, his dark Latin hair in a natty style.

"This is Gonzalo," Conrad said, and jutted his chin. "Slater."

"It's a great look you're working." Slater swirled a palm at him. "Classic fuckboy. The boxers provide just a hint that you might be stacked, but the rest is left to the imagination."

Gonzalo frowned, then his eyebrows shot up. "Oh—you're the crazy ex."

Conrad raised a hand. "Nobody said crazy."

"Too much?" Gonzalo said.

"It's not untrue," Slater said. "I'll cop to it."

"I just meant I know that's one of those words we're not supposed to say anymore."

"Right, because using a new word for it makes it completely different." Slater raised his eyebrows. "You don't have to explain it to me. And with tits like those, you don't have to explain anything to anybody."

"Why are you leaving your car here?" Gonzalo said.

"My handyman is painting the inside of my garage today. I live in Echo Park, so there's no street parking."

"Why would he do that if you don't have anywhere to put your car?"

Slater gestured helplessly. "Straight people are crazy." Looking to Conrad, he added, "I'll need your key."

He scoffed. "I'm not giving you the key to my garage."

"Fine," he said flatly. "Did you ever put in an alarm?"

"You're basically telling me you're going to break in."

"If you're not around," Slater said, "you're not leaving me any choice."

"Why do I put up with you?" Conrad glared at him for a moment. "Damn it," he muttered, and walked into the back of the house.

"You seem a little tightly wound," Gonzalo said.

Slater put his hands on his hips. "I don't know what you're on, baby, but you're buying from the wrong dealer."

He frowned. "I'm not on drugs."

"If you look closer, you'll see that I'm as calm as the placid surface of a pond on a summer morning. All smooth and methodical. The lamas down at the Buddhist meditation center call me up sometimes to ask how I manage to remain so unperturbed. 'How do you do it?' they ask. An island of serenity amid the perpetual raging chaos."

"That sounds far-fetched."

"What did he tell you about me," Slater said, "besides that I'm crazy?"

"Not much. How long were you together?"

"Way, way too long. I think I had Stockholm syndrome. I should have bailed long before I wound up in the gutter with his jackboot on my neck."

Gonzalo raised his eyebrows. "That sounds hot."

He scoffed. "If you're into that, he's got a pair of those fuck-me boots. The ones the motorcycle cops wear. Tell him to put those on. It actually is pretty hot."

Conrad stepped in and handed him a key. "This opens the side of the garage. Roll the door down when you go, and leave the key in the mailbox."

"Like I'm going to leave your garage door open."

"You're a lot of man, Ibáñez."

"Can I see the palm?"

"The palm is fine," Conrad said.

"I'll be the judge of that." Slater frowned. "What are you hiding?"

"What are you talking about?" Gonzalo said.

"The palm tree in back." Conrad gestured to the back door. "If you must."

Slater stepped out into the backyard. It looked good out here. The star jasmine had filled in, obscuring the cinder-block wall along the property line. Conrad had put in some decomposed granite under the patio furniture, and there was a new barbecue. Making detective must have involved a bump in pay. As he looked up at the palm, Conrad and Gonzalo followed him out.

"You trimmed it," Slater said. "It looks great."

"I didn't do it myself. I thought you'd be pissed. The guy only left a couple of fronds up there."

"You have to do that. It'll come back. By summer it'll be totally vibrant. And it's not a fire hazard anymore."

"I wanted to get it done before everybody sets off their holiday fireworks," Conrad said.

"There's so much freaking noise," Gonzalo said. "Christmas and New Year's both."

Conrad waved a hand. "It's better than it used to

be, peanut. People would fire handguns into the air."

"Peanut?" Slater said.

Gonzalo smiled. "It's a pet name."

"Really? I never would have figured that out."

"Slater's the one who planted the jasmine to cover the fence," Conrad said.

"I love that." Gonzalo glanced over at it. "In the spring all the flowers make it smell so nice out here. Are you a gardener?"

"I like to get my hands dirty." He eyed Conrad. "How far is it to the G Line?"

"Less than ten minutes' walk."

Gonzalo frowned. "You ride public transit?"

"I live in the city, peanut. City folks use transit."

"This is the city too."

"Keep telling yourself that, babe. No matter how many times you say it, that doesn't make it true." Slater walked toward the gate to the driveway.

"City people drive cars," Gonzalo called after him.

"Get a horse," Slater shouted back. It didn't really track, but that's all he could come up with in the moment as he went through the gate, and he needed to get the last word with that guy.

The G Line wasn't far, and soon he was riding the bus and then the metro back to his own neighborhood. At his house, he climbed the stairs and found Pike in the kitchen, wearing a plaid shirt and jeans. Embracing him, he met his mouth.

Pike's brow furrowed as he pulled back. "Who punched you?"

"A guy at those buildings on Broadway. It was a misunderstanding. We worked it out."

"Why did you need my car?"

"I had to transport something heavy. It made the Continental ride too low."

"What kind of something?" Pike said.

"It's part of my case. I haven't got it figured out yet."

He watched him for a moment. "Well, mystery man, we should get dressed."

"What's wrong with jeans?"

"It's a holiday. You know Doris will love it if you put in a little effort."

"She'll love it from you," Slater said. "From me she'll think I'm up to something."

They went down to the bedroom, and he pulled on a pair of dress pants and a collared shirt, and Pike put on his office drag. They climbed in the Continental, and as Slater was backing out of the garage, Pike spoke.

"Where's my rig, anyway? When you came in I thought you'd brought it back."

"It's safe."

"What kind of an answer is that?"

"It needed to be somewhere not connected to me."

Pike watched him for a moment. "What did you put in my car?"

"Nothing illegal, and nothing messy. Just something that somebody might be looking for."

"All this tsuris. I wish you trusted me."

"It's not about trust," Slater said, glancing left as he turned onto the boulevard. "It's about my case. You don't talk about your work either."

"That's different."

"You're legally obligated to your Uncle Sam, and I'm morally obligated to my clients."

"Moral," Pike said. "Now, there's an interesting word."

"I'll get your car back soon. Until then the Continental is at your full disposal."

Pulling into Doris's driveway, he saw that her stupid boyfriend Albert's stupid car was here, next to Doris's Buick. From the back seat he grabbed the little bag from Milena's store and they climbed out.

When Slater walked in, Doris stepped over. She was petite, and was letting her dark hair show the gray, today wearing a blue sweater and dark pants.

"It's my two favorite boys," she said.

Slater leaned in to kiss her, and Doris put a hand on his cheek, and touched his lip with a thumb. "Has my handsome son been brawling?"

"I walked into a door," he said, pulling away.

Her brow furrowed. "Is it the kind of door that's going to press charges?"

"Why would you assume that I started it? I'm the victim here."

Doris turned and embraced Pike. Albert was standing farther back. A frumpy guy with gray hair that was thin on top, his sideburns were way too long, and he wore a stupid grin on his stupid face.

Slater gave him a pointed once-over and said, "Albert."

Pike shook the guy's hand and clapped him on the shoulder. Why did he have to do that? He needed to keep his distance.

As they moved into the kitchen, Slater handed Doris the bag.

"A gift?" she said. "I'm the one who should be giving you gelt today."

"It's from both of us."

Setting it on the bar that fronted the kitchen, she pulled out the little box and held up the pin.

"It's lovely. It matches a piece I have. How did you know?"

"I remembered yours when I saw this in the store."

"So thoughtful. Both of you." She kissed him again. "Help yourselves to drinks. Then we should say the blessing over the candles."

She walked to the mantel, and lifted the menorah, and carried it to the bar.

"I love all this cultural stuff," Albert said, watching her set it down.

"Her culture isn't meant for your amusement," Slater said.

"He's participating, sweetie, not appropriating it," Doris said. "And it's your culture too."

He eyed Albert. "It just seems gauche coming from him."

Doris laughed. "No one in this house is an arbiter of that." She handed a stick lighter to Pike. "Do you know the blessing?"

Pike lit the main candle, and lifted it out to light the others, and chanted in Hebrew. It was just a couple of lines, and his voice was a little off-key, but he handled it like a boss. He knew Pike didn't really care about the ceremonial stuff, but it mattered to Doris. Watching him, he felt a lump in his throat. The guy even knew how many of them to light without needing to ask.

Albert opened a bottle of white wine, and eventually Doris had them help her set out the food on the dining table, tamales and rice and beans. They sat down to eat, and Doris pulled her napkin into her lap.

"It's not traditional, but this town is swimming in masa for the holidays. I saw these vegan tamales at the market. I couldn't resist."

"I love tamales," Pike said.

They were actually good, and as Slater dug into one, he eyed Doris. "So tell me about occupied minorities."

"That's the Hannukah story. The Maccabees overthrew an occupying army to reclaim Jerusalem."

"I'm talking about stuff happening in this millennium. Artsakh and Armenia. What's the skinny?"

"Did you read about it?" Doris said. "I raised you to be a critical thinker. You don't need me to interpret it."

"I also don't need a lecture on how to think."

"I don't know a lot about the conflict, so I can't give you an opinion about what's just and unjust," she said. "But one way to look at it is displacement. How long were people living there before they got occupied or pushed out? Did they push somebody else out when they got there? My understanding is that Artsakh was traditionally Armenian, and now it's occupied by somebody else."

"It's always about ethnicity," Albert said. "And all that matters in the end is who has the most troops and the better weaponry."

Pike waved his fork. "That actually sounds right."

They talked about it some more, then Doris had Albert gather all the corn husks, and she set out a plate of little jam doughnuts.

"This is a stand-in for latkes," she said. "I wasn't up for frying anything."

"Apparently the Israelis have gone hard for doughnuts," Albert said. "Latkes are unusual there."

Slater reached for one and frowned. "How would you know?"

"I boned up on Hannukah."

"That's the most *goyishe* thing I've ever heard."

"I think it's touching that he's interested," Doris said, and leaned over to kiss Albert.

Shaking off an involuntary shudder, Slater bit into a doughnut. That guy was relentless.

Eventually they got up to leave, and at the door he leaned in to give Doris a brief hug.

"Love you," he said.

She grasped his forearms for a moment to look him in the eye. "Put an ice pack on that lip."

TWENTY-TWO

F LICKING ON THE HEADLIGHTS, Slater backed the Continental into the street. "Albert sure can pack away the chow."

Pike laughed, his head back on the headrest. "I ate well too."

"I can't help but think the guy is playing the long con."

"From what I've seen, he treats her well."

"That's the only reason he's still breathing."

Slater navigated out of the neighborhood and punched the accelerator to merge onto the parkway. As he matched the speed of the traffic, his phone made a loud beep. That was an alert from Svetlana's tech, and it was loud because it was urgent. He grabbed the phone. The notification bubble said GARAGE INVASION.

"Fuck," he snapped.

Pike looked over at him. "What's going on?"

Before he could answer, the phone buzzed in his hand. Svetlana. He tapped to pick up and held the phone to his ear.

"Someone has tried to break into your garage," she said. "The tear-gas traps have deployed."

The sensors reported to her as well as to him, he realized.

"I'll be there in a few minutes."

"I don't think the invader will be around. They will need to decontaminate in the shower. I'm sending Garik to inspect the damage and reset the devices."

"I appreciate your conscientiousness," he said, and ended the call.

"Who was that?" Pike said.

"Someone tried to break into the garage."

"Who called to tell you that? You don't have an alarm."

"The sensors on the pepper-spray canisters alerted the Russian. She's sending her nephew to sort it out."

"That's much better service than any security company. What do you pay that woman?"

"Plenty."

He knew her motivation wasn't customer service. It was making sure her people were on scene in case the cops showed up. She didn't want anyone looking too closely at those canisters.

"Does she know it's illegal to booby-trap your house?" Pike said.

"I thought home security was a gray area."

He looked out the side window at the dark city rolling by. "It's not."

Pulling up to the house, he saw that the garage door was halfway up, the lights on inside. He parked at the curb farther up the block, and both of them jumped out and hustled back. Even from a distance he could see the lock on the garage door was broken, with a metal part dangling loose. He twisted his key in the front door and went into the little foyer. The side door into the garage was still locked. He flipped the thumb-turn on the bolt and stepped in.

A bulbous gray device was installed at either side of the wide door. When he looked up at them, the indicator lights on both were glowing red.

"The canisters deployed," Slater said.

"It's awfully thick in here. Can I roll up the door?"

"Go for it."

Pike hit the button on the wall, and the garage door ascended, smooth and quiet.

"At least the motor isn't messed up," Slater said.

"She told you specifically it was pepper spray?" Pike waved a hand. "It doesn't smell like capsicum. More like chemical weapons."

It was likely some Soviet-era chemical, Slater knew, and walked toward the back of the garage to check on his gear cabinet.

"It's probably a stronger version," he called back. "Maybe it's bear spray."

When he tried the handle, the cabinet was still locked. It looked unmolested.

"It smells like tear gas," Pike said.

Walking toward him, Slater furrowed his brow. "Have you actually smelled that before?"

"Yes, I have," he said intently. "In training for crowd control."

"Does it look like anything's missing?"

Pike waved at the room. "Not from here. The door to the house was still locked. The gas probably worked as an effective deterrent. Whoever broke in took off once they got sprayed."

Slater studied the tool rack above the workbench. It was mostly gardening stuff, and it seemed like nothing had been taken.

"Are you going to call the cops?" Pike said.

"There'd be so much 'splaining to do. The intruder didn't steal anything." He glanced toward the street as a white work truck pulled up across the garage door. "Let's see what Svetlana's guy has to say."

Garik climbed out of the truck and stepped around. Pasty and blond, he was wearing jeans and a heavy work shirt. His haircut was a lot better than the last time Slater had seen him.

Focused on Pike, he extended a hand. "I'm Garik."

Giving it a brief squeeze, Pike introduced himself.

The guy had changed, Slater thought, watching them talk. It was more than just the haircut. His demeanor was more confident, and his English had improved a lot. Svetlana had set them up when he was new in town, and Slater had quickly introduced him to other guys. He hadn't wanted to get entangled with someone in her inner circle. No way could he afford to lose such a valuable resource, and that would have happened when the guy inevitably got pissed off at him, so he'd avoided getting too sticky.

Eyeing Slater, Garik tapped the side of his own nose. "You have been fighting."

"You know how it goes."

"What happened here?"

"The lock on the garage door is broken," Slater said, "but I don't think anything was taken. The canisters deployed."

"Has anyone called the police?"

"We didn't. I don't think any of the neighbors noticed, or they'd be here."

Garik looked up at the tear gas traps. "The gas is usually enough to chase the invaders away. I can replenish the canisters, but I'm not sure about the mechanism on the door. I'll take a closer look at it."

He released the door from its track and then pulled it down manually until the broken lock was at chest level.

"Someone attacked it with a tool," Garik said, looking it over. "A crowbar or a tire iron. This is a simple repair."

Ducking under the door, he went to the back of the truck and opened a couple of the compartments, returning a moment later with a toolbox and a replacement lock. He spent a minute working on it, then pulled a stepladder from the side of the truck, and brought it in, and propped it next to the door. As he climbed up to the gas traps, Pike folded his arms and watched him work.

Eventually Garik put the ladder back, and reset the track, and walked over to the wall switch. When he hit it, the door rolled up and down smoothly.

"Everything is working again." Garik pointed to the gas traps. "The sensors are online. I set the gas release delay to six seconds."

"What's in those canisters, exactly?" Pike said.

"It's pepper spray," Slater said quickly.

Pike frowned. "Don't put words in his mouth."

"Slater is correct." Garik made his eyes wide. "It's pepper spray. All natural ingredients. A recipe from the old country."

"Do you want me to pay you for the work?" Slater said.

"You can talk to Sveta about the fees." He shifted on his feet. "Tonight there are other services I can provide, at no charge. I can help you reduce the stress of this traumatic event."

"Are you hitting on him?" Pike demanded.

"I'm flirting with both of you."

Pike guffawed, tilting his head back.

"Have I offended you?"

"Not at all. It just amazes me how Slater's life works."

"It's about you too." Slater waved his arm. "And I'm down for stress reduction."

"Well, there you have it," Pike said. "Come on up. Do you need to lock your vehicle?"

"It's secure." Garik followed them up the stairs and into the front bedroom. "May I wash my hands? I don't want to transfer the chemical from the security system."

"Even though it's just natural ingredients," Pike said. "Old-country capsicum, like what you'd put on your tacos."

"Sveta prepares the security devices." Garik held his gaze for a moment, then stepped into the bathroom.

As Pike pulled off his shirt, Slater unzipped his dress pants. Garik returned and started to get undressed, completely unself-conscious compared to when they'd first met. Once he was fully naked,

Garik stretched out on the bed and propped a pillow behind his head.

"One of you will fuck me, yes?"

Pike climbed up, and caressed his torso, and leaned in to kiss him, squeezing his cock. Sitting next to them, Slater pushed his face into theirs, into a three-way kiss, running his hands over both of them. It was intense, and exhilarating, their mouths warm and in turns firm and soft.

Pulling back, Pike was hard now, and he reached over to grab a condom from the bedside table.

"You are not using PrEP?" Garik said.

"I like the idea of multiple lines of defense."

"Let me do that." Slater took the condom and ripped it open, then growled, "Raskolnikov."

"What's the problem?" Pike said.

"It's dried out. The wrapper must have had a nick in it."

As Pike reached for another, Garik laughed. "You say this name like it's a curse. Raskolnikov was the main character in a Russian novel. *Crimes and Penalties*."

"It was translated as *Crime and Punishment*," Slater said, taking the little packet from Pike. "I didn't actually read it."

"Why is his name a curse in English? He did terrible things, but he knew he had made mistakes. The punishment for Raskolnikov was from his own conscience."

"It's from an old TV cartoon. The Soviet villain says 'Raskolnikov' when something goes wrong."

Garik frowned. "You're saying you learned this name from children's television and not from literature."

"Can we focus on the matter at hand?" Pike said.

Grabbing his cock, Slater rolled the condom onto him. Pike shifted closer to Garik, grabbing his ankles, and pressed into him. Running his hand on his chest, and squeezing his cock, Slater saw that Garik was getting into it, his head craning back, as Pike thrust. He wasn't jealous, exactly, but it felt weird to watch Pike with someone else.

After a minute Pike pulled back. He was breathing hard. "Your turn."

Slater rolled on a condom and shifted next to Garik, pushing inward, building up speed. Behind him Pike wrapped his arms around Slater, running his hands over his torso and his neck. Feeling his mouth on his skin was a turn-on, and Slater pounded Garik, and strained into him as he came, then sank on top of him.

"Don't move," Pike said, and pressed into Slater, and wrapped his arms around him, and started to pound him. Leaning close, his breath hot on his neck, Pike spoke in his ear.

"Your rig is safe, he says. Forget about it. Don't worry about the tear gas, he says. Just trust me."

Slater shifted sideways enough to look at him sidelong, then reached around and slapped his face.

Pounding him harder, Pike growled, "Fucking psycho," and then came, pulling him close and mouthing his neck.

He could feel Garik was hard, and Slater pulled back, and grabbed his cock, and stroked him.

"Yes," Garik said. "Just like this." A moment later he grunted and strained into his hand as he climaxed.

Rolling off, Slater tossed the condom on the floor.

Pike stretched out next to him, and he could feel the warmth of their bodies, one of them on either side. He could get used to this.

Eventually Garik rose, and he heard the shower go on. When he came back, Garik started to get dressed.

"I enjoyed your stress-reduction services." Pike sat up. "I don't think most security companies would provide that."

His expression somber, Garik said, "Thank you. I respect the seriousness of your passion."

He walked out, and a moment later the front door closed. Pike got up and went to shower. Lying there, feeling sated, Slater was glad Garik hadn't wanted to linger.

Thinking about it, it wasn't even obvious who had tried to break in. Clyde or Les or somebody stooging for one of them. Any of them might suspect Slater was part of the racket. Milena had basically accused him of robbing the storeroom, and that ape had chased him into the alley.

Whoever it was, the tear gas had slowed them down, but there was nothing to stop them from coming to search for that sunshine again. It wasn't even safe in Conrad's garage. If that set of tits Gonzalo went snooping around, or somebody happened to break in looking for copper to steal, it would be gone. But maybe there was a way to take the heat off until he sorted this out.

When Pike returned from his shower, he stretched out, and Slater caressed his belly.

"You were talking about trust."

Pike met his gaze. "It's a fundamental part of any relationship. Including our narrative complex."

"I need help with something, but it needs to happen without anyone asking too many questions."

"It sounds like I'm the one who needs to trust you." He chuckled. "What kind of help?"

"Carrying something heavy."

"How heavy?"

"About seventy pounds."

"Is it related to the break-in?" Pike said.

"I believe so."

"When would we be doing this?"

"You wanted to drive out to Amboy and Kelso," Slater said. "Let's do it tomorrow. This errand is on the way."

"On a scale of petty misdemeanor to class-A felony," Pike said, "how illegal is this?"

"Zero. Remember the part about too many questions?"

TWENTY-THREE

SLATER HAD CRASHED SOON after he'd gone upstairs for his quotidian snort, then got up hours before sunrise, and quietly got dressed in the dark. He walked to the bus stop on Sunset and rode to the metro station. The whole system was up and running by 4 a.m. Riding the train, he was kind of amazed that so many people were using it this early.

Eventually he got to Conrad's part of the Valley. It was still totally dark out as he walked up his driveway. Conrad was home, as his wheels were here, but he'd still be asleep. Letting himself into the garage, Slater opened the lift gate of the SUV. The black nylon bags were still here, and he zipped a couple open to double-check. Undisturbed, the contents gleamed bright, their extraordinary nature unmistakable even in the low light.

He backed the rig into the driveway, then climbed out and walked back in to lower the garage door. Once he'd locked the one on the side, he pocketed the key. Idiot Conrad wanted him to leave it, but he might need it again someday.

As he rolled back into civilization, the sun wasn't even on the horizon yet. He stopped to gas up the SUV, then pulled into the garage next to the Continental. Upstairs in the bedroom he found Pike was awake.

"Where were you?"

"I brought your rig back."

Stepping into the bathroom, he checked his nose. The swelling had gone down. His lip looked better too.

Pike soon got up, and pulled on a pair of jeans and a rumpled long-sleeved shirt. They went upstairs to make coffee and oatmeal, and ate at the dining table. As Pike grabbed his day pack and loaded it with bread and apples and oranges, Slater drained the last of his java and filled a couple of water bottles.

"We're taking your wheels."

In the garage he grabbed a couple of shovels from his gardening stuff, and Pike opened the lift gate for him.

"Those look heavy," he said, eyeing the nylon bags.

"I warned you." Slater loaded the shovels into the back and closed the gate.

"What's in them?"

"Nothing illegal."

Pike groaned. "And we're burying them, I'm thinking, since we're taking shovels. Where?"

"On my newly acquired desert acreage. We're

minimizing the questions, remember?"

They climbed into the vehicle, and Pike backed into the street, and got on the freeway. Soon the low winter sun was in their eyes, glaring off the pavement, and they both pulled on sunglasses.

"A redhead and a blond," Pike said.

"What are you talking about?"

"You brought one of each around this week. Almost like you're covering all the bases."

"That's mostly about you. The twink called you a smoke-show, and the Russian couldn't take his eyes off you."

"I'm not complaining. But it's definitely a major shift from how my life worked in the BS era. Before Slater."

"Things have changed for me too. One of my targets on this case accused me of being nice."

Pike laughed. "It sounds like that stung. I'd say it's not such a bad thing if it originated in our narrative complex."

An hour later, rolling through the Inland Empire, Slater's phone buzzed. It was a text from Clyde:

Where are you? We need to talk.

He thumb-typed a reply:

I'm not working today, boss. We can talk tomorrow.

His response came soon after:

It's urgent.

He ignored that. Slater knew exactly why he wanted to talk. Clyde had discovered the cargo had been taxed from the back of the Pacer, and it had happened without any of the doors or windows getting busted. Of course Slater would be a prime suspect. But he wasn't too worried about Clyde. If he was the one who'd broken into the garage, he'd need the day to recover from being tear-gassed.

As they rolled into the Coachella Valley, the light changed, and the landscape looked sharper in the dry air. Pike drove up into the high desert and onto a two-lane highway. They went through stretches of Mojave landscape studded with Joshua trees, but Lenny's acreage was a ways past them, on drier land, where the dominant species was creosote bush.

Slater pointed out where to turn off the highway, then when to turn onto a dirt road, and finally onto a double-track.

"I get it now," Pike said. "The Continental isn't the optimal vehicle to get out here. These aren't even roads. But it really is a beautiful landscape."

"There's something about the light. It's different from New Mexico or Arizona. Even Palm Springs. There's nowhere like this."

"I don't think you made a mistake buying it."

"It's yours now too."

"Not legally." Pike slowed down to roll through some ruts where water had washed across the track.

"If I get croaked, it will be. My lawyer got me to do a will a while ago. You'll have to give some jack to Doris, but the house is yours, and this too."

"You did that?" Pike reached over and squeezed the back of his neck.

"Don't be getting any wise-guy ideas. Have you heard of the slayer rule? You can't inherit somebody's stuff if you grease them."

He laughed. "I'm aware. I guess I should do that too."

"The thing is, I don't need your stuff. You should will it to your mama. The LA house is different. I'm not going to leave you homeless." Slater sat up. "Stop here."

Multiple tire tracks ran off the double track, into the landscape, toward the arroyo.

"Is this where my team went in to recover the bodies?" Pike said.

"Fricking idiots. They should have gone in on foot. It's only a couple of minutes' walk. Do you know how long it takes soil crust to recover from being molested like this?"

"The tracks are already starting to fade."

"It's not about that. Soil crusts are a delicate network of living things. Algae and fungi and bacteria. They collaborate and hang together so that the soil won't erode. Do you know how incredible that is? Three radically different kinds of life, all working together, unseen in the top few inches of ground."

"Well," Pike said, "my people were digging up corpses. They weren't about to hoof it."

"You might as well drive in too. The damage is already done."

"At least they mostly kept to the one path." He nosed in and drove on the tracks on the gradually rising land.

"There's no point putting up a fence," Slater said, "but I'm going to have to post some keep-out signs."

"More money, more problems."

"You know it, Biggie."

When they crested the rise, the arroyo came into

view, the land sloping down toward it. In several places the surface had been disturbed, the gritty gravel and darker earth left lumpy and uneven. At least the gravediggers had filled in the holes.

Pike made a three-point turn, and backed toward the arroyo, and they climbed out. It had been a long drive, and they both stretched, then Pike stepped away to piss on a creosote bush. Slater walked over to the disturbed patches.

When Pike came back, he looked over the site. "So this is where the bodies were."

"They're gone now. No residual bad vibes." He opened the lift gate and pulled out the shovels.

"I wonder if Lars would agree with that assessment."

Pike took one of the shovels, and they both started digging. After a few seconds Slater stopped, resting the blade of the shovel on the ground, and chuckled.

"What's funny?"

"I'm thinking you've never done this before. When you're working in the same place, you have to find a rhythm. Like the frug. When I'm tossing dirt, you dig, and I dig while you're unloading."

Pike briefly did the frug with his hips. "You know I've got rhythm, boss."

They started again, and found a rhythm, and made some progress. After a while Slater stepped back and rolled his shoulders to loosen up.

"The ground isn't hard at all," Pike said. "I suppose that's because it was recently dug up."

"I'm sure that's why Memo chose the arroyo in the first place. Because it was easier digging."

When they got about four feet down, and the hole was a few feet wide, Slater stood erect and slammed his shovel into the excavated pile.

"That's deep enough."

He scanned the horizon in a slow circle to make sure nobody was nearby, but there was no one in view, and nothing human-made, no structures or roads, just the desert and the creosotes and the distant mountains all around. Walking back to the SUV, he heaved out two of the nylon bags.

"It's a lot less hauling than I expected. I thought we'd be walking in from the double track."

Pike lifted out the other two, and set them down next to the hole. "These are heavy as hell. What exactly are we doing?"

"I know it's not really fair to keep you in the dark."

"I've held my tongue until now. But I can't let this go. Trust goes both ways, Slater. You have to show me."

"Go ahead." He waved at the bags. "Look inside."

Dropping to his knees, Pike pushed his sunglasses up into his hair, then pulled open one of the heavy zippers. He lifted out a couple of the bars and laughed, turning them over in his hands. Pulling out another, he gazed at the array.

"Fuck me," Pike muttered, then looked up at him.

"It's a lot of sunshine."

"How much is there?"

"Sixty-four of those bars. Each weighs a kilo."

He peered at the engraving on one, then turned it over. "I wish they all could be California boys."

"It's not just about me," Slater said. "I can see it in you. The treasure hunter instinct. It's what gold does to people. Like the conquistadores looking for El Dorado, and the dream that brought the forty-niners to the Sierra. The quest that drove people mad."

"In this equation you're the one planting the treasure, not the treasure hunter. Why are you doing this?"

"In the city it's too easy to steal. Out here nobody can take it from me. People know where I live, and what I drive, but nobody really knows about this land except you and me and Lenny. My name won't even be on the property records yet."

"Is this yours?"

"I'm not going to lie to you," Slater said. "I haven't completely figured out who the rightful owner is yet."

"It definitely explains things. Like our visitor last night. They were looking for this. I'm assuming it doesn't belong to them either."

"I don't know who that was."

Pike tucked the bars back in the bag and zipped it shut. "You are such a weirdo."

"And you can't get enough."

They put the bags in the hole, and filled it in with the earth and gravel, and smoothed out the surface. Slater scraped up some of the loose gravel from farther along the arroyo and scattered it over the excavation to make it look less disturbed. He found two ruddy rocks and put them close together on top, then photographed them, and copied the location coordinates into a note on his phone.

Mopping his brow, with the shovel in hand, Pike looked over the arroyo. "It's obvious that something happened here, but not that something's buried."

"Nobody's coming out here."

Pike loaded the shovel into the back of the SUV. "Next stop, Amboy? I don't suppose there'll be much traffic."

Tossing his shovel in the car, Slater stepped close, and put his hands on his neck. "It's you. *You* are the traffic." He mashed their mouths together, and lingered in it for a moment.

When he pulled back, Pike handed him the key fob. "Why don't you drive? You can be the traffic."

They climbed in, and Slater followed the path back toward the double-track.

"I wonder if there's gold on your land," Pike said. "Besides the stuff you just buried."

"There's traces of it everywhere, supposedly, but usually not enough to bother with. If there were, you'd have to do lode mining to get at it here. That's a lot of freaking work. Up in the Sierra they were doing placer mining in the rivers. It's still not easy, but it's way less destructive."

"You really are a forty-niner. Maybe you're the reincarnation of one of those guys."

"It feels like that potential is in everybody," Slater said. "I saw it in your eyes. Gold fever."

He drove back to the pavement and headed east. It was easy calm driving, and he knew they'd be on quiet back roads the whole way. After that shovel work it felt good to relax, with just the sound of the tires on the asphalt, the sunlight, and the wide-open views. He could feel the stress fading from the muscles in his neck and his arms.

Slater loved that he could be with Pike like this, contented and quiet, sharing the vibe, agreeing on everything. The silence meant as much as the talking.

Just being with this guy was a sustained low-level buzz.

Rolling past scattered homesteads and outposts for a while, they turned north, through a pass and into a fully desolate basin, with nothing in view but wildlands. They stopped at Amboy to look at the volcanic cinder cone, a massive pile of black rock that contrasted the surrounding sandy tan. Farther north they crossed the tracks at Kelso, a handful of railroad buildings that didn't even merit a place-name, and a little ways up the road Slater nosed into a pullout and parked. Pike grabbed his day pack, and Slater took the water, and they walked into the landscape.

They sat on the ground, and Pike zipped open his pack to unload the fruit, and a baguette, and a block of oat-milk cheese.

"So was Kelso everything you'd hoped it would be?" Slater said.

Pike chuckled as he tore off a piece of bread. "All that and more."

"Is there a knife in your hooptie?" he said as he ripped open the package of cheese.

Pike dug in his pants, and produced a pocket-knife, and handed it over.

"The man is prepared." He took it and pried it open.

"You keep me nimble," Pike said, gesturing with a hunk of bread. "I have to be ready for anything. Even buried treasure."

TWENTY-FOUR

THEY'D GOTTEN BACK TO the house in the dark, after driving into a brilliant blazing sunset. In the morning, when Slater woke, his head felt clear. He must not have overdone it on the apple-jack. The house was quiet, with Pike already gone to work. He hadn't even ingested any java yet but he felt awake, and present, almost energized. The desert air and the wide-open wilderness had effectively recharged him.

Grabbing his phone, he saw that Les James had texted a while ago:

I need to see you.

Even before that, Clyde had messaged him:

Where are you? Why are you avoiding me?

He lay there thinking about it. Taxing that treasure had definitely stirred the pot. First he texted Les:

I'll come by this afternoon.

Next he wrote to Clyde:

I'm not avoiding you, dumbass, I've got stuff to do. I'll come by your office today.

Pushing himself out of bed, he got dressed, and went upstairs. The deck looked wet. It had rained, finally, the first time this winter. When he backed the Continental into the street, it was overcast and gray, and he had to turn on the wipers on the way to Downtown.

Once he'd parked at the structure on Broadway, and stepped out onto the sidewalk, the rain was light, coming down in delicate little drops. He walked around to the alley to get a couple of Greek coffees, then went to Milena's shop. She was standing behind the counter, wearing a black turtleneck and one of her silver necklaces.

When he stepped in, she greeted him with a wan smile, and pulled the cap off the java.

"Your shoulders are wet."

"There's some kind of liquid falling out of the sky," Slater said. "I can't even remember what it's called."

She didn't react to that but said, "It's been months and months."

"It feels cathartic after so long." He put his hands on his hips. "You look tired."

"I'm under a lot of stress."

"Because of what happened in that storeroom on Saturday."

"I still don't understand what you were doing there," Milena said. "Why were you working on the weekend?"

"Erik called me and asked where I was, but he wouldn't tell me what was going on. Maybe you should explain it to me."

"Why should I tell you my business? I appreciate the coffee, but it's not much of a bribe."

"Maybe I'll have some insights," Slater said. "Maybe I saw something significant that day, or the day before. I won't know what's relevant until I know what's going on."

"How do I know you won't go gossiping to the Treasury Department?"

"You mean Agent Roscoe?" Slater frowned. "Why would I talk to that yutz? I think you can ignore him. If he had anything actionable, he'd be arresting people."

"Well, he's buzzing around for some reason."

"It seems to me he thinks you're trying to interfere in the conflict in Artsakh."

Milena's brow furrowed. "How would you know anything about that?"

"There's a lot of players involved in this. This woman I know says, 'Two people can keep a secret, if one of them is dead.'"

"You want me to believe that someone has already talked to you about it? No sale, Slater."

"Everybody in that storeroom was Armenian, and as far as I know, you're all in the jewelry business. And the feds are snooping around." Slater threw up his hands. "It's not hard to connect the dots. Do you think Les James is involved? Did she steal something from you?"

Her eyebrows shot up. "You're connecting the wrong dots."

"So sing, sister," he said, and waved an arm.

"I suppose it makes no difference now. It's all gone."

"What's gone?"

"Our little association has been working for years, sending aid to Artsakh. Clothes and used electronics. Strictly small potatoes. But we'd finally raised a significant amount. Enough to make a difference."

"That's what got stolen from the vault?"

"It wasn't cash," Milena said. "We're in the jewelry business. We work with precious metals every day. It's easy to amass value in that form. We were trying to figure out how to get it over there without people like Agent Roscoe interfering. But now it's gone. All of it. The sweat and tears of all these people."

"I know you and Erik are silversmiths."

"Gold has more value by weight." She sighed. "We had nearly four million dollars' worth. In bars."

He watched her for a moment before he spoke. It all aligned with what he already knew. Finally somebody was being honest with him.

"Who do you think took it?"

"We haven't figured that out. The lock wasn't disturbed, and there was no other way into that room. But someone got to it." She raised her eyebrows. "You had access to the building, and so did Clyde Park."

"That's true."

Milena looked away. "So did dozens of other people. Later that night, Saturday, there was a power failure. Just for a few minutes. Long enough that my cameras went out. Someone came into my shop."

"They broke in?"

"Nothing was broken, and nothing was stolen. But I know someone was here. I'm very detail oriented. It's an advantage in doing fine work on jewelry. Anyway, I know things were disturbed in my drawers and cupboards. The place wasn't rifled, but things were moved."

"The lock on your door wasn't damaged?"

"Someone either picked it," Milena said, holding his gaze, "or they had a key."

"Could it have been Les James?"

"You don't get it, Slater." She waved a hand. "Les is one of us. She contributed plenty to that stash. She's the one who set up the high-security lock on the door to the vault. Some of us are pointing fingers at each other now. Angry accusations about being careless. But nobody blames her."

She wasn't distorting the story, he decided. He could feel it in his gut. Nothing he'd seen in Les James made her look like a crook.

"Lo, she speaks the truth," Slater said.

"Do you know anything about it? Were there strangers around that day? Did you see anyone moving something heavy? Maybe with a handcart or a furniture truck."

"I didn't see anything like that."

The door to the street opened, and a woman stepped in, folding up a black umbrella. It took him a second to realize what it was. He never saw those. She gave it a shake, spattering droplets on Milena's carpet. Milena called out a greeting, then lowered her voice.

"If you think of something, you know where to find me."

As she went over to talk to her customer, Slater walked out to the street, ignoring the gentle rain. A few paces down the wet sidewalk he let himself into the building and headed upstairs to Clyde's office.

The door was closed, and he knocked, then pushed it open. Clyde was sitting behind his desk, and Slater had to turn away, taking a moment to close the door behind him so he could mask his reaction. The guy had a blotchy red rash on his forehead, and his ears, and the left side of his face. His eyes look watery. One glance at him said it all—Clyde is who had triggered the gas traps in his garage.

"What happened to you?" Slater said.

"I'm allergic to shellfish. I got a bite of some by mistake."

"It looks more like you got pepper-sprayed."

His brow furrowed. "Pepper spray wouldn't have messed me up this much."

There was anger in his eyes. It had to be frustrating, Slater realized. Obviously he suspected that Slater had jacked him, but he wasn't completely sure, as he had no real evidence. Clyde couldn't confront him about the tear gas traps without admitting that he broke into his place, and if he accused him of stealing from him, all the rest of it would unravel.

"Listen, did you see Milton on Saturday?" Clyde said.

"I was around that day. I parked in the structure, but I don't remember seeing the Pacer there. I thought you were in Beverly on Saturday with the hotel people." He raised his eyebrows. "Did you misplace it?"

"I know where he is, but somebody messed with him."

"They broke into it? That sucks. All that big beautiful glass. It must be a real bear to replace."

Clyde was watching him intently, his brow furrowed.

"I talked to some of your tenants that day," Slater said.

"Like who?"

"Milena, at the storefront with all the silver. She was an emotional wreck. Somebody broke into one of the jewelers' vaults. Maybe it was Les James."

"I hadn't heard about that."

"I'm telling you now."

"What was stolen from them?" Clyde said.

"Nobody would say. They're jewelers, so I'm thinking it must have been jewelry."

Clyde looked away, disinterested now. "That sounds like a tenant problem, not a me problem. They know damn well they're responsible for all their own locks and alarms and security."

"Isn't that what you hired me to watch for?"

"It sounds like you weren't able to prevent it."

Slater scoffed. "Did you know the power went out briefly on Saturday night?"

Raising his eyebrows, Clyde affected a weary expression. "No one mentioned that. It doesn't surprise me. The DWP is a perpetual mess."

He watched him for a moment. The guy was trying hard to look unconcerned.

"So I've been working for you for a week," Slater said. "I'm going to need more lettuce to keep digging into Les."

"No way. No more money." He shook his head and sat up. "We can wrap it up now. I'll need my keys back."

"That makes me think you already figured out what you needed to know." Slater dug in his front pocket, and pulled out the key ring, and tossed it on his desk.

"Just let it go, man. The situation has changed. There's other moving parts. Different things are in play."

"You're the client, so it's your call. But I'm definitely getting lowlife vibes from you right now."

Clyde scowled and jabbed a finger at him. "It's you. Take a look in the mirror, Ibáñez. You." And louder, "You're the lowlife."

"I'm not the one nickel-and-diming jewelry stores, and hock shops, and that quinceañera place."

His face red now, Clyde leapt out of his chair, fists swinging wildly. The guy had no idea how to brawl. Slater dodged one of his arms and deflected the other, then grabbed the guy around the waist and pulled him into a bear hug.

Struggling with him, Clyde pounded his fists on his back, and sank his teeth into his shoulder through his shirt. It hurt like hell, but Slater held on tightly. The guy needed to let it out.

Eventually Clyde went limp, and Slater let go of him. Grabbing his arms, he steered him back against the desk. Clyde sank onto it, still flushed and breathing hard, but the fight had drained out of him. He avoided Slater's gaze.

"There's no need to get steamed," Slater said, massaging his own shoulder. "If you don't tell me everything, you can't blame me for speculating."

"Let's just agree that the case is closed." Finally he looked up. "Right now I've got things to do."

"All right. Maybe we can take your drop cloth into that hotel wing again. Once you've busted into the rest of the bricked-up hallways."

Clyde frowned and looked away. "Sure."

There wasn't the remotest spark of interest, Slater saw, and zero trace of the vulnerable ingenue, or the cock tease, or the wolf. At least he'd worked out some of his frustration. Slater was going to have the bruises and bite marks to show for that.

Walking out, he rolled his shoulders and twisted his back. It still hurt, but it was superficial, just skin and muscle, and he hadn't bitten through his shirt. Trotting down a few flights, he stepped into the hallway, and walked to the end, and used one of the keys he'd copied to let himself into Sackett's dining room. Mounting the stairs to Greenleaf, he walked through the club to Les's office.

The door was open, and sitting behind the desk was Lars, his feet up, gazing at his phone. There were a couple of coins on the carpet, and Slater stooped to pick them up.

"Pennies from heaven," he said, and tossed them to Lars. "Does Les know you hang out in here?"

Lars slapped his shirt to grab the coins when they landed, then sat up. "I've got a better one for you. What are you up to?"

"Les wanted to see me. Not that it's any of your damn business."

"It doesn't even matter." He huffed and tossed the coins on the desk. "It's all blown up."

"What are you talking about?"

He stood and stepped toward him, brow furrowed, and jutted his chin. "Are you spying on me?"

"Why would I do that?" Slater demanded.

"I've kind of been spying on you."

"Do you even realize you're not making any sense right now?"

That look on his face. Belligerence, hostility, a taunt. Slater couldn't resist. Stepping closer, he slapped him hard, left and then right, a rapid kovac.

"Snap out of it," he growled.

"Stop it," Lars shouted, and shoved him off. "What is wrong with you?"

He lunged at him again. "Why do you make me do this to you?" He yanked his arm away from his face and managed to land another blow.

"Slater, stop."

Stepping back, he spoke intently. "What do you mean you were spying on me?"

Lars's face was red, and he was panting. "I can't believe you hit me."

"It was open-handed." He raised his voice. "Sing, brother."

"We couldn't figure out why you were hanging around. Les asked me to keep an eye on you. It was easy because you're hot."

"Is she paying you to do that?"

He frowned. "It's just a favor. We're friends."

"Are you sure about that? She's your boss."

"Les treats me well. How many people can say that they like their boss?"

"She's also not here. You can tell me the real story."

"That is real. I'm not playing." Lars rubbed his

cheek. "Did anyone ever tell you that you were kind of rash? Pike seems a lot more stable. I asked him why he was even with you."

"I haven't figured that out myself. I know he's way too good for me. You don't have to explain it."

"He told me you were nothing but trouble, but you were his."

Les walked in and frowned at the sight of him. She was wearing jeans and a Breton top with her hair pulled back in a clip.

"You," she said.

Slater gestured to Lars. "Why did you tell the twink to spy on me?"

Les stepped behind her desk. "Why have you been hanging around here? I know it's not about fire doors. Clyde wouldn't have hired a ruffian for that. The fire department does it." Rolling open a desk drawer, she grabbed her pistol and leveled it at Slater.

TWENTY-FIVE

SLATER INSTINCTIVELY FLASHED HIS palms. "Don't point your gun at me."

"I think you were casing the place," Les said. "I think you figured out what we were doing, and then you stole something from me."

"I did not. But I might know who did. We can talk about it without the rod. Why are you playing the gun moll anyway?"

"So you admit it." She raised her voice. "What do you know about it?"

Slater winced, and wiggled his fingers to point to one side. "At least just aim that thing somewhere else for a minute. You're making me nervous."

She huffed but then adjusted her aim just past his arm. The way she was holding the weapon, with her finger on the trigger guard, implied that she knew how to use it. That actually made it safer. She was far less likely to ventilate him by mistake.

"So where is it?" Les said.

"First, what exactly went missing?"

"Stop fucking with me," she shouted. "I know you talked to Milena today. I know you know about the gold."

"Last week she told me she didn't really know you. But you two obviously compare notes." He waved a hand. "Clyde Park is the one who robbed you."

Les gestured with the weapon. "How? He doesn't have the key."

"There's a back way into that storeroom. I'm surprised none of your cohort spotted it. I did. Although they were all pretty stressed out that day."

Her expression shifted. "Are you telling me the truth right now?"

"Do you have a better explanation?"

"So where did he take it?"

"I know exactly where it is. When I found the back door, I figured it was either you or Clyde. At the time I didn't know you were allied with the jewelers. I went looking for it, and I took it from him. He doesn't know for sure that it was me, but he broke into my house Saturday night trying to get it back, and it sounds like he broke into Milena's shop too."

"Somebody went into at least half a dozen different shops and offices that night," Les said. "But nothing was stolen. We couldn't figure it out."

"I'd bet cash money they're all places that hadn't put in their own locks. Clyde still had the keys, and he was looking for the hoard."

"But you took it from him. You're admitting that

you stole three and a half million dollars from me."

Lars folded his arms and frowned. "Slater, that's so not cool."

He heard a soft tap on the carpet. Glancing down, he saw a nickel next to his feet, glinting in the light. It was heads up.

"I didn't steal it," Slater said. "I'm holding it until I figure this out. I didn't know who it really belonged to. I was told you were the thief."

Les scoffed. "Like I'd steal from myself. How did Clyde know about it?"

"That might have been my fault." He groaned. "Clyde hired me to gather intel."

"So you were collaborating with him."

"He lied to me about what he really wanted. If I'd known he was planning to jack you, I wouldn't have taken the job."

"Before that, though. Before he hired you, how did he know we were amassing that collection?"

"Who knows? He's here all day. Maybe he over-heard somebody, or saw something. He didn't know exactly what was going on. I think that's why he hired me."

"And you have it now," Les said. "What exactly do you need to figure out?"

"In my business I don't believe anything anyone tells me. Not unless I can verify it. You already know I talked to Milena today. She's pretty guileless. I know she told me the truth about a lot of it." Slater shifted on his feet. "And beyond what I know for certain, I know you're all Armenian, and that fed is sniffing around talking about foreign policy. So it all fits."

"I saw that guy too," Lars said. "I absolutely hate that suit he wears."

"Preach, brother." Slater eyed him. "It's like something you'd find discarded at a homeless encampment."

Lars chuckled at that, and Les raised her voice. "I don't care about his suit."

"The truth is so elegant, isn't it?" Slater said. "No distortions, no contradictions. It's the golden thread that stitches the world together."

Les raised her eyebrows. "So where is it?"

"I buried it in the Mojave Desert."

"Why would you do that?" she demanded.

He matched her volume. "So that none of you lowlifes would burgle my place, or steal my whip, or bust it out of my office." He gestured helplessly. "It seemed like a reasonable solution at the time. I didn't know who it belonged to and who the gonifs were."

"You know, gold makes people crazy," Lars said. "It's a whole thing. Maybe you got infected with that."

"So what were you planning to do with it?" Les said.

"I'm thinking you want it back."

Her eyes narrowed. "Yes, Slater, we want it back."

"So I'll go dig it up. It might take me a day or two."

"Tell me where it is, and I'll go dig it up."

"Fine, but you'll need a high-clearance vehicle, and a shovel." He gestured to the weapon. "If you'll put the heater down, I'll show you on a map."

Les took a breath and dropped the gun in the desk drawer. Once she'd rolled it closed, she sat and pulled open her laptop. Slater stepped around and leaned in next to her. At the side of the desk, Lars stood watching them, but he had the good sense not to look at the screen.

Tapping the touch pad, Slater zoomed in on a map and dropped a pin. "See the double track? You have to turn here, and stay on the established tire tracks." He dropped another pin. "The bags are buried right about there. In the arroyo. About four feet down. I marked the site with a couple of rocks. I'll text you a photo of them and the exact coordinates."

Les pointed at the screen. "Why can't I just drive in from the dirt road right here?"

"Because it's pristine land," Slater said. "I just bought it. I don't need you tearing it up."

She turned to look at him. "You are such a nut job."

"I get that a lot."

"If it's not there, I'm coming for you."

"It's there."

When he stepped around the desk, Les sat back. She looked tired now.

"I assume you arranged to keep a percentage of the collection as your fee?" Les said. "A kilo or two? How much of it is missing?"

"I don't want your fucking money," he snapped. "It's all there."

"Come on, Slater," Lars said. "Be nice."

"Don't make me out to be a chiseler, and I won't get riled." He frowned at him. "And knock it off with the crosstalk."

Lars eyed Les. "It sounds like you've got a Clyde problem."

"A serious Clyde problem."

Slater took a breath and dropped into the guest

chair. "There's a way to deal with Clyde. A way that you could remove him from the equation."

Les frowned. "How?"

"You've met Agent Roscoe, I'm thinking."

"That guy is just trying to intimidate us."

"Roscoe was pretty tits-out about why he's snooping around. He told me Americans weren't allowed to conduct their own foreign policy."

"Blah, blah, blah," Les said flatly.

"We don't know what Roscoe knows about you, but logically he has some idea about the gold, don't you think? You could tell Roscoe that Clyde asked you to arrange to buy a bunch of gold bars through the jewelers in these buildings. Clyde thought you'd have connections with them because of the shared language and culture. He's just the landlord, and nobody really trusts him, so he needed a go-between. Exporting the gold was his thing."

"Why would Clyde be concerned about Armenian politics?"

"Maybe it's for some other purpose. All you know is that he was planning to send the bars to some conflict zone."

Her brow furrowed. "It wouldn't take long for the feds to check on that, and figure out it's bogus."

"Maybe," Slater said, "but it'll keep Clyde out of your hair while they go through it. The last thing he'll want to do when the feds are sniffing around is come after you again. You can get on with your own project. Move your stuff before he can come back to interfere."

"I need to go," Lars said. "I'm supposed to be rehearsing right now."

"I thought musicians took Monday off," Slater said.

"We're not performing tonight, but we have to learn the songs."

"Toy-toy-toy," Les called after him as he walked out.

Slater leaned ahead to pick up the nickel from the carpet, and found another one nearby. It was heads up too.

"What the hell does toy-toy-toy mean?" he said.

"It's like wishing him good luck."

He set the coins on the edge of the desk and met her gaze. "Are you sleeping with him?"

"Good god, no. He's not into women. I know you have firsthand evidence of that." She sat up. "How would you feel about talking to Roscoe? It makes more sense that you'd have that intel about Clyde, since you were working for him. And that would keep it all away from me."

"I don't know. Cops make me nervous."

"You owe me, Slater, after you absconded with sixty-four of my high-value items."

"I didn't actually abscond. I deftly prevented someone else from jacking you."

"Fair enough." She looked away. "Do you have a number for Agent Roscoe?"

He closed his eyes for a second and took a breath. He hated this stuff, the social give-and-take, the obligations, the unspoken debts. It was what Talisha had seen in him. That he was getting soft. He wasn't working for Les, but she was right. It would work better coming from Slater.

"Fine," he said. "I'll call him."

Les grinned. "Brilliant. I hope it works."

"If nothing else, Roscoe might be distracted for a minute, and give you some breathing room."

"Maybe he'll arrest that trash bag. If I never see Clyde again, it'll be too soon."

"You know," Slater said, "Clyde told me something about the accordion. He said it's the best musical instrument of all. It's like the voices of a thousand angels all singing at once. I wonder if you need to smash some of your biases around it."

Her eyes went hard. "Who would say something like that? The man is a sociopath."

"I was also thinking about your logistics issue. Moving all the sunshine overseas."

"You mean getting the gold bars to where they're needed."

"Milena said you've been shipping other stuff as aid."

"Besides clothes, it's mostly used computer parts," Les said. "Nothing worth more than ten grand at a time. That number is a flag for busybodies like Agent Roscoe to start to question things."

"Do you know what a two-stroke engine is?"

"Enlighten me."

"It's like the small engine on a lawn mower, or a leaf blower, or those old-school chainsaws you were talking about the other day. You don't see them much anymore because they're noisy and polluting. They're also simple, easy to fix, no electronics. I bet they'd be useful in a place like Artsakh."

"Machine parts are totally doable."

"Those jewelers work with metal," Slater said. "So you cast two-stroke engine parts out of the gold.

Paint it or dip it in something to disguise it, make it look old and used. You could even just replace the piston and the internal parts. Then ship it over there and tell them to melt it down."

She pursed her lips and then nodded. "It's an interesting approach. You've got some seriously deceptive thinking going on. You figured out how we'd been robbed, and then you did your own thievery, and now smuggling."

"It's how my mind works." Slater rose. "I'm immersed in the cesspool."

"It's not a bad idea. We already have an established history of shipping used items as aid."

"Gold is a lot heavier than steel, so you'd have to make thinner components to get the weight right."

"Some of my squad could figure out the weight. They work with gold every day." Les waved a hand. "Listen—you need to show me how Clyde got into that storeroom."

He stepped into the hall and waited for Les to lock her office door, then led the way through the club and down to Sackett's dining room. Digging out his keys, he opened the connecting door into the next building.

"Clyde said you had keys to this," Slater said as they stepped through.

"There was no deceit involved in that. I got a set when we renovated Greenleaf. I wasn't the one who keyed all the doors the same. But it comes in handy."

They walked to the stairwell, and down to ground level, and around to the stairs leading down.

As they walked the hall, Les waved a hand. "This is a different building from where the incinerator and the storeroom are."

"I know that." Slater stopped at the unmarked door, and glanced back down the hall to make sure no one was watching them. "This must have been a way out to the alley at one time, but the back door is sealed up now." Finally he found the right key, and unlocked it, and pulled it open.

"I get it," Les said, following him down the steps into the hallway. "There are no office doors. It's totally disused."

When they got to the hatch-shaped door, Slater gestured to it. "If my reckoning is accurate, this connects to the storeroom."

"It's odd. It's not really a door."

"I think maybe it was put in during Prohibition. A hidden exit from a speakeasy or an illicit still. Or maybe it's more prosaic. Maybe it was just a trash chute to move stuff to the incinerator."

"Did you open it?"

"That didn't seem like a good idea on Saturday. Emotions were running high. Erik had already clobbered me."

"So let's try."

Slater grabbed the handle and pushed on the door. It took some force, using both arms, but the door swung inward, its hinges creaking. They were looking into the storeroom. The bottom of the hatch was flush with the floor inside. As he pushed it he could feel the door scrape the concrete—not enough to bind on it, but just enough to leave that perfect arc.

Inside, Erik stepped into view, and peered out at them, his eyes wide. "Are you fucking kidding me?"

TWENTY-SIX

ES STEPPED UP INTO the room, and Slater followed. Erik was alone here. Walking around the door, they looked at the other side of it. The horizontal boards and the studs over them were attached to it. From inside, it looked like part of the wall had come unglued.

"This explains things," Les said, looking it over. "See where the boards on the door meet the ones on the wall? It's made to look like a natural seam. It was definitely hidden on purpose."

"A minute ago this was invisible," Erik said. "Why the fuck is there a hidden door here?"

"Prohibition," Les said. "It's the only explanation that makes sense. This room must have been a speakeasy or a distillery, like you said. If there was a raid, you'd get everyone out this way and close it. The police wouldn't know anyone had even been in this room."

"There's a direct route to the alley from here," Slater said, gesturing to the hatch, "and the other end has a door into a completely different building. The boozers could just fade into the city."

Erik waved an arm. "You knew about this?"

"Not until Saturday. I went looking for it after you rinsed me."

"That never happened. Those were rabbit punches." Stepping to the door, Erik looked it over, and grasped the handle on the outside, giving it a tentative tug. "There isn't even a lock. Anybody could have come through." He hopped down into the hallway.

"We know who it was," Les said.

Erik climbed back in. "Who?" he demanded. "Let's go get them. Me and Slater'll mess them up."

"We're not going to do that," Les said. "Strategic thinking and strategic action, remember? We'll talk about the next steps. Come to my office in an hour or so. You're going out of town today."

"Tomorrow," Slater said. "If you go now, with the traffic, it'll be dark by the time you get there. Start early in the morning. You'll need the daylight."

Erik stood staring at the gap in the wall. "I can't fucking believe this."

"You should keep quiet about it for now," Slater said. "Until everything shakes out."

"Excellent advice." Les eyed Erik. "Erik knows how to be discreet."

"I'll close the hatch," Slater said, "if you two want to stay on this side."

Stepping down into the hall, he pulled it shut,

and walked up to street level and across to the parking structure. The rain had let up but it was still overcast, the streets dark and wet. He sat in the Continental, and dug out his phone, and dialed Agent Roscoe.

"I'm surprised you picked up," Slater said. "Can we talk? It has to be in person."

"I'm working today. I can come by your office."

"No way. All that G-man energy makes people jittery."

"Innocent people don't need to be afraid of the authorities," Roscoe said.

"That's what they all say, right before they slam my face onto the hood of a prowl car."

"My office is in the Civic Center. You can come here."

"How about that coffee place on Main?" Slater said. "There's fewer cameras and metal detectors and handsy security guards."

Pulling into the street, he drove north, flicking on his wipers for the residual mist in the air. By the time he walked into the coffee place, Roscoe was already parked at a table, far from the window, with his back to the wall. Of course that's where he'd sit— not exposed, and with a view of the exits. Typical cop.

Once Slater had an espresso in hand, he took the chair opposite the guy.

"I was surprised to hear from you," Roscoe said.

Slater met his eye and tried to look earnest. "You asked why I was hanging around Greenleaf and the historic buildings."

"I remember."

"The property manager hired me."

"Clyde Park."

"That's the guy." Slater leaned toward him and lowered his voice. "He wanted me to keep an eye on Les James and the jewelers."

Roscoe frowned. "Why?"

"He was buying something from them. Something expensive. I assume it was diamonds or gold. Whatever they deal in. There's so much bling in the shops up and down that block. Clyde was going to ship the stuff abroad. It sounded like it was a complicated transaction, and he didn't trust them."

"Why was he going to export diamonds or gold?" Roscoe said.

"I overheard him talking about somebody named Park."

"That's his name."

"So maybe it's a relative. I also overheard the words 'North Korea.' I know Clyde isn't from there. He's from the south. Maybe he needs to send money to them for this other Park person."

"You think the North Koreans are holding one of his relatives hostage?"

"How should I know? All I can say is what I heard." Slater sipped his coffee.

"When and where did you hear this?"

"Sometime last week. I was in his office and he took a call. It was mostly in Korean, but there were a few parts in English. Bilingual people do that, right? Switch in and out of the language."

Roscoe folded his arms, his brow furrowing. "Why are you telling me this?"

"That thing you said. It's illegal to mess with foreign stuff. It feels like I'm getting too mixed up in other people's bullshit. That's why you're snooping around, isn't it? Hanging out at Greenleaf and bringing that pill-popper to my office. Somehow you got wind of Clyde conducting his own foreign policy."

He chuckled. "Why do you think Ramírez is a drug addict?"

"My office is basically on Skid Row. I know what dopers look like. You should make him empty his pockets. I'd bet money you'll find vitamin R, or goofballs at least." Slater raised his eyebrows. "Don't leave your medications lying around."

"What did you learn about Les James and the jewelers when you were keeping an eye on them?"

"Nothing, really. Clyde wanted me to snoop around, but they're totally security conscious. It's not surprising, right, with all that jewelry. I told Clyde today that I was done working for him."

"Why would I believe you about any of this?"

Slater sat back and frowned at him. "You can believe whatever the fuck you want. I'd rather be a witness than get charged with something. Aiding and abetting those dirty commies, or illegal misuse of jewelry, or whatever you come up with. Now I can tell a judge I came to you first and gave you the dope."

"I guess that follows."

"I'm also deeply embroiled with a G-man," Slater said.

"Zebulon Pike."

"That's the one. I don't want to jeopardize our narrative complex."

"Which is what, exactly?"

"It's what squares would interpret as a relationship." He raised his eyebrows. "But it's much, much deeper, and more intense, and more meaningful. It's

operating on multiple levels and in unseen dimensions."

Roscoe frowned. "OK."

"Pike said I should come clean." He drained the little cup.

"He's right." He gestured vaguely. "We'll see if this leads anywhere. You do know it's a crime to lie to a federal agent."

"Why would I lie to you?" Slater scowled. "I'm bringing you a potentially big bust, you ingrate."

Rising, he walked out to the slick wet street, and took a deep breath. It didn't feel like the guy bought it. He wasn't worried about lying to him, but at the very least maybe it would slow Clyde down.

———◆———

A FEW DAYS LATER, sitting at his desk in his office trying to make stuff up for his expense reports for O'Dowd, Slater's phone buzzed, and he dug it out. It was a text from Les James:

Can you come by the club tonight?

He texted her back:

Are you going to try to grease me?

Setting the phone down, he looked back to his computer screen, and picked it up again when her reply came:

I don't need to. The complete set of items has been recovered from the desert. I wanted to thank you for doing right by me.

Thinking about it, he had no reason not to believe that. He sent a quick response:

I'll be there.

A while later he pulled the red-and-purple suit out of the wardrobe in Max's office, and put it on, and walked over to Greenleaf. It was still early in the evening, and a few people were eating at the tables and hanging around the bar. The band was on stage, playing a sweet slow song. As he strode through the room, he saw Lars at the drum kit, and nodded to him, eliciting a smile.

The office door was open, and he knocked as he stepped in. Sitting at her desk, Les was wearing the dark-red dress he'd seen her in once before, and evening makeup, with her hair down. She sat back.

"I love that suit."

"This seems promising," Slater said, standing in front of her desk. "There's no pistol aimed at me, and there's a smile on your face."

"I have a small gift for you."

She rose and handed him a little cardboard box. Folding it open, he found a thick gold chain, and lifted it out. It had a necklace clasp.

"It's nice, but I don't really wear stuff like this."

"Then you can sell it," Les said. "If it's not obvious, it's made of gold. Take it to Milena. She'll turn it into cash."

"Don't you have better uses for it?" He raised his eyebrows. "Like Artsakh?"

"I won't take no for an answer. You helped me a lot."

"I appreciate this." He looped it around his neck, and fastened the clasp, leaving it on top of his shirt.

Les sat down and gestured to the guest chair.

"You found my land without any trouble?" he said, dropping into it.

"The missing items were right where you told me they'd be. I sent Erik. He said it was a lot of work digging in the hot sun."

"The weather is beautiful out there right now. That guy is such a piece of work."

"That's what he said about you."

"At least he brought it back," Slater said. "Where did you put it?"

She laughed. "You want me to draw you a map? It's in a safe place. Nowhere near this neighborhood. Not that it matters as much now, since Clyde is gone."

"What kind of gone?"

"Whatever you told Agent Roscoe, it worked. Roscoe came around the next day asking questions about what Clyde was doing in the building besides managing it. I'm almost certain Clyde got scared and went to Brazil."

"Seriously?" Slater said. "Why would he do that? And why Brazil specifically?"

"For one, Agent Roscoe asked me if Clyde had ever mentioned having friends or family in São Paulo."

"I'm surprised he'd bolt. The story I fed Roscoe was pure fiction. Clyde would have laughed in his face."

"Roscoe was pretty reserved about the whole thing, but he was working with a forensic banker."

"Ramírez. I met that wastoid too. He's the kind of guy you just want to punch in the face."

"Ramírez came here on his own to ask me some questions," Les said. "Punchable or not, he doesn't really have law enforcement training."

"What does that mean?"

"People like Agent Roscoe collect information. They don't distribute it. Ramírez isn't a cop. He was gossiping like a costermonger."

"What did he tell you?"

"Apparently he went to interview Clyde early this week. Clyde thought the feds were looking into the hotel renovation project up the block. He said Clyde kept talking about it, so Ramírez asked him all about it. In hindsight, Ramírez thinks the questioning spooked him. Ramírez mentioned Brazil too. He said they can't extradite people from there."

"I'm pretty sure Clyde was impersonating one of the hotel landowners," Slater said. "I saw the paperwork. It looked to be straight-up fraud. If he was worried about the hotel, it means he stole money from his partners. He must have scored big."

"Ramírez said if Clyde really did flee to a place without extradition, he must have done something felonious enough to make it worthwhile." Les raised her eyebrows. "But I don't think Roscoe and Ramírez knew anything about the hotel project until Clyde brought it up."

"It was pointless for Clyde to upend his life if nobody was on to it. That guy is kind of snakebit. I feel a little bad for him. He wanted to be a big shot but ended up taking a long-term powder."

"He's a crook, Slater," she said intently. "You can skip the sympathy. I'm just glad to be rid of him."

"Are you sure Clyde faded?"

"Roscoe was still looking for him this morning, and there's no sign he's been in his office."

"You broke in?"

She laughed. "I've done some questionable things,

but I don't operate the way you operate. There's someone else working there now. A woman. She told me
she'd been sent in by the building owners, and that
Clyde had 'abandoned his position.'" She waggled
her fingers to put air quotes around the words. "But
he left something for you in his office."

Les handed a lumpy manila envelope across the
desk. It was labeled in Sharpie in big letters: SLATER
IBÁÑEZ.

As he reached for it, he saw that it had been torn
open. "It looks like the new manager got curious."

"That was me," Les said.

"No static." He met her gaze. "Dealing with all
these lowlifes, I would have done the same thing."

Pulling out the contents, he saw that it was the
keys and the pink slip for the Pacer. Clyde had signed
it over to him. He must have done it in a hurry, as he
hadn't sent the DMV its part. Attached to it was a
sticky note with a handwritten message:

Take care of Milton. You're worthy of him.

There was no signature, but Clyde had drawn a
heart at the bottom.

"The little heart implies you had some kind of
romantic connection," Les said.

Slater eyed her. "I don't kiss and tell, sister."

Les chuckled. "Milton is the car?"

"Milton is a whole lot of car."

———◆———